CARPE DIEM JULIET

CARPE DIEM JULIET

CLAUDIA VELASCO

Published by Florid Romance
an imprint of LMBPN Publishing
PMB 196, 2540 South Maryland Pkwy
Las Vegas, NV 89109

Version 1.00 April 2023
eBook ISBN: 979-8-88878-327-6
Print ISBN: 979-8-88878-328-3

THE CARPE DIEM JULIET TEAM

Thanks to our Beta Readers:

Kelly O'Donnell, Malyssa Brannon

Editor
SkyHunter Editing Team

PROLOGUE

Juliet is a Latin name. It comes from the *Roman gens* Julia and means "of strong root." That's what is explained in books dedicated to onomastics and in Wikipedia, and what she had been told once by a professor and even by a doctor fond of the study of names.

A bit old-fashioned but a classic—the name chosen by William Shakespeare for his most romantic female protagonist, Juliet Capulet. A girl with too much passion and too much bad luck in love. Why deny it? The name suited her perfectly.

About to turn thirty-two, Juliet Miller, born in Gibraltar but living in London since the age of four, was perfectly aware that her romantic life was never going to be put back together again. When it came to true love and all those other chimeras she had been dreaming of for as long as she could remember, things were going badly for her. Like Shakespeare's Juliet, she fell in love with constancy, tenacity, and devotion, but unlike the Capulet girl, she had never had it reciprocated. Never been loved madly, much less had someone die of love for her. She had never been loved.

However, she had learned to live with that feeling of emptiness and constant frustration. She had resigned herself that love with a capital letter happened to other people, was only experienced by others who were more fortunate and that, in the end, let's be honest, it wasn't that bad that way.

Her life, then, was limited to a wonderful job which she did marvelously and enjoyed very much. To her hobbies, to which she devoted herself with passion and almost scientific thoroughness. To her few friends, to her solitary walks in London, and to her cat Romeo, of course, who was the true love of her life.

As we can see, Juliet was not an official romantic heroine, but she was one at heart and in spirit. An elegant and subtle and loving personality who had not yet been lucky enough to experience the romance she deserved. On this morning, when this story begins, the day her eternal love, whom she called privately and publicly LOML, Love Of My Life, the guy to whom she had devoted attention, energy, work, hope, to whom she had given wings and who she had helped in every imaginable way since they had met, sent her his first book. It was dedicated, on the first page and in big letters, to a certain Carola. Everything had exploded, had blown up, making her come out of a deep, heavy sleep that had never led her anywhere, that had weighed her down for years, and, at last, she had woken up.

The blow of reality had been hard. She could never forget that feeling of absolute stupidity, of wasted time, of lack of love, of sheer frustration when she read that dedication. She could never forget this Carola of whom LOML had never spoken but whom he now called "my partner," and she had wanted to die. She had blamed him for everything, for being an idiot, for giving more than necessary without thinking, for making a fool of her.

A few hours later, as always, she had consoled herself, gotten up, and dusted herself off to move on, a little lonelier than before but with her dignity intact. That guy might have a "partner" to dedicate books to and be very happy with, but he would no longer have her, and that was an irreparable loss.

He knew it, she knew it, everybody knew it. Even lucky Carola would come to know it. Without her and her support, without her admiration and powerful and constant love hovering around him, he would be much more alone, much sadder and less brilliant, and that certainty gave Juliet immeasurable comfort. Forgetting about LOML forever was the best thing that could happen to her. Without him, she had a lot of blank chapters to start, and although she didn't know it yet, that was exactly what he was about to do, and that was the best thing that could happen to her.

PART I
JULIET

CHAPTER ONE

"Do you know how many students enter the School of Drama at the Royal Conservatoire in Glasgow each year? The Royal Central School of Speech and Drama in London, the American Academy of Dramatic Arts in New York, the Academy of Dramatic Art in Stockholm, and the University of the Arts in Korea. Do you know?"

Iona McCameron stood up. Juliet held her breath because when her boss, who was the most famous actress and actor agent in the UK, got up from a table and addressed people in that tone, anything could happen. Anything, but mostly bad things. She swallowed as she looked at her cell phone.

"I know," the boy in front of her mumbled. He was as handsome as he was insecure. Iona approached him with her hands on her hips.

Juliet glanced sideways at Fabio, her partner in crime, and saw he was as worried as she was.

"If you know that, how the fuck do you dare show up here saying you don't give a fuck about training because you're a born actor who doesn't need that shit?"

"My mentor says—"

"Your mentor says? What does he say?"

"That theater schools spoil and restrict talent, and that mine is too evident to—"

"To lower yourself to study drama?"

"I only want to do movies and television. John Wayne or Cary Grant never set foot in a theater school until—"

"Fuck, man, this guy is so dumb," Iona blurted in her strong Scottish accent. She turned to Juliet and Fabio, laughing her head off.

Neither dared to say anything and finally, she thought better of continuing to martyr the poor kid with movie-star aspirations. She blinked, touched the emerald necklace she was wearing, and turned to him.

"I received you personally, Saxon, because Robert Burton asked me on his knees, swearing that you were going to charm me with your talent. However, I don't give a damn about your talent. It's not enough for me if it doesn't have a solid background behind it. I would never send an untrained actress or actor to an audition.

"If theater schools exist, it is to sift through the trash, find talent, and then train it. I respect them, and that's the least I demand from those I represent—respect for their work and for the hard training it entails. A little effort, for God's sake. I'm sorry, but I can't work with you. Find yourself another agent, one who is worthy of your perfect body and your perfect face, or else study. Prepare yourself, and in three years, you will be able to work with me."

She turned her back on him and looked at Fabio. "Honey, what do we have now?"

"Goodbye, Miss McCameron."

She dismissed the poor boy, who was almost trembling but looking at her with all the contempt he could muster. Iona ignored him, then turned to follow him with her eyes.

"Just so you know, Cary Grant had walked halfway across the

UK with a street theater troupe before he set foot in Hollywood and got Mae West to notice him. Don't spout all the bullshit you hear out there, Saxon. Brainless pretty boys went out of fashion a long time ago."

Juliet got up from the chair and looked at the floor with that feeling of total embarrassment that her boss sometimes caused. Iona was the best at her job and a person she sincerely admired, but sometimes it was impossible to justify her actions. She gathered her things and felt Fabio's hand on her neck.

"How can he come in here and say he doesn't need to study drama? Is Robert out of his mind?" he whispered, pulling her out into the hallway, and Juliet nodded. "First sentence, first screw-up. She wasn't going to give him the slightest chance, poor kid."

"It's incomprehensible. I don't know why he didn't warn you."

"I'll call him back and explain it to him."

"You don't need to. Just skip Robert Burton, Juliet. He's looking for younger and younger assholes every day. It's his fault if he has no judgment about who he promises to make the next Netflix star," Iona spat, overtaking her from the right and jumping into the conversation as always because nothing was being talked about or commented on in her office that didn't interest her.

Fabio said goodbye and walked hurriedly behind her as she headed for her elegant office on the second floor.

Juliet watched them for a second and glanced at Andrea, her assistant, with utter disgust on her face. She walked over to her desk and slumped in her chair, looking for the phone number of Robert Burton, who was a fantastic casting director and a good friend, to explain what had happened with the recommended one, who had screwed up as soon as he said good morning.

"They've called twice from Pinewood. Raven still hasn't shown up."

"I'm sorry?" She raised her head to look at Andrea, and the assistant shrugged. "Raven Lee Westings. She arrived last night from Los Angeles, but she hasn't shown up at the shoot today. Neither she nor her assistant is answering the phone."

"Why didn't you tell me before?"

"Because I just found out, and you were involved with that guy. By the way, how did that go down?"

"Iona asked him to tell us about his training, and he told us that he didn't go to drama school. She almost ate it. You know how sensitive she is on the subject. Who called you from the shoot?"

"Susan, one of the producers, and Rachel Newman, the director's assistant. They're beside themselves."

"No wonder. They lose a lot of money if the star starts delaying the work from the first day."

She picked up the landline and called the Ritz Hotel, where Raven Lee Westings had asked to stay. She dialed the extension for Elis, the head of the hotel's public relations department, and asked about her actress. Elis confirmed that she was there, holed up in the Arlington suite with her assistant, and had given strict orders that she was not to be disturbed. Juliet was counting on that, but she intended to skip over it as usual.

"Please connect me to the Arlington suite. Forty people are waiting for Raven at Pinewood Studios, and I need to wake her up."

"Juliet, seriously?"

"I take full responsibility."

"Okay, wait a second."

"Thank you. I owe you one."

She waited three minutes, and then a woman's sleepy voice greeted her with a cough.

"Who is it?"

"I'm Juliet Miller from Shaughnessy & McCameron. I need to speak to—"

"Juliet, this is Annie, Raven's assistant. How are you?"

"Annie, what's up? What are you still doing at the hotel? They were expecting Raven over an hour ago at Pinewood."

She opened the computer to check the shooting schedule for that particular film and looked at the time. "She was supposed to be at the script reading at ten o'clock in the morning. It's been scheduled for a month."

"I beg your pardon. Was it today?"

"Of course it was today. That's why you arrived last night."

"Fuck!" she exclaimed in her thick American accent. "Fuck, it's the jet lag. I'm so sorry, we overslept. I'll wake Raven, call Richard to apologize, and we'll be on our way in no time. Have we lost the whole day?"

"No, maybe something can still be salvaged. I'll take care of talking to Richard, and I'll send Andrea, my assistant, to help you and accompany you to the studio. I'm going to call for a helicopter, or these people will chop us all to pieces."

"Thank you very much, Juliet. Hug."

She hung up and dialed the number of the film director, looking at Andrea out of the corner of her eye.

"You heard me. Go to the Ritz and make yourself available to Raven Lee and her assistant. They're in the Arlington suite. Order a car, take them to Battersea, and I'll order a helicopter to take you to Buckinghamshire. Don't leave them alone until you see them in their dressing room at Pinewood, okay?"

"Me with Raven Lee Westings?"

Juliet replied, "Didn't you want to go out in the field? This is your chance. Don't let me down. Come on, run."

She smiled to see Andrea so excited, then concentrated on talking first to the assistant director and then to the director, apologizing for Raven's unforgivable absence and assuring her that she would be at the studio as soon as possible to try to salvage something from the first day of shooting.

He went on a rant and threatened her with lawsuits and

contract cancelations before hanging up on her in indignation, but she ignored him because getting reprimanded was the bread and butter of her trade. She continued working steadily until seven o'clock in the evening. Raven Lee Westings had been at Pinewood for hours, and there was hardly anyone left in her office.

CHAPTER TWO

"Take an avocado salad with you, Juliet. Give it a try."

"I don't like avocado, thank you very much. I'll take the usual Mediterranean salad."

"I have wonderful feta."

"Great. Give me a double portion, please."

She smiled at Amadeo, the owner of the Italian takeout place that saved her life almost every night, and he winked at her before concentrating on her Mediterranean salad.

One of the best Mediterranean salads in London, she thought, recognizing that she was very hungry because she hadn't eaten anything since breakfast. She averted her eyes from the bottles of wine on a shelf and thought about buying one for dinner and to have at home, although she also thought of her mother, who would kill her if she knew she was about to buy an Italian wine instead of a good Rioja or...

"Excuse me," said a man next to her. She moved to let him pass, but he made no move to approach the counter, so she turned slightly, looked up, and met spectacular dark eyes. "Excuse me, are you Juliet?"

"Yes. Do we know each other?"

"How do you do? My name is Michiel. We are neighbors," he said, clearing his throat when he saw her bewilderment. "During the lockdown, I used to have lunch or dinner with Mrs. Stuyvesant, Audrey, on our terraces. She talked to me a lot about you. You substituted for me when I was away, and you also did her shopping."

"Oh, of course!" she exclaimed, delighted to see him for the first time in person, and he relaxed his shoulders. "You are the famous Mike!"

"Michiel."

"I beg your pardon?"

"Audrey calls me Mike, but my name is Michiel."

"Like Michiel Huisman, the actor?"

"Exactly, he's from Amstelveen, and I'm from Amsterdam."

"I know he is from Amstelveen. I work with him."

"Oh?"

"I work with your agent. He's one of my company's clients." She picked up her salad, paid for it, and looked back at him. "I thought you didn't live in the building anymore. Audrey told me you had left."

"I left for Holland when I was able to work online, but I'm back now, and I'm really worried about her. Someone told me that she disappeared overnight, and no one has gone to pack up her apartment or pick up her things, and since I saw you, I wanted to ask you if you know anything about it."

She stood still, thinking that it was a long time since she had heard from the charming Mrs. Stuyvesant, a venerable lady of eighty-three she had "adopted" during the first weeks of confinement because she reminded her so much of her grandmother. She looked at her neighbor, the "other guardian angel," as Mrs. Stuyvesant called him, feeling guilty.

She replied, "God, the truth is that I don't know anything. I haven't seen her for a long time because I've been traveling and working a lot these last few weeks. The last time I spoke to her, she was waiting for the city council to send her home care, and then one of the neighbors told me that she had gone away with a nephew or a relative."

"A nephew?" he asked. "She had no one, not from her family nor her husband's family. That's why she had asked for home care. I helped her to fill out the online application from Amsterdam."

"You're right; she had no one. Maybe her social worker decided to move her to a nursing home."

"No, I asked by email, and they told me that they have not heard from her for at least a month. I've made an appointment for a personal consultation."

"You've got me worried. My friend Rocío started to visit her for me when I went back to work and stopped when she disappeared without warning. It was very strange, but we let it go because we both thought it was a good idea to go back to work." I had been certain that she had left with a relative, as the neighbors said. The truth was that I did not stop to think about the details.

"Misha, haven't you ordered yet?" A girl came up behind him and interrupted them by grabbing him by the arm and kissing him on the cheek. Juliet smiled at her, and she smiled back.

"I've been waiting in the street for fifteen minutes."

"I'm sorry. I just needed to talk to Juliet. Juliet, this is Laura."

"Lovely, and sorry to have kept you waiting."

Michiel admitted, "It was me who kept you, so it's my fault."

"Anyway, nice to meet you, and if I find out anything about Mrs. Stuyvesant, I'll let you know, Michiel. Can I have an email address or…"

"Please write down my phone number so we can communicate. I know you were the only one besides me who spent time with her."

"Of course. We can call each other."

She pulled out her cell phone, exchanged numbers, and then walked away from the couple. She was worried, thinking he was right. It seemed rather unlikely that an eighty-three-year-old lady who lamented daily that she had no family would disappear overnight to move into a supposed relative's house.

It was very strange. Alarming, to say the least, but she thought she would find out what was going on as soon as possible.

CHAPTER THREE

S he felt her cell phone vibrate and glanced at it out of the corner of her eye and opened the message from LOML, who had reappeared after several days of no contact.

How are you doing? You're very quiet.

She snorted, unable to believe he would write to her after what had happened with his little book and his blissful dedication to this Carola. She ignored him since she knew the next message would ask her for a favor. She turned the screen black, took a deep breath, and looked at the meeting table where they were going over the avalanche of work they could barely keep up with.

"We've signed forty contracts today alone," said Bill from the legal department. "We've been averaging thirty a day for the last two years."

"It's wonderful. That's what our job is all about. Our clients keep signing contracts," said Iona happily. "All our actors are working, we don't have any of them unemployed, and that's a dream for any agent."

"I know, but we need extra help. We need to hire a couple more people, even if they are interns."

"Right now, we have six interns, and they've given us nothing but trouble," said Betty from Human Resources. "I have to put a junior in to train them, and we're wasting time and money. Don't bring me any more bureaucrats. Please hire qualified and experienced people. We can afford it, can't we, Sandra?"

"We can pay for it," Sandra replied.

"Juliet, what do you think?" Iona looked her in the eye, and she sat straighter in the chair.

"With the demand from the platforms, there has been a five-fold increase in work, Iona. That's wonderful for our actors, but we can't cover the flood of work with the same people you worked with before Amazon Prime, Netflix, and HBO. Of course, we need new additions."

"We've been telling you this for many years, my dear," Andrew Shaughnessy, the company's president, intervened.

Iona snorted, stroked her pearl necklace, and shrugged.

"If it's just an administrative and management issue, get a lawyer and a couple of secretaries."

"That's fine, but it's not just an administrative issue." Deborah, the manager, finally spoke up. "Our valuable and unsustainable personalized assistance to each client means that Juliet, Kevin, Malcolm, and Rose have to travel all the time. That leaves us with insurmountable gaps. We also need staff in your department, qualified people able to read and approve a script or a contract and deal with the actors, directors, or producers on duty. In short, I need a paralegal and two administrative assistants for the legal department, yes, but also about four other employees for multipurpose tasks."

"Six new employees?" Iona asked. "There are already forty of us working here."

"We need more if you want to continue providing optimal

and luxurious service to your famous and elite clientele. You'll see, Iona. It is urgent to expand the staff!"

"We can't delay signing a contract or supporting a client on a shoot because we're short-staffed," Juliet murmured. "It's already happened, and we've looked terrible."

"Sandra?" Iona looked at the CFO again. She nodded.

"We can pay for it, and we should pay for it. It's not a question of money, Iona. It's about growing and getting stronger before someone else steps in and eats our piece of the pie. We have prestige and a name to maintain, and for that, we have to invest."

"Well said, my dear. I agree," said Andrew Shaughnessy, standing up. "I have to go. Judi Dench is waiting for me."

"Okay, do whatever it takes. Hire whoever you want." Iona relented at last and adjourned the meeting. Juliet got up, but before she left the room, Betty grabbed her by the arm to go out into the hallway with her.

"Let's start breathing for once," she said. "It's unbelievable that this woman is so stingy. Thank God Andrew was able to come and support us."

"Let's see how long it takes to find people."

"We already have a selection, Juliet. We have been working for months on this staff expansion. We only needed the boss's okay. Don't worry. Do you think Andrea can take on more responsible tasks?"

"I think she's great. She's very efficient, but if I have to do without her, I'll have a fit."

"You won't do without. You work well in tandem. It's just something to keep in mind when we need extra coverage."

"She'll do well. She's been with me for two years. She's ready."

"Great. How are you?"

"I'm fine, and you?"

"Fine. With an unbearable teenage daughter, but fine. I'll leave you, we'll talk later, and I'll call you for the final screening of the applicants. I could use your clinical eye."

"Anytime."

She said goodbye. Juliet arrived at her office, went inside, and saw that she had new messages on her cell phone. She ignored them all, thinking they were from LOML, and asked Andrea to update her. Andrea told her what they had pending and handed her the script for a new Amazon Prime series she had been approached about for one of her clients. She glanced over it, walked to her desk, and suddenly felt the irrepressible urge to read the cell phone messages.

She slumped in her armchair, thought about going to make herself coffee, and opened the phone screen. To her surprise, she discovered that she did indeed have an unopened message from LOML, but she also had another one from her Dutch neighbor, Michiel, Mrs. Stuyvesant's friend.

She clicked on the text, very interested to know if he had any news for her.

Hi, Juliet. It's Michiel. I've been with Audrey's caseworker. You might be interested to know what she told me. I hate communicating through text messages. Please, if you have time, give me a call or let me know what time I can call you so we can talk.

It's normal that he hates texting, she thought and immediately replied.

Hi, Michiel, thanks for writing to me. Of course, I want to know what the social worker told you. I'm working. I'll call you when I have a little free time. See you later.

She left her cell phone on the table without reading LOML's text and saw Fabio enter with a huge cup of coffee. She smiled at him and offered him a chair.

"You read my mind, Fabito. I love you, and you know that? I was dying for a cup of coffee."

"I can't stay long. Iona's on a rampage. She's made me call her guru. She's talking to him by video call, but it won't take too long."

"Does it bother her so much to hire people?"

"She is a millionaire, her company is wealthy, and she doesn't mind paying for a helicopter or bringing mineral water from Tibet for a five-star client, but when it comes to paying a measly salary to a little worker, she gets sick."

"My grandmother says that greed is one of the worst deadly sins."

"What are the deadly sins? Are there many?"

"Seven: pride, greed, lust, anger, gluttony, envy, and sloth."

"I think I practice them all. Listen," he said as he approached her, resting his hands on the desk, "I've heard from the beautiful Saxon."

"The born actor who doesn't need to go to drama school?"

"Exactly. He's signed with Gloria and Peter Fleming. They're representing him now, and within a week, he's already signed his first contract for a Starz historical series. He's going to be great on screen."

"I hope he does well, poor guy. He's got a lot of hurdles ahead of him."

"Yes, but he's very handsome and will go far in his career."

"For a while, yes."

"What are you doing on your afternoon off?"

"First I'm going to the hairdresser because Nadia wants to cut my hair, and then we're going to the Barbican to see Damian Hastings' play."

"Are you going to swallow that nonsense?"

"I couldn't go to the premiere. She begged me, it's two steps away from home, and Nadia wants to go."

"If you get a chance, bang that Damian Hastings before he gets too famous. He's so hot."

"Wait, my mother is calling me." Juliet picked up her cell phone and greeted her in Spanish. "Hi, Mum, is everything okay?"

"All good. I just wanted to hear from you. It's been a month since we've seen you, Juliet."

"I'm leaving. On Monday, you'll tell me if you fucked Damian," Fabio whispered to her, wiggling his hips, and she waved goodbye.

"Mum, what were you saying?"

"Where are you?"

"Working in the office in London."

"Your brother told me you were in Northern Ireland."

"I got back yesterday. How are you?"

"All well, thank God. When are you coming?"

"Sunday."

"Don't let me down. Your grandmother is crazy to see you and crazy to go back to La Línea. You know how intense she gets. If you don't hurry, you might not see her."

"Of course, I'm coming. Don't worry. Tell her to stay there, or put her on the phone, and I'll tell her."

"She's not here. Your father has taken her to do the shopping."

"Okay, so you can rest a little."

"How are you getting to Willesden?"

"By train. Don't worry. I'll be there around noon."

"Okay, sweetheart, see you Sunday."

"Until Sunday, Mum."

She hung up and saw Michiel's response.

Perfect, call whenever you want, and if you have time, we'll have a coffee in the neighborhood. It's on me.

She replied **Okay** and opened the script in front of her. She still had a couple of hours of work to do before she could take advantage of her first Friday afternoon off in months, so she settled back in her chair and concentrated on the script. Sure enough, it was for a medieval historical series with lots of sexy warriors and damsels in distress.

CHAPTER FOUR

"Mrs. Stuyvesant hasn't shown up at the doctor's, hasn't picked up her prescriptions from the pharmacy, hasn't opened the door to the home help volunteer, doesn't pick up the phone, and doesn't answer the letters from the city government. I could have guessed the last because her mailbox is full."

Michiel suddenly looked up at the sky, and Juliet found, to her surprise, that his eyes were not dark as she had thought in the takeout place. They were very dark blue, and his skin was tanned. He was a very manly guy, very handsome, although quite a mess, dressed in old jeans, a plaid flannel shirt, and worn, unpolished boots. He did, however, have beautiful hair, the sort that many of the men she knew would pay for, especially in the world of movies and television, where a good head of hair easily catapulted you to stardom. Obviously, hair wasn't everything, but it helped a lot.

She nodded, listening to his account of the frustrating visit to Mrs. Stuyvesant's caseworker, and she couldn't help but watch him carefully. She was used to scrutinizing people, men and women, with a clinical eye, and she was an expert at picking up on beauty or charisma in people. Her boss said she had a gift because as soon as she met someone, she knew how to find their good side—if they had one. If they didn't, even if they were a Greek god descended from Olympus, she was capable of detecting that. Magnetism was not always found in perfect looks. It was something much deeper. It was what is called charisma, angel, or *duende*, as her mother, who was Andalusian, used to call it.

Juliet Miller was considered a good discoverer of charisma. Of course, some beautiful people also had overwhelming charisma, but they did not always go hand in hand. You had to be able to spot it.

Her job, which often prioritized people's physical appearance, had made her immune to good looks. She didn't faint if Idris Elba, with all his imposing size, hugged her to say hello, or if Henry Cavill showed up at her office with one of his advert smiles to say good morning. Nor was she intimidated by Angelina Jolie's overwhelming beauty or Margot Robbie's incredible figure. Fortunately, she had outgrown that. She now valued other things. She saw people far beyond the obvious, and everyone trusted her objective opinion on the matter.

"Objective opinion on the matter," she repeated to herself, calmly looking at Michiel, the thirty-something Dutchman she had met for coffee on a terrace next to her house and who, according to her professional criteria, had it all, natural beauty and charisma. A twenty-five on a scale of one to ten.

"Juliet?" he asked, pulling her out of her professional musings. She looked him straight in the face and opened her mouth, but what came out had nothing to do with what he was telling her.

"Are you related to Michiel Hiusman? You look just like him."

"I don't know. I don't think so."

"Do you know him in person?"

"No."

"You've got his hair and his eyes, and..." She waved her hands, and he frowned. "All in all, come on! You could be his double."

"I'll keep that in mind, thank you. What do you think about what Kate, Audrey's caseworker, told me?"

"I think we should go into Mrs. Stuyvesant's apartment and see if we can find out anything. Did anyone see her leave her house?"

"Yes, Mr. Harris saw her and says she was in a wheelchair. Of course, she never used a wheelchair. We can't enter her house without permission. That would be breaking and entering. We need the police or the fire department to open the door."

"The building manager is very nice. I know him well. I've gotten him tickets for several premieres, and he owes me one. I'll ask him to open the apartment with his key."

"Really?"

"Sure, I'll call him on Monday. If we have to wait for the police to listen to us and open the door, that will take forever. It's about finding out if Audrey is all right as soon as possible, isn't it?"

"Great! Thanks for understanding. Everyone tells me I'm nuts for caring so much about a neighbor I barely knew."

"If you had known Audrey Stuyvesant better, you would know she wasn't the type to leave without saying goodbye, let alone miss a doctor's appointment or not pick up prescriptions from the pharmacy. I'm with you. Something has happened, and the least we can do is try to find out what."

"Thank you, Juliet." He looked over his coffee cup at her, and she winked. He continued, "So, you work with celebrities, get tickets to premieres, and you've seen Michiel Huisman in person?"

"Yes. I work in an actors' representation agency. What do you do?"

"I am a teacher."

"Of what?"

"I'm a primary school teacher. I work with children from six years old."

"Really?"

"Yes."

"How interesting."

"Not as glamorous as what you do with all those movie stars."

"I usually work with the newer actors. As soon as they become stars, they move to the first division and work with my bosses directly."

"After you've done all the work?"

"We work as a team, but yes, after a lot of hard work and a lot of dealing with them, we put them on track for the big leagues. To be fair, some who also make it to the top reject the new privileges and still count on me." She took a deep breath, waiting for the usual question, but he kept quiet and looked at her very attentively.

"What?"

"Nothing, it's just that it's at this point in the conversation that people usually ask me for the names of my clients."

"Are you going to ask me for the names of my students?"

"No!" She laughed, and he laughed with her.

"I guess you have to be discreet about it, and besides, I'm terrible at matching names and faces, especially those of people I don't know."

"I think it's perfect."

"How does one get to work in a representation agency?"

"Not in a very honorable way. I'll tell you about it if I get to know you better."

"Do you promise?"

"I promise." She took a sip of coffee. "Do you work at a school near here?"

"I work at the American School in St. John's Wood, about thirty minutes by bike or twenty minutes by Underground."

"Wow, great center. Lots of people want to send kids there."

"Yes, it's great. I feel privileged to work there. In Amsterdam, I was at the International College, and it's the same teaching philosophy."

"Now London. How long have you been here?"

"I've been here for three years, and I came for my son. His mother moved to London, and I came behind. The normal thing in these cases." He looked into her blue eyes and Juliet nodded, thinking that it was not the most normal thing to do, but she did not open her mouth.

"How old is your son?"

"Daniel? Eight years old."

"Does he live with you?"

"No, he lives with his mother and stepfather next to the school in Regent's Park, but I see him every day because he is a student at my school."

"Ah, how fortunate."

"You are very young, and I know you live alone because of what Audrey mentioned."

"Yes, I live alone with Romeo, my cat, and I have no children. My family lives in Willesden, northwest London, about five miles from Charing Cross."

"Parents and siblings?"

"My parents and my older brother live there. I live here in the center, and my younger sister lives in Scotland."

"So, Romeo lives with you. How lucky I am! I didn't know I was Romeo and Juliet's neighbor."

He smiled at her, and Juliet laughed and stretched her legs, realizing that she had no trouble talking to this nice man. He was a family man and a nice elementary school teacher. She leaned against the back of the chair and looked at the bright blue sky.

"I love these breezy, clear days at the end of the summer."

"The truth is that it's a spectacular day," he replied.

Juliet observed the peculiar landscape that surrounded them. They were in the heart of the Barbican, her neighborhood. It was one of the most ancient in London, but it had been devastated by the Blitz, the bombing of the city by the German Air Force during World War II. Therefore, what was in front of them was new, rebuilt from the ground up since 1959.

She shook her head and gazed at the impressive Barbican Arts Centre, home of the National Theatre. The huge, modern space with theater and concert halls was at the foot of her home, a cute little flat on the second floor of one of the concrete towers that housed the 2,113 apartments of the Barbican residential area, the Barbican Estate.

She took a deep breath, noting that her companion enjoyed the silence as much as she did and didn't need to break it to talk nonsense. Out of the corner of her eye, she saw a figure completely alien to the landscape appear in her field of vision: LOML, dressed in his leather jacket and walking next to a young blonde girl carrying some shopping bags.

At first, she tensed, and her stomach contracted. She wanted to hide under the table, but she didn't move. She just watched as he walked along with his friend, chatting animatedly. He passed in front of her doorway without even looking at it. He was like that. He had no attachment to anyone or anything and did not even bother to take a look at the doorway of her house, the house where she had welcomed him and fed him hundreds of times.

Shit. She hated to think like that. She hated to remember how many times she had taken him in, cared for him, and pampered him because she had done it voluntarily and for pleasure, out of pure and authentic love. She couldn't help it. She couldn't because he had broken her heart. He had broken it about four hundred and fifty times since she had known him. She followed him with her eyes until he disappeared down a staircase behind that blonde girl who was probably the famous Carola...or not. She couldn't know and didn't care. She only hoped that she was not the girl's neighbor because it was no fun for her to start meeting them on the street or in the Underground corridors.

"Hello!" a woman exclaimed in front of her face. She jumped

up and saw Michiel's girlfriend, the woman who had been with him when they had first met. He smiled at her and stood up to greet her with a couple of kisses.

"Hello! What's up?"

"Have you finished?"

"Yes, we've already caught up," Juliet replied because Michiel hadn't said anything. She stepped back and picked up her back-pack. "I'm going to leave you two. I have a lot of errands to run."

"Are you up for brunch? Laura and I were thinking of going to..." Michiel started. His girl grabbed his arm and kissed him on the cheek.

"Leave it, honey. I'm sure a pretty young girl has better things to do on a Saturday than go to brunch with a couple of fogies."

"You're not fogies at all. I appreciate the invitation, but I can't. It's my first weekend off in months, and I have a thousand things to do."

"Sure, another time," Laura replied, and Michiel smiled at her with a little wink.

"When you hear from the building manager, please get in touch."

"That's done. See you later."

She waved goodbye to both of them and turned her back to walk to the supermarket, trying not to think about LOML but about everything she had to do. First shopping, then a visit to the pharmacy, and finally, to the dry cleaners before returning home, ordering Chinese food, having a quiet meal, and spending the rest of the afternoon reading and watching movies with Romeo.

CHAPTER FIVE

S he rushed into her office and stopped in the doorway when she saw that she was the first to arrive, as usual. She stopped and took a sip of the coffee she had bought. She glimpsed the cleaning staff at work, among them Rocío, her guardian angel, and he waved at her. She returned his greeting and approached him.

"Did you do anything interesting over the weekend, Juliet?" he asked in Spanish, and she shook her head.

"I went to see my parents. My nephews and nieces were there."

"I meant something else. Weren't you going to the theater on Friday?"

"Yes, and then straight home, Nadia was working on Saturday, and I wanted to be with Romeo. He spends a lot of time alone."

"He doesn't spend much time alone, and in any case, he loves to be alone and at ease."

"That's true. How about you? Did you go out with the Kensington guy?" She walked toward her office. Rocío, who was an

English student from Seville who made a living working at a thousand things, followed her, protesting.

"Yes, but I was a fucking mess in bed. I didn't know what to do with my hands. A waste of time. At least he invited me to a cool place for dinner."

"Wow, I'm sorry."

"I have a full schedule, don't worry."

"I think I can get you in as an extra in the movie being shot in Leavesden next week, but you know it's thirty kilometers from here. Can you make it?"

"If necessary, I go by bike, they pay very well, and I see celebrities."

"Could you get Pili? Her brother has a car."

"Sure. Tell me how many of us you can use, and I'll fix you up."

"I can use all three, but I don't want to spread the word about the subject of the shoot, or they will drive me crazy."

She looked at her freshly cleaned and tidied desk and opened the computer, remembering Michiel. "Hey, have you seen a neighbor named Michiel, a tall, handsome guy with nice hair? Has a little boy and lives two doors down from me?"

"Sure. He's dreamy! Why, are you smitten?"

"No, he's not my type, and on top of that, he has a son and a girlfriend," she replied. "He asked me for help in locating Mrs. Stuyvesant. He's very worried about her sudden disappearance, which I didn't know about."

"I don't know if it was sudden. Everyone says she left with a nephew, right?"

"That's the crux of the matter. She had no nieces, nephews, or relatives that we know of, and, according to Michiel, who has spoken to her social worker, she has disappeared as if by magic."

"I hope nothing happened to her. She's so nice."

"I'm sure it's nothing, but let's do some research."

"Mrs. Stuyvesant talked a lot about him, the neighbor Michiel. She said that you and he were the best things that had happened to her in years because of the company and the errands you ran for her during her confinement."

"Ya, poor thing. She was very grateful. I don't know why I'm talking in the past tense. Anyway, send me the names of the people who can go to the shoot and the ID, passport, or residence card numbers as soon as possible, okay?"

"Okay, I'll send them to you by WhatsApp later. I'm leaving. I'm late for another place. See you tomorrow."

"See you tomorrow."

"Juliet."

"What?"

"Let's see if next weekend you go wild a little bit and get laid. *Carpe diem*, Juliet."

She laughed, and Rocío blew her a kiss and disappeared down the hallway. She slumped in her chair and concentrated on the computer to answer emails before the daily ruckus began.

They had a lot of projects going on that involved many clients spread all over the world. Some were working on various first-class productions, others not so important but equally interesting, that used to have repercussions on their agenda because there was always some setback that had to be solved.

Fortunately, she was no longer stressed by those stories, so she worked quietly until Andrea and the others showed up. The office began to fill with voices and comments, with busy people coming in and out of her office asking her questions or leaving folders on her desk. It went on for a couple of hours until a message from LOML broke her out of her routine and forced her to pay attention.

Are you okay? I need to consult you about something impor-tant. Can I call you?

She read it but didn't answer. She threw her phone on the table, and the next thing she heard was her boss's voice from the door.

"Juliet, look who's here to see you."

"Kit, hello! What's up?"

She jumped up to greet that wonderful, adorable actor. He was a big star who had started working with her ten years ago when they were both inexperienced kids. She went over to hug him.

Kit had just become a father and he'd come from Los Angeles, where he was working on whatever he wanted. He gave her an overview of his life, told her what was new with his wife and family, asked about hers, and in the end, offered her a job as his personal assistant. She declined the offer as usual and accompanied him to Iona's office, where they were waiting for him for an important meeting. Juliet said goodbye, promising to meet him later, and returned to her office. Andrea was waiting for her, standing with the headset of the landline in one hand.

"It's Caden Brown. He says you haven't answered his messages for weeks, and he's starting to worry."

Caden Brown, LOML, textbook ballbuster, she thought, nodding and picking up the landline on her desk. It was typical. As soon as you stopped paying attention to him, his defenses went down or something, and he remembered her. It was either that or, more likely, he was calling because he needed her to do him an urgent favor.

"Caden," she greeted him.

He replied in his sexy Australian accent. "Hello, missing. Are you all right? Are you trying to get rid of me?"

"Do you need anything? I'm in the middle of rush hour."

"I know. I just wanted to say hello. Is everything okay?"

"Yes, thank you."

"Okay. It's just that you don't reply to messages."

"I've been traveling and busy, you know."

"How is Romeo?"

Romeo? Was he asking about Romeo? Him, the guy who didn't like cats? *The favor is a big one*, she concluded and took a deep breath.

"Do you need something, Caden?"

"I just wanted to say hello and talk to you about the presentation of my book. We want to do it in Camden, and I don't know if you know a nice place where I can get a good price or, better yet, for free. Besides presenting the book, we will do a small exhibition of my work. It will bring a lot of people."

"Do you think so?" she asked nastily since she remembered perfectly well the very poor attendance at his exhibitions. So poor that it had kept her awake for a long time.

He kept silent for a second but then went on talking as if nothing had happened. "You have to take advantage of the effervescence of the city at this time of the year. Of course, you are invited, and you can bring whoever you want. If they are celebrities, all the better." He giggled.

"Okay."

"Do you know a location?"

"No, not really."

"Ah, wow. I thought you..."

"It's been years since I've been in charge of organizing company events. That's run by someone else now, and I certainly never held them in Camden."

"Oh, okay. When I get the site, I'll send you an invitation."

"Great, thank you very much."

She hung up on him abruptly, not intending to continue this absurd talk and wishing she had the ovaries to have told him to ask his girlfriend Carola to get him a nice place in Camden and not her. She sat down indignantly, looked at her cell phone, and saw that she was being called by Robert Whitehall, the manager of her building, whom she had emailed earlier that morning.

"Hello, Robert."

"Hi, Juliet. How are you? I just saw your email asking me for the keys to Mrs. Stuyvesant's flat. As you can imagine, that's very irregular."

"Of course, I know it's irregular. It's just that her neighbor on the left and I, who took care of her during the confinement, are very concerned about her disappearance and would like to check."

"Disappearance? What disappearance? She just went to live with a nephew out of town."

"She has no family. She never spoke to us about a nephew. On the contrary, she constantly complained about her loneliness and spoke of having no family. It has been more than a month since she stopped going to the doctor and picking up her prescriptions at the pharmacy. We know this from her social worker, the one who was assigned to her when she asked for home support. When the social worker went to visit her, she was no longer there."

"Old ladies often complain about loneliness."

"Believe me, Robert, Audrey Stuyvesant was not complaining for nothing. She is all alone in the world since she became a widow. She was not exaggerating anything or trying to get our sympathy. That's why we are so worried about this sudden move. She left without saying goodbye to us to live with a relative she had not told either of us about."

"Not you or Michiel Lezer?"

"Exactly," she replied, learning that Michiel's last name was Lezer, something she hadn't thought to ask.

"It is illegal to enter her home without her consent. What do you expect to find there?"

"Nothing specific. Just check that she took her things and see if she left any address. I don't know. Once we're there, we'll know what we're looking for. Listen, if it wasn't really important, I wouldn't be asking you for this favor, Robert. I assure you that both Mr. Lezer and I take full responsibility for it."

"I hate to deny you this, Juliet, and if you take full responsibility in writing, I'll give you the keys and wash my hands of it."

"Of course. We will sign anything."

"Great. Come by and pick them up whenever you want."

CHAPTER SIX

She looked at the time, thinking about getting going, and at that precise moment, the doorbell rang. Romeo jumped up and settled in her arms, and she stroked his head, taking her keys from the dresser. She opened the door and found Michiel waiting for her in the hallway with his hands in his pockets.

"Good afternoon."

"Hello. How are you? Is this the famous Romeo? A Russian blue? He is beautiful."

"Yes, he's a Russian blue. Are you allergic to cats, or are you afraid of them? I was thinking of taking him with me. He loves to get out of the apartment from time to time."

"I don't have allergies, and I like cats very much. I grew up with cats, dogs, and all kinds of pets. Hello, Romeo. You are very handsome." He reached out and stroked Romeo's soft little head. The cat purred and allowed himself to be petted.

"Wow, he seems to like you. Have you got the keys yet?"

"I just picked them up after signing the declaration of responsibility. He's a real stickler, that guy."

"Yes, he is. He's posh, picky, and a bit fearful, and he gets upset by anything."

She felt the cold wind on her back since the corridors in the Barbican Estate towers had roofs but no walls and were open to the air. She followed him as he opened Mrs. Stuyvesant's door and passed into the foyer, turning on the lights.

It smelled closed, but it didn't smell bad, which made her assume they wouldn't come across a dead body. She saw the two glass vases in the entryway with at least a dozen wilted roses, which was very unlike Audrey Stuyvesant, who loved plants and kept the vases in her house filled with fresh flowers.

Michiel took a step into the living room and let out an exclamation that made Romeo jump to the floor, ready to explore the apartment on his own. Juliet followed him and saw what he was seeing: everything was in perfect order and in its place. Not a thimble or a book was missing, and that was a bit disturbing. Neither the blanket on the sofa nor the remote control, which was always on the coffee table, had been moved, which was very strange if you were supposed to have moved out. A shiver ran down her spine.

"Didn't she take anything?"

"Apparently not," Michiel replied, pointing at the TV, the laptop, and the pictures on the walls. He turned to the master bedroom. "Maybe she just took her clothes. I'll check it out."

Juliet nodded and approached the door to the terrace, which was ajar. She glanced sideways at a half-finished embroidery work on Audrey's favorite armchair. The cushions were neatly arranged, and the table where she dined many a night during confinement had a magazine.

She went into the kitchen to take a look in the refrigerator, opened it, and saw that there was quite a lot of old food in it. She closed it and went to the cupboards to look for her friend's greatest treasure, a valuable Royal Copenhagen China set that she kept wrapped in cloths. She tiptoed to locate it and found it immediately.

"Look at this," Michiel said from behind her, and she jumped.

"She didn't take her Royal Copenhagen China. That's strange."

"What did you find?"

"Everything is tidy, with clothes in the closets and in the drawers of her dresser, an empty jewelry box on the bed, and these photos hidden in a safe in the floor next to the bedside table."

"Was the safe open?"

"Wide open."

"What pictures are those?

"During the lockdown, she showed me her photo albums many times, but never these. And look!" He pointed at several pictures of a young Audrey, dressed very elegantly, on the arm of a military man. Juliet looked at them carefully and then shrugged her shoulders.

"It's Gregory, isn't it? Her husband?"

"Yes, but she had never, ever told me that her husband was an American. Look at the uniform! Behind the pictures, it says, *'Audrey Glenn and Peter Gregory Stuyvesant III, Captain, United States Air Force. New York, December 1955.'*"

"I didn't know it either, but she was always talking about her beloved Gregory."

"Don't you know about the Stuyvesants from New York?" Michiel asked.

Juliet shook her head.

"They are one of the richest and most powerful families in the United States. The Stuyvesants descended from Peter Stuyvesant, who came to Manhattan in the seventeenth century. They are the most prosperous family in Manhattan. They are elite, a sort of American aristocracy. Perhaps our lovely Audrey was married to one of them."

"I don't think so. There are other Stuyvesants in the United States, aren't there?"

"Yeah, but this guy looks like he had money. Why didn't

Audrey ever tell us that her husband, who she kept talking about, was American?"

"If she were a rich widow, she wouldn't be living in the Barbican in a ninety-meter apartment. At the very least, she would have moved to Mayfair or even Manhattan, don't you think?"

"I don't know, but I'm going to find out."

"How?"

"The first thing I asked her when I met her was about her last name. If she came from the Dutch in the United States or directly from the Netherlands, and she was speechless. She even stopped talking to me for a while. Then she forgot, and we went back to having dinner together on our terraces."

"The Dutch in the United States?"

"Manhattan's first Stuyvesant came from the Netherlands to take over the Dutch West India Company, then went on to become the governor of New Amsterdam in 1647. That was the beginning of his family's fortune."

"I knew the Dutch arrived before the English on the island of Manhattan and that they christened it New Amsterdam, but from then on, I know nothing."

"It's a short period, spanning only forty years, but it is exciting. I majored in history and did my dissertation on New Amsterdam, the Dutch West India Company, and Peter Stuyvesant."

"Really!"

"That's why I started talking with Audrey. Because one morning, she approached me in the hallway to introduce herself, and when she told me her last name, I was stunned. It was too much of a coincidence. I couldn't let it go, and we became friends. Then came the confinement and the endless chats on our terraces, conversations in which we talked about everything. She especially liked me to tell her the story of the Stuyvesants in New York. That's why I was blown away when I saw these pictures of

Peter Gregory Stuyvesant III, a captain in the US Air Force. Why didn't she ever tell me he was an American? Why didn't she show me these pictures? Why did she keep them hidden in a safe on the floor of her bedroom?"

"I don't know. It's all pretty weird."

"You're telling me."

"What happened to the Dutch in Manhattan? Could you give me a summary?"

"Of course."

He walked over to the sideboard and leaned on it, petting Romeo, who had approached him for a closer look. Juliet sat on the armrest of a couch and gave him her attention.

"The first Dutch settlement in New York was founded in 1625 as New Amsterdam and occupied the southern part of present-day Manhattan. That settlement was the trading outpost of the powerful Dutch West India Company and survived for only thirty-nine years until the English conquest in 1664. You can see the Dutch influence in the toponyms that remain in the city, Brooklyn, Harlem, Yonkers, Staten Island, and so on.

"During those almost forty years, the Dutch West India Company did as it pleased with the long-suffering inhabitants of that prosperous colony in the so-called New Netherlands. They administered their law with tyranny, so much so that some employees demanded full citizenship in their new country. Among those 'rebels' was the lawyer Adriaen van der Donck, who wanted a representative government for New Amsterdam and went so far as to file a lawsuit in Holland to demand it."

"Wow. Go on."

"In 1647, five years before the Anglo-Dutch war, the Dutch West India Company was worried about the insurgent movements in its best-located, most prosperous, and strategic colony. Instead of negotiating with its rebellious employees, they decided to appoint a new general manager of the company—a ruthless ex-military officer, Peter Stuyvesant. He landed on the island to take over with an iron fist and confronted Adriaen van der Donck personally. They were irreconcilable enemies. In 1650, van der Donck compiled the claims of the colonists in writing and presented a formal complaint eighty-three pages long against Stuyvesant and his company before the Government of the Hague."

"Did they get anything?"

"Unfortunately, no. In 1653, the trade war with England broke out, The Hague rejected van der Donck's proposals, and he returned to Manhattan without having achieved his dream. Finally, to make a long story short, in 1664, Charles II of England decided to cede a large portion of land in the New World to his brother James, land that arbitrarily included the New Netherlands. It was at that time that four English ships with several hundred soldiers onboard arrived in New Amsterdam's harbor and demanded that the Dutch surrender. They did.

"The Dutch colony was finally taken by some five hundred men commanded by Richard Nicolls. On August 30, 1664, a letter was sent to Governor Stuyvesant, requesting his surrender and promising to respect the life, property, and liberty of all those citizens of Manhattan who submitted to the authority of King Charles II of England. Stuyvesant, seeing that they were lost, signed a peace treaty a week later. The Netherlands surrendered New Amsterdam, Richard Nicolls was declared governor, and the city was renamed New York."

"What happened to van der Donck?"

"Van der Donck apparently died around 1655 during an Indian attack."

"What about Stuyvesant?"

"First, he traveled to Holland to report the loss of New Amsterdam, but he didn't stay there. He returned to Manhattan and spent the rest of his life on a huge, beautiful farm called Great Bouwerie, which at the time was far from the center of the city. Today, it would go from First Avenue to 16th Street, and it had a beautiful view of the East River."

"He lived as he wished."

"Exactly. He lived as he wanted to. He knew how to live with the Church, so he prospered and made his family one of the most important in New York and, over the years, in the United States. He is buried in St. Mark's Church, which is the oldest continuous place of worship in Manhattan and the second oldest public building in New York City."

"He has a street very close to Second Avenue," Juliet suddenly remembered. "Is it named for him or one of his descendants?"

"For him. The land covering Tenth Avenue between Second and Stuyvesant Street was purchased by Peter Stuyvesant in 1651 to enlarge his farm. There he built St. Mark's. Do you know New York?"

"I've been there a thousand times for work, but I don't know St. Mark's. I'll go there as soon as I get back to Manhattan. Does the current Bowery Street between Chinatown and Little Italy have anything to do with Great Bouwerie?"

"Yes, the land originally belonged to Stuyvesants. Bouwerie means cottage in Dutch, and the English called it Bowery. He also built a great wall to protect the settlement from Indian attacks and the neighboring populations. That became Wall Street. He built the governor's mansion on Whitehall Street, the original one that was more in the center of the island."

"A very proactive man, I see."

"There is the famous pear tree."

"What famous pear tree?"

"What are you doing here?" Suddenly, a man's powerful voice startled them from their chatter. Juliet stood up and turned to face him, putting herself on guard as Romeo jumped into Michiel's arms.

The huge guy, dressed in a suit and with very bad manners, entered the apartment and addressed them in a British accent.

Juliet didn't blink and folded her arms before looking him in the eye.

"Excuse me, who are you?"

"What are you doing here?"

"Good afternoon. My name is Juliet Miller, and this is Mr. Michiel Lezer. We are neighbors in the building and friends of Mrs. Audrey Stuyvesant, who is absent at the moment, as you can see. Your name is?"

"How did you get in?"

"With a key."

"Who provided you with a key?"

"She…" "Audrey…" They blurted in unison without looking at each other, and Juliet took a step and narrowed her eyes.

"Who are you? Please identify yourself."

"Lynch, Jack Lynch. I'm the real estate agent in charge of the property."

"Are you going to sell it?" Michiel asked, and the guy nodded, looking around. "Mrs. Stuyvesant hired you?"

"I would ask you to leave the apartment, please. We have to appraise it."

"Do you know where the owner is?" Michiel insisted, and Lynch turned away.

"I have no specific information about the owner. I am only in charge of selling the apartment."

"She didn't hire you, so who did? Could you provide us with a contact, please? We need to speak to Audrey."

"I can't give you any contacts."

"What if I want to buy the apartment?"

"Michiel," said Juliet, approaching him and grabbing his arm.

He hadn't noticed, but two more guys had appeared at the door. They were just as bad-tempered as the first one, and all the alarms went off in her mind.

She grabbed him firmly by the sleeve of his sweater and pulled him toward the exit. He resisted a little, but, realizing the situation, he followed her. The men stared at them until they stepped onto the landing, at which point the two guys entered the apartment and slammed the door in their faces.

"Juliet," he whispered, pointing at the door of his apartment. "Let's go to my apartment. Let's stay together until those people get out of there.

"What happened in there?" she asked in bewilderment as she followed him.

"I don't know, but at least I kept the photos of Audrey. Romeo helped me camouflage them."

CHAPTER SEVEN

Julia looked at the social media traffic report for one of her clients, most of which was controlled by a team of her company's advertising and community managers. She saw the trending topic for that morning, photos of one of their most famous international stars walking the streets of London with his new girlfriend.

"Fuck," she mumbled, seeing the repercussion of the news, the comments on Twitter or Instagram from the millions of fans who had not reacted well at all to the images. She was sorry for him. He was the most discreet guy in the world with his private life. Even more, she was sorry for his girlfriend, who was being trashed.

The comments were indescribable, mainly from women who felt betrayed by their idol as if he somehow belonged to them or owed them something. She read the note that Beatrice, the marketing management director, had enclosed on an attached sheet.

The advisable thing to do is to contain with silence. Officially, we will not comment, but if he wants to talk, let him talk. I don't think he deserves this kind of bashing. It is embarrassing.

They usually did not engage in absurd wars through social networks, in denial or defense. It was considered unnecessary and even vulgar, but she felt so bad for her actor, who was also a good friend, that she reached out to call him on the phone. Before she could do so, he called her cell phone.

"Hello, Henry. How are you?"

"Hi, Juliet. Have you seen the report and everything else?"

"Yes, congratulations on your girlfriend. What's her name?"

"Her name is Natalie. You've seen her. She's my physiotherapist. Listen," he added, clearing his throat uncomfortably.

Juliet kept silent.

"I've talked to Iona, and she thinks I should ignore everything these fucking photos have triggered. Ignore the negative reactions, but it's impossible for me. I've been putting up with digital harassment for centuries, being hated, loved, asked for children, threatened with rape, or getting locked up in a cell to be sexually abused. That is my daily bread, even in press conferences, in a premiere, or a TV interview. You are a witness, and you know that I always keep calm and respond with humor, but this time it is different because it is not about me. It is about my girl, who is an anonymous person."

"Of course."

"Who do these crazy bitches think they are, calling my girlfriend fat, a monster, a troll, and a bunch of other bullshit? Where's the sorority? What do they think, that I give a shit about their bullshit opinions?"

"It's a shame, and I'm sorry."

"What can I do? What do you advise me to do?"

"The agency's official response is to maintain our silence, but the director of marketing management and I will support you if you decide to fight back as you see fit. You have every right to do so."

"My initial impulse is to close all the official accounts and tell everyone to go fuck themselves, but before that, I'd like to do something other than a press release or an official defense. Natalie doesn't want to make things worse, and neither do I. What would you do?"

"Me?" She took a deep breath, gauging the playground that Instagram had become, and gave him her honest opinion. "I'd fuck it up a little bit."

"How?"

"Post a romantic picture with you and Natalie doing something cool, like having dinner in a nice place. In the kitchen of your house, maybe. I don't know…something idyllic like that, and in the text, confirm that yes, she is your girlfriend, that you are happy, that you think she is wonderful, and that you love her very much. Don't mention the messages and the embarrassing comments that are everywhere. You ignore them and slap them without hands."

"I think it's a great idea. Thank you, Juliet, you're the best," he said in a livelier voice. "Thank you so much, and anytime you want to, join us for dinner and bring your boyfriend."

"I still don't have a boyfriend, but I'll gladly join you for dinner."

"My goodness, girl, get a move on! I'll have to introduce you to someone proper."

"No, thanks. Let me take a break from screwing up."

"We'll see. Thanks again, and stay in touch."

She hung up, feeling terrible for poor Henry, who was nice and deserved to be happy with whomever he pleased. She emailed Beatrice to tell her about her talk with him and the advice she had given him. Then she went through the rest of the mail, and her mind flew to her latest obsession: the Stuyvesants in New York.

It had been four days since they had entered Audrey's apartment and been surprised by Jack Lynch and his friends.

Curiously, someone had once told her that "Jack Lynch" was the alias most often used by the CIA and the FBI to camouflage their agents. She had even read it in a script, and she and Michiel were convinced that this guy, the supposed real estate agent, was American, not British, much less an apartment salesman. They had put two and two together, and everything had fit.

They believed they were facing a mystery worthy of the CIA, and they needed to unravel it. Michiel was an interesting and restless guy. He had her fascinated and had managed to pull her out of her strict routine to push her to track down a mind-boggling mystery. He had spent the last few days researching Audrey's husband, Peter Gregory Stuyvesant III, and had found his pilot's card through the US Ministry of Defense and other official archives.

Peter Gregory Stuyvesant III was born in Manhattan, New York, in 1928. He attended Harvard College from 1945 to 1947, entered the prestigious West Point Academy in 1948, and the United States Air Force in 1950. There was no more public data, but they were still researching. She was jotting down hypotheses and Googling everything that popped into her head because, as was often the case with her, she was becoming obsessed and needed to find answers.

"Hello," she answered her cell phone without looking.

"This is Robert Whitehall, your building manager. Juliet Miller, what have you done?"

"Excuse me?"

"A Jack Lynch, who identified himself as Audrey Stuyvesant's real estate agent, has just left my office. He wanted to know the situation of the apartment, outstanding bills, etc., because he told me that they want to sell it, and he also told me that he caught his neighbors, that is, Michiel and you, searching everything. Weren't you going to be discreet?"

"We were discreet until that guy showed up out of nowhere with two bouncers and threw us out on the street. Don't worry. We told him that Audrey had given us the keys."

"Thank goodness."

"Did you ask him about Mrs. Stuyvesant? Did he tell you about her or where she is?"

"No, and he was quite rude. I warned him that I had an endless waiting list to rent something on the Barbican Estate and that if the apartment was going to be put up for sale, I'd buy it myself because people would kill for a property there. He didn't even flinch, just turned and walked away."

"It's all so weird."

"Be that as it may, it's none of our business, and don't try to enter the property again, or your hair will fall out."

"We won't, don't worry."

"Okay, honey, we'll talk. Take care of yourself."

"You too, and thanks for calling. See you later."

"Hello, beautiful!"

Someone greeted her in Spanish from the doorway. She jumped up, hung up her cell phone, and smiled.

"Damian Hastings, what are you doing here? Were we supposed to meet?"

"No, Juliet, we didn't have a date. It would be very disappointing if you had forgotten about a date with me, you know?"

"I'm sorry, I don't even know what day it is. How are you?"

The talented and gifted man, whom she had been with for two years, hugged her to his chest and then looked at her.

"You promised to call me for dinner. That was more than a fortnight ago at the theater, and I'm still waiting."

"I'm sorry, I've been busy."

"You haven't moved from London, Andrea told me."

"No, but I've had other things to do besides being a little tired and being with my cat. What are you doing here?"

"I don't know. Iona called me to tell me about a secret project. She didn't tell you anything?"

"No, and that's strange." She frowned because he was her client, not the boss's, and looked toward Iona's office. "Come on.

I'll walk you to her office, and we'll find out what this is all about."

"Okay." He grabbed her by the neck to pull her into the hallway. "Your little friend, Caden, sent me an invitation to his book launch."

"Really?"

"Really, through Instagram."

"Did he tell you he was my friend?"

"Of course, I know him from you, and he reminded me who he was. It's okay. Are you going? We can go together."

"I'm not going. I don't care about their stories."

"I'm glad, but I'm still going. He has invited many people from the agency, and he will have an open bar."

"From this agency?" she exclaimed, indignant, and Damian laughed.

"Yes, from this agency. Ask around, and you'll see."

"Fuck, the guy's so two-faced."

They arrived at Iona's office, and Fabio jumped to his feet when he saw them both there. First, she looked at them a little uncomfortably. Finally, she walked over to speak to them in a low voice.

"What are you two doing here? I only summoned you, Damian."

"Yes, but he is my client, and if he is called for a business meeting, I come."

"It's not a business meeting, my dear. It's a personal matter. Didn't you read the email all the way through, Damian?"

"Yes, but I don't see why I can't stop by and say hello to Juliet and have her walk me over here. What's the mystery?"

"I did not want to involve more people. Come on, you can come in. Juliet, I'll buy you a coffee."

"I can't. Damian, I'm in my office, if you need anything, call me. Goodbye."

She said goodbye to both of them, fearing that Iona would ask him to accompany her to some event or on a vacation in the Bahamas, but she concluded that Damian was old enough to face Iona and fifty like her and returned to her office thinking about Caden and his lies. She stood in front of Andrea's desk.

"Andrea, did you get an invitation from LOML?" she asked directly, and Andrea nodded. "I can't believe it. Damian says he's written to him and some other people here. Could you find out who they are? Maybe this guy hacked my address book. If so, I'm not amused."

"Caden?" Juliet nodded and looked at her vibrating cell phone, saw that it was Michiel, and greeted him while entering her office and closing the door.

"*Goede morgen!*"

"You speak Dutch? You kept it to yourself!"

"Just hello, but I'm in the process of learning more. How are you doing? Any news, my dear Watson?" she joked.

"Yes, I achieved something extraordinary at Chelsea City Hall."

"Really? Do tell!"

"I have a copy of the marriage certificate of Peter Gregory Stuyvesant III, born in Manhattan, New York, April 20, 1928, to Miss Audrey Rose Glenn, born January 18, 1938, in Hampstead, London. They were married on April 10, 1956."

"She was very young."

"Eighteen years old. The photo we have from New York is dated four months before the wedding when she was still seventeen."

"Maybe they met in New York."

"She told me in detail how they had met at the cinema in Leicester Square, where she worked as a ticket-taker."

"Yes, but she also told us details about her husband without mentioning that he was an American or a pilot, so maybe she lied. Maybe she went to New York and met him there, at the box office of a movie theater in Times Square," Juliet replied.

"Which makes me wonder again. Why would she lie to us when she used to repeat that you and I were the only friends she had in the world? We will have to investigate further."

"About that. I thought I'd ask my brother James for help. He's a journalist for *The Guardian.*"

"You have a brother at *The Guardian?* How interesting."

"Yes, he's very interesting. He's an investigative journalist, and I thought we could ask him to help us find out more information about Audrey and her husband. He has more means and contacts than we do."

"I would prefer not to involve the press in this."

"It's not the press; it's my brother. If I ask for discretion, he will give it. He's a very reliable guy."

"I do not doubt that he is a thorough and reliable person. It's just that I think we're getting into an important story, and I'd like to keep it private until we can get it in order, all right?"

"Okay," she answered. She was offended by his doubts, but she didn't want to get into an argument. They were not solving the Watergate case. It was just a matter of reconciling the past and present of a nice neighbor they both knew. It was not worth getting upset over.

"I have nothing against your brother, Juliet," said Michiel after a few seconds of silence. "On the contrary, if he is your brother, I'm sure he's a great and reliable guy. But I think this is a personal matter, and before going to a professional, we should continue investigating on our own. I think it will be fun."

"If the certificate says Audrey was born in Hampstead," she said, ignoring the comment, "maybe there is someone who knows her there. Maybe she has family or friends in the neighborhood. We could look at the Municipal Board. Maybe she has moved there, and we are being foolish with all this."

"It's a good idea." He offered, "I'll look it up online. With any luck, we can order a birth certificate to see her old address, or we can look up the Glenns in the area in the phone book and call them."

"Perfect."

"Great, I'll do that. You stick with the Stuyvesants in New York. If we can get the affiliation with Gregory, we'll make some more progress."

"Great. What are you doing this weekend?"

"I'm going to Willesden. It's my mother's birthday. Why?"

"Congratulations to your mother. I was telling you because I have Daniel, and I wanted to introduce him to you. He is obsessed with meeting Romeo."

"I'll be back on Sunday. If I'm early, I'll give you a call."

"Great, we'll keep in touch. *Doei!*"

He said goodbye in Dutch.

She took a deep breath, looked at everything she had pending, and concentrated on her work.

CHAPTER EIGHT

Juliet rushed to the Red Lyon, her parents' favorite pub in Willesden, where her father had organized the birthday lunch for her mother. Just outside the door, she stopped to read a message from Henry, her actor client, who sent her the romantic photo he had posted on his social networks with his girl. It confirmed that she was his girlfriend, that he was very happy, and that she was wonderful.

Thank you so much for everything, Juliet.

He added a bunch of smiley emoticons, and she replied with just as many before entering the pub with a firm step and finding herself face to face with her brother. He was running after his sons, the twins James and Harry, who, at three years old, were real whirlwinds.

"Mother of God, where are you little demons going?" he asked them in Spanish. They stopped dead in their tracks to hug his legs.

"Hello, Aunt Juliet. Are you here with Romeo?"

"No, sweethearts. I didn't bring him because I came by train, and he doesn't like the train. You have to come to see him at my house. Okay?"

"Okay!" They screamed, turned, and raced back inside the pub to lose themselves between the older boys' legs. Juliet looked at her brother. He had huge dark circles under his eyes, and she reached out and hugged him.

"What's up, Jamie? You look tired."

"What do you think? I don't know how long since I've slept through the night."

"The joys of parenthood, right?"

"Juliet!" Siobhan, her sister-in-law, came up to her and hugged her too, looking her up and down. "How pretty. Who made it?"

"From Zara. How are you?"

"Has James told you that we have an appointment in a fortnight with the notary about the will?" she blurted. Juliet took a deep breath. "We shouldn't keep putting it off, and I'd like to know if you're prepared to be the twins' guardian in case we… you know. I don't want to press, but…"

"Honey, let her breathe, will you?" Her brother grabbed his wife by the neck and kissed her forehead. "She just got off the train, and she'll want to have a drink. Then we'll talk."

"Okay, I'm sorry. I'm just a little paranoid."

"Don't worry."

Juliet stroked his arm and said nothing more because she was not yet ready to. Being the first choice to act as the legal guardian for their two children in the event of the death of James and Siobhan was an immense compliment but also a tremendous responsibility. Considering that at the age of thirty-one, she did not have a very stable life and showed no signs of getting one and that she could hardly take good care of her cat because she spent her life traveling, that decision was colossal. So, she was thinking about it a little more than usual, although, deep down, she knew she would say yes in the end because very few people would deny their family such a thing.

She smiled at them both and walked away from them, looking for her mother. She located her and hugged her and presented her with a gift. Her mother thanked her and asked her to take care of her grandmother, who was grumbling in a corner because she neither understood nor enjoyed English pubs. Juliet nodded and went to look for her grandmother while greeting and hugging friends and neighbors who had gathered there to honor the birthday girl, who was looking great, happy and smiling as always.

Her mother was like that. She shone because she was a beautiful and very loving woman, and that day even more, because she was turning sixty-two in "the best moment of her life," she said, and she was delighted to have so many people to attend and greet, among them her two grandchildren who had her crazy with happiness.

She found her grandmother in a booth opening a lunch box. "Yaya, what are you doing?" she asked. Her grandmother frowned and gestured for her to sit down.

"Sit down and eat. You're very skinny, and no wonder, with the food in this country. Do you ever cook anything proper, daughter?"

"Better not ask. Did you bring an omelet to a pub, Yaya?"

"Yes. I wasn't going to eat pickles and refried potatoes," she replied in her Cádiz accent and showed her a second bag full of croquettes. "They are ham. Your father and Jamie have already eaten a dozen. Eat them before your sister comes and wipes out the rest."

"Is Sarah here yet?"

"Yes, and she has brought a handsome guy. He's blond and blue-eyed like her. They look like two cherubs."

"Oh, my goodness! It must be the famous Jonathan, the one from Newcastle."

"I don't know where he's from, but he's very tasty. You didn't bring anyone?"

"Who would you have me bring, Yaya? Except Romeo, and he doesn't like to ride the train."

Her yaya gave her a questioning look and Juliet squinted, then popped a croquette into her mouth. She swallowed slowly, waiting for the usual speech, but against all odds, her grandmother sighed and set about cutting her omelet into perfect squares.

"What about that tall guy from Australia, Caden or Kayden or whatever his name is?"

"It's spelled Caden, pronounced 'Kayden.' He is no longer a friend of mine."

"He came to your mother's birthday last year and to your brother's birthday."

"Don't remind me. It hurts my soul to have introduced him to you and brought him to Willesden."

"The kid was nice."

"Sure, for a while, but I assure you that by now, he doesn't even remember Willesden and how well he was treated here."

"We treated him well, as we treat everyone."

"Exactly, but there comes a time when the bag breaks, and you get tired of being shat on."

"Has he behaved badly to you, my life?"

"Actually, no. It's my fault for putting him on a pedestal and thinking he cared about me. Can we talk about something else? When are you going back to Spain?"

"Your mother used to tell me that you spent the whole day lowering the moon and doing favors for him."

"Thank God he didn't ask me for a kidney because if he had asked me, I'd have given it to him." She shut up, feeling like an idiot again because she had behaved like a complete jerk with Caden. She looked at her grandmother with a shrug. "It doesn't matter now."

"It's his loss, my girl, because there is no one better and prettier than you," she told Juliet with conviction.

"That's because you look at me with good eyes, Yaya."

"Maybe you should do like your cousin Triana and get a girl-friend. They're doing great, and they're going to look for one of those sperm banks to have a baby."

"Oh, Yaya, what a heart you have." She sat up to kiss her. "Don't worry about me. I don't need a partner to be well. In fact, I'm great. I love my life just the way it is."

"You're right. You go about your business. You have a very nice job."

"I'm going to get something to drink. What can I get you?"

"Nothing, honey. Jamie brought me a beer a while ago, and I don't want any more."

"Okay, I'll be right back."

She left her there, quietly eating her omelet, walked over to the bar, and ordered a soft drink, waving at the bartender, who was the son of the pub owner and a former high school class-mate. He was like a train, she thought inadvertently, giving him a full sweep and remembering that Bill Richardson, the bartender, had been another of her countless platonic loves. She sighed, recognizing that she had spent her whole life missing the mark.

She had always had a thing for the unattainable, which a woman psychologist she had visited when she was in college had called an "unconscious attitude of self-sabotage." Dr. Hill had told her to her face that she was self-sabotaging by choosing impossi-bilities since, in reality, she was terrified of entering into a stable, adult relationship. She had left the office shocked and offended and had never seen her again, even though, deep down, she knew the doctor was right.

"How's life, Juliet?" Bill Richardson asked, looking at her with his big green eyes. She smiled at him. "I hear you work with a lot of celebrities."

"I'm just another little worker in an actors' agency. How about you? How about Jennifer?"

"We have separated. I am free as the wind."

"Ah, gee, I didn't know that. I'm sorry."

"Maybe you and I could catch up. I've always liked you a lot."

"I'm sorry?" She blinked, blushing up to her ears, but before she could answer, her sister came screaming up to hug her from behind.

"Juliet, how I've been looking forward to seeing you!" Her sister turned her around and kept hugging her and jumping up and down until Juliet pulled her away to look at her face. "Jo, how beautiful you look. You get more beautiful every day."

"When did you arrive? Are you staying for many days?"

"We're staying the weekend at Mum and Dad's house. Look, this is Jon. Jon, this is my beautiful, brilliant, and successful older sister, Juliet."

"Hi, nice to meet you. I'm the middle sister," she joked, greeting the famous Jonathan. He was in the military like Sarah and looked a lot like her, blond with blue eyes, as her grandmother had pointed out.

He stayed chatting with them for a while, catching up, until his father appeared and joined the conversation. Thus it went for hours, seeing a succession of faces and smiles, hugging and kissing many people until, on the verge of succumbing to boredom, she received a message that saved her from being overwhelmed and allowed her to go out into the street to read it in peace.

A friend of mine at the Dutch embassy in New York has obtained a complete family tree of the original Stuyvesants, from Governor Peter Stuyvesant to the present day. There is a Peter Gregory Stuyvesant III born in Manhattan on April 20, 1928. It looks like he's ours. I'll talk to you later. I hope you're having a good time. Congratulations to your mother.

She was delighted to read a message without any typos or abbreviations, and she called him back after looking at the time.

She had been in the pub almost all day, talking nonstop and smiling. She thought that, with any luck, she could slip out at that moment to get back to London in time to see Michiel if he didn't have other plans with Laura and her son.

"How are you, my dear Watson? What news!"

"What's up? What are you doing on the phone? Is the celebration over?"

"I've been here since noon. I don't know if it's over for the others, but it is for me. I'm going to call an Uber to go back to Barbican right away. Maybe we can meet up, and you can tell me in detail about your friend's discovery. By the way, how did you get the family tree?"

"It was provided by a member of the New York Historical Society. It has been secret since the 1950s for security reasons, so he couldn't find it in any public archives."

"It looks like Peter Gregory III is our guy, doesn't it?"

"I would bet on that, yes. It would be too much of a coincidence otherwise."

"No record of Audrey?"

"No, and that is the most interesting thing about all this. Peter Gregory Stuyvesant III, firstborn of Peter Gregory II and Candace Stuyvesant, disappears from the family tree in 1956 when in theory, he marries Audrey Glenn in Chelsea. There is no notation of his death. He simply ceases to appear and is never spoken of again. The official heir of this marriage becomes Charles Irving, who was the fourth child and second son."

"It keeps getting better."

"Are you coming now?"

"Yes, I'll say goodbye and leave."

"Okay. Daniel and I will make you dinner if you want, and you can bring Romeo."

"Great, thank you very much. I'll see you in a little while."

CHAPTER NINE

They cleared the dining room table, put the dishes in the dishwasher, and continued chatting about everything while Michiel pulled his notes on the Audrey case, as he called it, from a shelf and laid out before her eyes the very long family tree of the Stuyvesants of New York.

Folios and folios of names and relationships beginning with Peter Stuyvesant, the last general manager of the Dutch West India Company in Manhattan and last governor of New Amsterdam, and his wife, Judith Bayard, with whom he had only one son. Nicholas William Stuyvesant was born in 1648 and married Maria Beckman.

From then on, everything began to grow, divide, and bifurcate until it became a tangle of husbands, wives, and children that reached into the twenty-first century. They were interested in the first half of the twentieth century, specifically 1928 when Peter Gregory Stuyvesant III was born in Manhattan, the first-born son of Peter Gregory and Candance Stuyvesant and supposed husband of their dear neighbor, the lovely Mrs. Audrey Stuyvesant.

"This is incredible. I have never seen such a large family tree.

At least, one that is not royal." She ran her finger over the papers, and out of the corner of her eye, she noticed her research partner was looking at them with the same affection. He was as excited as she was. She was very glad to have left the celebration at the Willesden pub to come home and spend the rest of the afternoon with him and his son, who was a very nice boy.

"I've already put on my pajamas and brushed my teeth. Can I play an online game with Marcus before bed?" asked Daniel at his back, and they both jumped.

Daniel, who was a very handsome, lanky boy with the same hair as his father, put his hands on his hips and waited with raised eyebrows for his father's answer. Michiel looked at his watch and began speaking to him in Dutch, though he suddenly remembered her and very politely switched to English.

"Okay, you have one hour to play. Now say good night to Juliet and Romeo."

"Can Romeo come to my room, Juliet?"

"I wouldn't force him," she replied. "But if he follows you, that's fine with me."

"Thank you, good night. Let's go, Romeo," he said confidently. Her cat, the most independent feline in the universe, got off the sofa and happily followed him to his room. Juliet watched him and then looked at Michiel, who was laughing his head off.

"It's the first time I've seen him obey! The first time!"

"You seem to like my house. Would you like a glass of wine, tea, or something stronger?"

"Tea would be nice, thank you."

She watched him fiddle in the kitchen and then admired the living room, which was the same size as hers and full of books. It was very nice but austere, but it had hundreds of books and vinyl records, a beautiful wooden desk by the terrace, and an electric guitar in one corner, as well as a couple of paintings that looked like the real thing.

He was a guy with very good taste, Michiel Lezer, she

thought, picking up one of the books that rested on a low table next to the most comfortable sofa in the room.

"Have you lived here since you came to London?"

"Yes, from the beginning. It was rented to me by a friend who went to live in Australia. I was very lucky."

"How is it that we never met, living so close to each other?"

"We did meet several times, Juliet. I knew perfectly well who you were—Audrey's neighbor to the right. She kept talking about you."

"Really? I'm not aware of..."

"You don't usually enter the building from the hallway that suits me best, and I've always seen you in a hurry, focused on your phone or your stuff, so I guess you never noticed me."

"Wow, what a bad neighbor I've been. I'm sorry."

"Well, that's settled." He held the cup of tea out to her. "I'm sure Audrey will be delighted to know that we've become friends because of her."

"I'm sure she will. She also told me a lot about you. Just a moment." She looked at her cell phone and, seeing that her mother was calling, she apologized. "Sorry, I have to answer it. Hi, Mum, what's up?"

"Billy Richardson asked me for your phone number. Can I give it to him? Your brother says he doesn't like him, but I think he's a handsome boy."

"I don't know. Okay, why not? But tell him that I'm always on the road and that maybe I can't answer him the first time."

"Okay, honey. Tomorrow we're having lunch at the center with your sister and her boyfriend. Don't forget that."

"I won't forget. I'll see you later." She hung up and turned her attention to Michiel, who was watching her with a smile. She took a sip of tea and gestured for him to speak. "What's wrong?"

"Do you speak Spanish?"

"My mother is Spanish, from La Línea de la Concepción, province of Cádiz, and at home, we only speak Spanish."

"Repeat the name of the city, please."

"La Línea de la Concepción is in the province of Cádiz, in Andalusia."

"I know. I know where it is. I love to listen to Spanish. I think it's a beautiful language. It's very musical."

"That's nice."

"Have you lived in Spain?"

"Yes. I was born in Gibraltar, next to La Línea de la Concepción. My father is English, and he met my mother there. She worked on the Rock, they fell in love, got married, and my siblings and I were born there. Then, when I was about four years old, they moved back to London, and we stayed here."

"Is he in the military?"

"No, civil servant. He worked for the Ministry of the Interior. He was posted to Gibraltar at a very young age. He was assigned for two years, but he met my mother and stayed there. He loves Spain."

"Doesn't an Andalusian woman miss the sun and the heat, living in London?"

"No. My mother is very determined, intelligent, and strong. She adapted immediately. Now she is more from Willesden than anywhere else. She raised us here, founded a catering company, and has hundreds of friends. They go back to Cádiz a lot because they have a little house in Puerto de Santa Maria, so she doesn't miss anything. I've never heard her complain. She only misses her mother, but she brings her over whenever she can. Right now, my grandmother is here."

"I love Spain. I've been going there on vacation since I was seventeen."

"Ibiza and the Balearic Islands?"

"Yes, and many other places. I love Barcelona, Madrid, Granada, all the south."

"Okay, I'm glad. Most of the people I know go to Ibiza or

Mallorca and don't move from the islands. They have too much fun to go to Madrid to see the Prado Museum."

"I will be an exception because I have been to the Prado Museum a dozen times, the Reina Sofia, and the Sagrada Familia in Barcelona."

"I'm glad to hear it." She smiled at him and returned to the table where they had the Stuyvesant family tree, then sat down. "How is Laura? I thought I would find her here."

"She never comes if Daniel is here."

"Ah, normal."

"Normal?"

"I don't know. I have no idea, but I know a lot of divorced people who don't introduce their new partners to their children. I guess that's the norm."

"First, I'm not divorced. Daniel's mother and I never got married. We never even lived together. Second, Laura is not my exclusive partner. If she doesn't come when Daniel is here, it's not because she doesn't know him. It's because he dislikes her."

"Exclusive partner?" She smiled because she used to hear that from her friends under thirty or from people in her work environment who were super modern, but never from a full-fledged gentleman, a primary school teacher and the father of an eight-year-old. She laughed with a shake of her head.

"Laura and I have a sporadic open relationship. We both see other people as well."

"Have you signed up for polyamory?"

"I wouldn't call it 'polyamory' because it has nothing to do with love. It's about sex and free and uncompromising relationships. I think it's the healthiest and most honest way of relating."

"How does one arrive at this type of relationship?"

"In my case, when I entered college."

"So, practically your entire adult life?"

"Yes."

"Even with the mother of your child?"

"She and I were close friends when we decided to have Daniel, but parenthood didn't make us a stable couple, and neither of us was up for it."

"Hmm."

She turned her attention back to the family tree, concluding that he was light-years away from her way of looking at life, but she liked him just the same. She continued scanning the documents in silence until she felt his eyes on her for too long and had no choice but to look him in the face.

"What about you, Juliet?"

"About my relationships? I'm quite conventional. I believe in commitment, fidelity, and loyalty. I believe in the loves of William Shakespeare and Jane Austen. However, all other options seem great to me, even open relationships, although I would be unable to cope with them."

"What a pity."

"Why?"

"Because you just closed all possibilities with you."

"Very funny." She laughed and pointed at the papers on the table. "Can I see Audrey and Gregory's marriage certificate? I'd like to look at the address they put down as a reference."

"The address is for a hotel in Mayfair. I checked, and it no longer exists." He got up to look through his papers for the certificate and glanced sideways at her. "Now that you know us a little better, are you going to tell me how you started working for a prestigious actors' agency?"

"Really?"

"You promised."

"Wow, you don't miss a beat."

"No."

"All right then. When I entered university, I started studying English because I had always dreamed of being a writer, but King's College also has a very good drama program, and, encouraged by my classmates, my family, etc., I started taking drama classes. I didn't give up my career, fortunately, but acting is like a drug. Although I had no talent at all, I kept dabbling as a stand-in, as the last actress without a line or whatever, until one fine day, an audition was called for a summer job at Shakespeare's Globe. Imagine! It was a dream.

"I went there, and while we waited for the test, I dedicated myself to giving water, candy, and comfort to my classmates and all the people who swarmed nervously in the waiting room until it was my turn. I entered that rehearsal room full of people, and they asked me to read my text. At that moment, the tragedy unfolded."

"No," Michiel whispered, and she nodded.

"I opened my mouth. After a very long pause, not a syllable came out, so I burst into tears. I cried so much that they took me out to the Globe courtyard. That was the end of my acting career."

"I'm so sorry."

"Thank you, but now comes the good part because, as my grandmother says, 'When God closes a door, he always opens a window.' That happened to me because, among all those people organizing the audition was Iona McCameron, the most important actors' agent in the UK and maybe the whole world. She came up to me, waited for me to calm down, then said, "You'll never be an actress, honey, but I've been watching you, and I like what I see. I like you. If you don't have anything to do this summer, come to my agency, and I'll give you a job."

"Wow!"

"I swear, it was a miracle. Over the years, I learned that she is like that. That she does these inexplicable things and changes people's lives."

"What happened then?"

"The next day, after staying up all night, embarrassed by what I had been through, I showed up at Shaughnessy & McCameron, prepared to be the best scholar of the century. Iona interviewed me personally. She talked to me for a long time. She loved that I was studying philology and that I was bilingual.

"She repeated that I would never be a good actress but that she was sure I would understand actors. That I seemed very empathetic and that something told her we would work very well together. So it has been. This year I have been with her for ten years, and I still think that that afternoon, as they say in Spain, 'God came to see me.'"

"It's a beautiful story. Not dishonorable, as you told me."

"It's a little embarrassing. Every time I go to the Globe, I remember what a fool I made of myself, and I want to die."

"How old were you?"

"Twenty-one."

"What exactly do you do at the agency? What does your job consist of?"

"I started as Iona's assistant and the go-to girl for everything. Then I went on to read scripts and cover for her on trips. I got a master's and a Ph.D. in a couple of years by observing how she works. After two years, I started to be assigned to new actors, and they let me supervise small projects.

"Anyway, it's a very long story, but today I have my own portfolio of clients. When necessary, I travel with them, I read the scripts they are offered, and I advise them. I'm aware of auditions, casting calls, shoots, rehearsals, press, and their life in general. Most of them have personal assistants, but they always end up calling their agent, says my boss, and that's the truth."

"You take care of the stars."

"Less than five percent of actors manage to become superstars. The rest fall by the wayside or work in huge film or television casts, make up almost anonymous theater casts, or do publicity. I know the situation is not the same as stonecutting or working in a mine or a hospital, but it is a very difficult profession, very hard, because it plays with emotions, with self-esteem, and brutally and continuously judges those who get into it. We just accompany them along the way and try to smooth it for them. We can't get them all the role of a lifetime or transform them into Brad Pitt or Kate Winslet, but at least we work hard with them to try to make the right choice. To try to get that big break, and once they get it, we get to work again to help them get it right."

"You love your job."

"The truth is, I do."

"Do the actors and actresses appreciate that work?"

"My experience tells me they do. I can't complain. I still keep in touch with most of those who started working with me and who, today, are the great stars in the firmament, as well as with those who didn't make it. The truth is that they are usually very vulnerable and very sensitive people, and bonds are built more easily than in other professions. There are all kinds, but I'm not one of those who bothers to think about whether they appreciate my work. There will be people who love us and a lot of people who hate us. It's an occupational hazard."

"What about being a writer?"

"I'm still writing, but my energy for the last few years has not been focused on writing a novel but on writing a good screenplay."

"The Audrey case could be made into a great movie."

"I keep thinking about it."

They had been talking for a long time. Romeo had come back to the living room and climbed into her lap to sleep. She thought it was time to say goodbye and go home.

"I don't know what it is about you that I can talk for hours and hours and I don't get any sleep, but it's getting very late, and Romeo and I need to go to bed."

"Of course." He waited for her to take Romeo in her arms, picked up her keys, and walked her to her door. He stayed until she opened it and turned on the light, then paused.

"I'm serious about the script. I think you should seriously consider writing Audrey and Gregory's story."

"The bulk of the research is being done by you, and in my world, these things are sacred. You wouldn't mind if I..."

"Of course, I wouldn't mind. On the contrary, there is still a lot of work to do. We have to continue investigating until we close the circle and get answers, but it seems to me that you already have enough material to start working."

"I would love to."

"Then it's all yours. Now to rest, and if you need me, whistle!"

CHAPTER TEN

"Juliet, Phillip Glenn is calling you. He says it's personal."

"Phillip Glenn?" She looked at Andrea, puzzled.

"Yes. He says you left a message on his answering machine last week."

"Oh, my goodness! Yes, of course. Phillip Glenn. Put him on, please."

"Line one," Andrea whispered.

Juliet sat up in the chair, remembering that this gentleman, Phillip Glenn, was one of the twenty-five people with the Glenn surname, residents of Hampstead, whom she had called over the past two weeks to ask if they were related to Audrey Stuyvesant.

"Mr. Glenn, good morning. This is Juliet Miller. Thank you very much for calling.

"Are you looking for Audrey Rose Glenn?"

"Yes, she was my neighbor, and we are trying to locate her."

"Born on January 18, 1938?" He continued to speak, and she stood up.

"Yes, exactly."

"Is she still alive?"

"Do you know her?"

"I think so. She was my father's little sister, but the family hasn't heard from her for decades."

"Are you sure?"

Her heart started pounding, and she grabbed her cell phone, intending to call Michiel, but at that hour, he was at school and teaching classes. She gave up and calmly waited for the man, who had the voice of a very old person, to continue talking.

"According to the information you left on my answering machine, I think it's my aunt. My father died last year, but my mother was very close to Audrey. So, she's still alive?"

"We haven't seen her for two months. Apparently, she moved suddenly. That's why we are trying to locate her, but until two months ago, she lived in Barbican Estate."

"Wow."

"So, you don't know anything about her either?"

"No. My mother says they stopped seeing her in the 1950s when she disappeared with her American husband."

"Disappeared?"

"He vanished. My father always said the husband was hiding something. His last name was Stuy or something like that."

"Stuyvesant."

"That's right, Stuyvesant, but my mother swears that before long, they changed their last name."

"We know her as Audrey Stuyvesant, but if she had changed her last name, how strange!"

"Look, I don't know what happened. All my life, I've heard about Aunt Audrey as a mystery. I was born in 1952, and shortly after that, she left London, so I didn't know her personally."

"Mr. Glenn, I don't want to abuse your kindness, but do you think you could talk to your mother about Audrey? We have some pictures and memories of her."

"I'll ask her. Wait a moment." He went away from the handset. Juliet began to hyperventilate, and when he returned, he was clear and concise. "Miss Miller, my mother is crazy to talk about

Audrey, but she is eighty-eight years old, and I don't know if it is good for her. However, if you promise it will be a short talk, you can come to my house this afternoon at about three o'clock, and we'll receive you."

"Thank you very much. I give you my word of honor that I won't be more than half an hour."

"All right. Write down the directions."

She hung up, very excited, and the first thing she did was text Michiel to tell him the news. Then she canceled everything she had for the afternoon and tried to resume work with some normality until he called her, just as excited about the news as she was.

"I had to sit down. I can't believe it, Juliet."

"Me neither. I'm still shaking."

"If they give us so little time, the best thing to do is to bring some prepared questions."

"Can you come with me?"

"I wouldn't let you go to a strange house alone, even if that man says he's Audrey's nephew. I'll meet you at Hampstead, shall I?"

"Great, I'll wait for you at the door. I'll send you the address."

Phillip Glenn's big house in the beautiful neighborhood of Hampstead was very nice. A typical English red brick house with white windows, black iron railings, a little garden, and a dark, tiled roof. A real luxury, she thought as soon as she got out of the cab because everybody knew that Hampstead was one of the most expensive neighborhoods in London and Europe, and if you had such a property there, things were going very well for you. Personalities like Lord Byron, Charles Dickens, Robert Louis Stevenson, Agatha Christie, and Elizabeth Taylor were born or lived in Hampstead. She fidgeted nervously, waiting for Michiel, who appeared in an Uber five minutes later, wearing his worn jeans and flannel shirt, but with a very nice blazer and polished shoes.

He smiled at her, and, without speaking, they approached Mr. Glenn's door. Juliet rang the doorbell and, a few eternal minutes later, it was opened by an older man who was dressed very neatly. He took off his glasses to look them up and down.

"Miss Miller? I didn't know you would be accompanied."

"Mr. Glenn? Good afternoon. This is Michiel."

"Come in, come in," he ordered, turning away from the door to let them in.

Juliet walked down a carpeted hallway, feeling Michiel's safe, protective presence clinging to her back. For a second, she thanked God he was there because the house was a dark and sinister mausoleum. They didn't stop until they reached a large, book-filled room overlooking a wonderful back garden.

"Mum, the young lady I told you about has arrived with her husband."

"No," Juliet managed to whisper, but Michiel stopped her by putting a hand on her waist. He stepped forward and greeted the venerable old woman, who was watching TV in her warmest clothes, with the sweetest of his smiles.

"Good afternoon, Mrs. Glenn. Nice to meet you. My name is Michiel, and this is Juliet. Thank you so much for seeing us so quickly."

"Delighted!" she exclaimed enthusiastically and pointed to a double sofa in front of her, turned off the television with the remote control, and then turned to her son. "Phillip, please order tea. I told Doris to have it ready. Would you like a cup of tea?"

"Of course. Thank you very much."

They sat next to each other and looked puzzled before Mrs. Glenn spoke to them again.

"What a beautiful couple you make!" she commented, observing them with great attention.

Juliet was speechless, but Michiel reached out and took her hand. He stroked her fingers and, for a split second, she forgot everything—why she was there, who these people were, and what their names were—because the soft, warm touch of that big, manly hand sent a sharp and very pleasant electric shock through her body.

"Thank you very much. How are you, Mrs. Glenn?" Michiel asked calmly, and she smiled.

"I am very happy to receive visitors who talk to me about Audrey. It has been extraordinary to hear about her. She left about sixty years ago, and we never heard from her again."

"Do you know why she left?"

"Because she married an American who, from the very beginning, made her half-stoned."

"Excuse me?" Juliet asked, regaining control of her actions, and the lady looked at her with surprised eyes. "Didn't you know Gregory?"

"No. When we got to know her, she had been widowed. Very recently, but she was alone. That must be why she returned to London, because of her husband's death. Did they have children?"

"No, unfortunately, they had no children. As far as we know, she had been living in London for a long time, at least twenty years, in his apartment in the Barbican Estate."

"The Barbican Estate? That hideous mass where the cultural center is?

"Exactly."

"It doesn't suit him at all." She paused as her son came in with the tea service and concentrated on pouring the cups. Since Juliet was still holding onto Michiel's hand, she let go.

"Audrey was always a rebel. Her parents and my late husband, who was older than her, never managed to bring her to heel. At sixteen, she ran away from home because she didn't want to study, and my in-laws wouldn't let her go back, so she settled down to live in some dingy boarding house in the city center and started working as a box-office girl in a cinema in Leicester Square. An embarrassment to the family. My father-in-law was a very respected man in London, you know. He had a printing press that didn't stop working even during the war."

"The business is still going," Phillip Glenn commented, but his mother motioned for him to shut up.

"I would go to see Audrey at her work, and we would go out for coffee or a walk because I felt sorry for her and I loved her very much. One day, she introduced me to that Yankee, Gregory Stuyvesant, who took a fancy to her. So much so that he took her to New York."

"That was 1955," Michiel said.

"Yes, that was because I was pregnant with Billy, my second son. Phillip would have been about three years old."

She squinted her eyes. "Yes, it was 1955, and only a few months later, she called me and told me that she was pregnant. She said she was in London, that she had married Gregory in a civil ceremony in Chelsea, and she wanted to say goodbye to me because they were going to live in the Antipodes."

"Australia or New Zealand?" Juliet looked at Michiel because she hadn't told them that, and he stroked the back of her hand with his thumb.

"I do not know. I could not delve into the question because I could not see her. I had just given birth and had no one to leave the children with. She didn't want to come here, and I never saw her again."

"No news?"

"Yes, she sent me two very strange letters, but I never saw her in person again."

"Why were they strange, Mum?" her son wanted to know.

"Because his name was no longer Stuyvesant, it was now Mc-something. He explained to me that they had changed the last name for security because Gregory worked for the US government in a top-secret position, and they were living incognito."

"Good God." Phillip Glenn snorted, got up, and left them alone.

"We didn't know that," said Michiel. He let go of her hand to take out some notes he had in his jacket pocket. Juliet suddenly felt like an orphan and wanted to grab him again, but she didn't. She concentrated on Mrs. Glenn, who was a very beautiful and elegant woman. "We know Audrey married Gregory on April 10, 1956, and that his name was actually Peter Gregory Stuyvesant III. Juliet and I believe that he was from one of the wealthiest families in New York. She didn't tell you any of that?"

"When she started dating him, she bragged that he was a good boy from Manhattan, but suddenly she didn't want to talk about it anymore. He controlled her and wouldn't let her talk about anything. He was very handsome and very polite, but you could tell that he was a domineering, manipulative guy. If you knew him, you'd know what I'm talking about. He was overwhelming like many Americans, you know? She was very young, and she respected him so much, loved him so much, that I even thought she was afraid of him or his family, but this is my perception. I cannot assure you of anything."

"Didn't he ever tell you anything about what he did in New York when he was there in 1955?"

"Nothing, not a word."

"You don't have those letters he sent you from the Antipodes?"

"No, that was a long time ago. Can you tell me why you are so interested in Audrey?"

"During the months of the harshest confinement, we shared a lot of time with her. We brought her groceries, we had dinner or shared a chat and coffee across our terraces, and we were both very close to her," Juliet explained. "Two months ago, she disappeared overnight. She didn't say goodbye to us, left no clues, and left all her things inside her house."

"We are very worried about her and are just trying to find out what has happened to her," Michiel continued. "One of the options is that she had moved with her family to Hampstead, and that is why we have contacted you."

"I wouldn't worry about Audrey. That's her modus operandi. Is that how you say it? Disappear overnight, and don't say goodbye."

"Perhaps, but she is now eighty-three years old and seemed very much at home and at ease with her life in the Barbican."

"Did you tell them about us?"

"Not really. That's why Juliet called all the Glenns in Hampstead, asking for her. It was fortunate that your son responded to her message."

"She was ungrateful. She was very much loved here, but she was only looking out for herself. She didn't mind making her parents suffer when she was sixteen years old and ran away from home, and then she didn't mind marrying a stranger and disappearing without a single farewell note. I repeat, I wouldn't worry about her. I'm sure she's gone because she felt like it, and she's forgotten about the two of you like everyone else."

"Well..."

"Anyway, will you let me know if you manage to find her? I'm curious to know what happened to her this time."

"Of course."

The two stood up, sensing that the visit was over. Phillip Glenn appeared at the door to escort them out.

"If you talk to her again, let me know and tell her to call me. That I am still alive, and she still owes me an explanation."

"Of course, and thank you very much for speaking with us, Mrs. Glenn. It has been a pleasure."

"Goodbye."

She smiled at them, turned on the television, and seemed to forget them immediately. Michiel took Juliet's hand again, this time interlacing his fingers with hers, and walked out into the hallway with a firm step. Juliet followed him without opening her mouth until they stepped onto the street, and they both turned to say goodbye to Phillip Glenn, who bid them farewell very politely.

"Wow! Audrey never ceases to amaze us," he said. He walked down the sidewalk, and Juliet let go of his hand.

"Antipodes, a top-secret position in the US government, a change of last name, and an anonymous life? Who was Audrey? I'm freaking out. Either she was a compulsive liar, or she had a very interesting life."

"Maybe she was lying to her family to reassure them."

"I don't know if she cared much about her family." He looked up at the sky and saw that it was about to rain. "What do we do now? Where do we go from here?"

"Australia or New Zealand? We'll have to see if we can locate her there. Of course, if they changed their last name..."

"They had been in London for at least twenty years, and here they were Audrey and Gregory Stuyvesant. There's no doubt about that because it's on their mailbox and their medical records and at the pharmacy, and with Social Services. From then on, we don't know what he did, but maybe it's not important now."

"It is not unimportant if we want to complete the story for your script."

"True."

"We'll get to the Antipodes," he joked, imitating Mrs. Glenn's accent, and winked at her. "What are you doing now? I don't think I can lock myself in the house."

"I have an engagement in Soho, a birthday party for a friend. Come with me if you want."

"Great. Should we change?"

"I think so. It's in a rather posh club. Let's get a cab, go home, get something to eat, change, and go out. I think we deserve it today, my dear Watson." She stood in the middle of the street and raised her hand to hail a cab. Michiel didn't move, and she gave him a sidelong glance. "What is it now?"

"I've loved being married to you for forty-five minutes, Juliet. Maybe I'm becoming monogamous."

"Very funny. Come on, let's go."

CHAPTER ELEVEN

She didn't know if it was the white wine she was drinking, the stress she was under, the excitement of her intrepid advances in the Audrey case, or because he had held her hand and it had been a thousand years since anyone had done that, but suddenly Michiel Lezer, her adorable neighbor, the Dutch elementary school teacher with the beautiful hair and fondness for open relationships with whom she was sharing the greatest adventure of her life, seemed tremendously handsome and sexy.

He was very attractive, manly, and edible. He was delicious. On top of that, he was friendly, intelligent, cultured, educated, bold, and steady. He was a ten in many ways. She liked him a lot, and she loved talking to him and spending time with him. For that reason, she wouldn't spoil it by developing romantic fantasies about him.

She would never again allow herself the luxury of having romantic fantasies about a guy, not after years of having them with LOML, who had used her and squeezed her emotionally until she was exhausted and sad. That was not going to happen again, she had sworn to herself, because she was not going to suffer again for anything, to let her imagination take her to impossible and unrealistic romantic scenarios. They only ended up hurting her, no one else, because no one had ever shared them in real life with her, and that was tremendously painful.

She preferred never to fall in love again in her life to going through unrequited love once more. She had tried it several times in her almost thirty-two years, and she did not need to experience it another time. Her commitment to herself was to keep a cool head and a frozen heart, especially concerning Michiel Lezer, who had made it clear to her that he was into open and multiple relationships. In other words, he was more dangerous than she could handle.

The logical and rational thing to do, the most mature thing to do at that precise moment in her life, was to make this precious friendship grow—a friendship that had begun with a very quick spark and had put them into an investigation worthy of Sherlock Holmes. That was giving her some great moments, a natural trust with him, and a great and fun companionship that made her feel very happy.

"Why didn't you tell me your friend was a celebrity? There are a lot of famous people here," he whispered against her neck, and she jumped and turned to get the glass of wine he had fetched from the bar.

"Because I didn't want you to be scared. What are you drinking?"

"An Old-Fashioned. The server insisted."

"Okay."

She took a step back and observed how great he looked, dressed in black. He was tall and lanky and had great style, just like his near-double Michiel Huisman. He looked great in the dress pants and shirt open to the second button that he had worn to accompany her to Lily James's birthday party.

A hottie, she thought and glanced at the club full of famous people, mostly actors, who had gathered there to celebrate the birthday of Lily, a successful movie star, a friend, and a client she had been working with for over eight years. She waved at those she knew and turned her attention back to Michiel, who seemed very amused.

"You've never dated a famous actor?" he asked.

She shook her head. "Not seriously, no. You shouldn't mix work with pleasure, don't you know that?"

"What does 'not seriously, no' mean?

"I've gone out for dinner or a drink with someone, but I haven't had an actor boyfriend."

"I'm sure you get hit on a lot."

"Don't think so. You want something to eat? The food looks great."

Damian Hastings approached her from the right and kissed her on the cheek before hugging her. "My goodness, you look beautiful."

"Hi, Damian. This is Michiel."

"Oh, I didn't know you had company. Hi, nice to meet you."

"Enchanted."

"You didn't call me to ask me what Iona wanted to propose," Damian asked Juliet, ignoring Michiel.

She shrugged. "I've been very busy, Damian. I've got a lot on my plate."

"What's wrong with you? Am I missing something?" He looked at Michiel out of the corner of his eye, and she snorted.

"What did Iona propose to you? Can you tell me, or is it still a secret?"

"She wants me to accompany her to the Tokyo Film Festival."

"Are you going to be a toy boy, Damian?"

"She wants to introduce me to some people, and no, I won't be her toy boy. It's just work."

"You'll see, but we'll talk about it calmly later. Okay, I need to disconnect tonight."

"Do you know who's here?" He approached her, and she took a step back. "Your worst nightmare."

"Caden?"

"No, love, Jennifer Davies."

"I didn't know she was around."

"Juliet!" Andrea appeared on the run and stood in front of her, looking at her two companions curiously. "We need to talk. She came!"

"Jennifer Davies. Damian is telling me, but it's okay. I don't care if she comes to London."

"I don't like her. I'm going to avoid her as much as I can. Excuse me, you are?" she asked Michiel flirtatiously, and he smiled at her.

"Michiel. I came with Juliet."

"How nice. I'm Andrea, her assistant. Nice to meet you."

"I'm delighted, Andrea."

"Damian, come with me to get something to drink. Come on."

She grabbed Hastings by the arm and dragged him across the club. Juliet felt a shiver run up and down her spine at the thought of Jennifer Davies being so close, but she didn't bother to get pissed off and motioned Michiel to sit on some sofas by the terrace.

"So you have an assistant?" She nodded. "Who is Jennifer Davies?"

"My nemesis."

"Do you have your own Moriarty, Sherlock?"

"Yes, exactly. Very good."

"Tell me about it."

"She's a colleague from our New York office who has wanted to work in London for years and, if possible, in my position, so she's been screwing with my life, or trying to screw with my life, all that time."

"Mmm."

"Yes, my dear Watson. Nothing is perfect."

"Why does she want your job?"

"Because I work directly with Iona, the big boss, and, in

theory, it is a prestigious position with a certain importance that she feels is more appropriate for her. She is older than me and has been with the company for more years."

"I understand."

"I even like her because, although she has given me a hard time and has tripped me up a thousand times, she is very competent and super-efficient. She is one of the best at her job. She is one of those relentless people who, despite everything, you are happy to have on your team."

"Is that her?" he asked, nodding at an imposing African-American woman who was approaching with open arms to greet her, and she nodded and stood up.

"Juliet Miller, look at you! You look fantastic."

"Hi, Jennifer. How are you?"

"Not as well as you!" She looked Michiel up and down and stood for a couple of seconds with her mouth open.

"What are you doing in London?"

"Me? I've only been here forty-eight hours. I was in Paris, and I stopped by to sign some contracts and meet with Andrew and Iona. This big man? What happened to your Aussie boy?"

"Hi, what's up?" Michiel held out his hand very politely, and Juliet sighed.

"You have something to do with Michiel Huisman? You look a lot alike."

"No, it has nothing to do with it," she answered for him and searched for his hand.

"Do we have any pending contracts with your office?"

"No, don't worry. Everything is in order. It's my business. Are you coming to the buffet to eat something?"

Jennifer winked at Michiel and sensually touched the silver pendant she wore over her perfect, expensive silk blouse. Michiel looked at her with a half-smile Juliet had never seen, which she assumed was his seductive smile, and took a deep breath. She thought that she might have to leave them alone, but he stopped holding Jennifer's gaze, reached out, and took Juliet's hand.

"Thank you. Now I'll take this young lady to go dance," he said.

He forced her to leave the wine glass on a server's tray and took her to the center of the dance floor, where everyone was dancing to Beyoncé's best songs.

She loved Beyoncé and dance music, and she threw herself into dancing and singing and jumping with Andrea, Michiel, and all the friends and colleagues who joined in the revelry. Later, after passing up the buffet, people went to a private karaoke bar in Camden Town.

The plan was great, and she was a little tipsy because of the wine, but since it was midnight, it was Thursday, and she had to go to work very early the next day, she decided to go home alone, as usual. To her surprise, Michiel, who was the most fun-loving and friendly guy in the universe, decided to go with her.

"In Spain, at this hour, the party would be just starting," she told him as they arrived at their building. He nodded, laughing.

"I'm a disgrace to my Spanish half, and you didn't have to come back with me."

"Why not?"

"Because I didn't need you to. I'm used to walking alone. I've traveled half the planet alone. I don't mind."

"I do mind, and that was enough. Afternoon to midnight is perfect."

"Okay, suit yourself."

She stuck the key in the lock a little dizzily and looked at him out of the corner of her eye. So handsome, waiting with his hands in his pockets to leave her safe and sound in her quarters. She straightened and looked him in the eye.

"Would you like some tea, my dear Watson?"

"Please."

He followed her into her apartment and they greeted Romeo,

who barely paid them any attention. She took off her heels and went to the kitchen to find some non-caffeinated tea to drink.

As she heated the water, she watched out of the corner of her eye as he perused her bookshelves very attentively and as he lingered over her collection of *Romeo and Juliet*—one hundred and two copies in different languages, editions, and quality. Finally, she approached him from behind with a mug of hot tea.

"Do you want sugar?"

"No, that's perfect. How many times have you read *Romeo and Juliet?*"

"I don't know. Not many, maybe ten, but I have seen the play hundreds of times, anywhere in the world and in any language. If it's in the theater and I'm nearby, I go to see it."

"You are missing a Dutch edition."

"I know. When I've been in Amsterdam, I've never had time to buy one."

"I'll take care of it, okay?" He turned to her and smiled.

"Sit down. I don't know about you, but with the excitement of meeting Ms. Glenn and all, I'm worn out."

"Who's your 'Aussie boy?'" he asked, making the quotation mark gesture, and Juliet blinked. "At least six people asked you about him tonight. Are you going to introduce me to him?"

"I doubt it. He is no longer a friend of mine."

"Was he your boyfriend?

"No, although I treated him as such for about eight years."

"How?"

"When I met him, I fell madly in love with him. We had a text-book co-dependent relationship. I spent eight years adoring him and letting him in and out of my life whenever it suited him. I've given him everything but my blood because we're not the same blood type," she joked and shook her head.

"Anyway, I'm not very proud to have put him at the top of my priorities and to have devoted so much love and time to him. The good news is that three months ago, he left my life for good, and I feel great."

"Did you live together?"

"No, no way. Caden liked everyone but me. We were never formal boyfriend and girlfriend. On my side, yes, but not on his. It was a weird relationship. Nice at times, but most of the time, it only brought me frustration and helplessness, jealousy, and other things I hate to admit."

"Wow, I'm sorry."

"It's over. It took me a while, but finally, my instincts reacted. I don't want to know anything about him anymore. The thing is that everyone around me knew him. That's why they ask me about him. People liked him, including my family."

"Is he an actor? Did he work with you?"

"He is an artist, a painter, or he wants to be. I met him because my company hired him eight years ago as an accent coach."

"Accent coach?"

"An accent coach is a person who helps an actor or actress with a particular accent. In this case, Australian. We needed a person who was willing to work regularly with our actors when they needed it, and someone recommended this guy from Sydney, Caden Brown, who was very nice and needed a stable job so he could stay in England.

"That's how we met, and from minute one, I started protecting him, and, you know… I don't know what happened to me because I'd never been like that before, but I went out of my mind. I didn't see anything wrong with him, not even when after three months, he started missing work or doing it badly and reluctantly, and when after four months, he decided to leave us hanging. That was intolerable, but I was still there, justifying it.

"He jumps from job to job because he is not fond of routine or schedules, although he never stops painting. That's where the second part of my disaster came from."

"What disaster?"

"My personal disaster, when I began to move heaven and earth to pull contacts and ask for favors that I had never asked for myself to get them to let him exhibit in fashionable places and super-clean art galleries, everywhere. I had no idea about that business, but we made inroads. For a while, we were the perfect team. I was very happy until I started to see him with other girls and, what the fuck, it all went to hell. Do you want a bite to eat?"

"No, thank you. I want you to unburden yourself to me."

"Thank you." She looked him in the eye and was touched because he was the first person to ask her, openly and honestly, about her history with Caden. She sighed with the urge to jump up and hug him, but she held back and kept talking.

"He never took me to a party or one of 'his' places. Everything was confined to my home, my office, my friends, my surroundings, and even my family, who welcomed him with open arms. We never traveled together, nor did he spend a weekend with me. He bullied me as he pleased. He was all over me, or I didn't see hide or hair of him, but he never let go fully. He would disappear for months, not remember my birthday, not call to find out if I was okay. He had no idea about my life or what I was doing or what was happening to me, but when he would text or call me, I would forget everything and succumb again, so many times I can't even count."

"What has happened now to make this time the final breakthrough?"

"I had been away from him for about six months without seeing him, and I didn't talk about Caden until, three months ago, he called me to ask me for a favor. Logically, because he always calls to ask for favors. He wanted me to help him with the launching of his first book, a picture book, and he needed guidance on the subject of promotion. I, being an idiot, called a friend who is a literary agent, got my bearings, asked my marketing colleagues for help, and spent a whole weekend studying the options and talking to him on the phone to see what I could do until it occurred to him to send me the book. When I opened it, on the first page, I read in big letters, *For Carola.*"

"Seriously?"

"I swear."

"How tactless, man."

"Look, I don't care if he dedicates it to his neighbor's dog. I don't care; it doesn't matter. He has the right to dedicate his book to whomever he wants. What I will never understand is why, after being friends for so many years, he didn't tell me he had a girlfriend. Why he called me to involve me in his affairs. He didn't need to pull the string again. He didn't need to trick me to ask for my help. If he ever cared about me at all, he should have left me alone long ago. It's as simple as that; disappear, man! You're great at it. Forget about me, especially if you already have a partner to dedicate books to. I couldn't digest that, and my head clicked for good."

"There's no bad thing without a good thing."

"Yes, thank God."

"He hasn't contacted you again?"

"He's tried, but I pass. I don't even dislike him. Seriously, I don't know how I could keep such an emotional vampire by my side for so many years. I know it's all my fault because I always miss the mark. I give myself completely, and I don't see that they don't love me until I've emptied myself. At least, I've realized it; a little late, but I've opened my eyes."

"They say that the first step to overcoming it is to recognize it."

"Exactly. I've told you something very humiliating that I don't usually tell anyone. Now it's your turn."

"I don't find it humiliating. It seems to me that a scoundrel landed on his feet when he met you. He didn't deserve you, and he stayed longer than necessary. You are only guilty of wanting and giving. That's not bad. That speaks well of you."

"Thank you."

"I'm serious."

"Tell me, how has love treated you?"

"I can't complain. I've already told you that since I was very young, I've maintained open relationships, and it's the best decision I've made in my life. Unlike your Australian, I don't go after people, and I don't take advantage of anyone's feelings. I don't possess anyone, and that is beneficial for everyone, starting with me."

"Doesn't that imply giving up on true love?"

"No. As I told you once, I don't think this option has anything to do with love, neither true nor surrogate."

"Of course. How old are you? I'm thirty-two."

"I just made forty."

She was silent, and they stayed like that until he stretched out his legs and asked without looking at her, "What do you expect from love, Juliet?

"I just want to be someone's priority."

"That is the best and most concise definition of love I have ever heard in my entire life."

She looked him in the eye with a smile, excited because she had never delved so deeply into her feelings out loud. He held her gaze for a few seconds, then she took a deep breath and pulled back her hair.

"I could spend ages chatting with you, Juliet, but I should go. I have an eight o'clock class."

"Of course, it's very late. I have to get up early too." They jumped up. He stroked Romeo's little head and reached the door holding his jacket. Before opening it, he turned and leaned down to kiss her. Juliet moved in to say goodbye, and in the middle of the maneuver, they brushed their noses. Neither avoided the other. His breath mingled with hers, she felt the proximity of his mouth, and she held her breath, closing her eyes. He leaned in and gave her a soft kiss on the lips, innocent. She opened her mouth to his and kissed him eagerly.

He shivered, and his legs buckled. Then he was aware of her taste, so rich, so sweet, and of the warmth of her mouth and tongue. She was anxious but a wonderful kisser. She made an attempt to grab him by the neck, but she stopped in her tracks and froze.

He, noticing her tension, stopped kissing her and stepped back. "I'm sorry, Juliet, I..."

"No, no, no, no. It's fine. It's perfect. It's just..." She looked into his dark blue eyes and smiled at him. "You're the best friend I've had in years. I love being with you and talking to you, and I don't want to lose you. I don't want to ruin it. I don't want you to..."

Michiel sighed. "I think it's perfect. You're very special to me, and I don't want to... I know I'll never be able to give you what you expect. You know how I see relationships, and..."

"I know. It's okay."

They looked at each other, then he opened his arms and embraced her. She clung to him tightly, closing her eyes, inhaling his scent, and thinking that in those arms, she could live peacefully for the rest of her life. After a few seconds, she separated from him, stroked the breast of his shirt, and laughed. "A timely withdrawal is a victory, my dear Watson."

"Good night. We'll talk tomorrow."

He gave her a quick kiss on the cheek, opened the door, and left. Juliet felt her chest tighten and her pulse pound in her ears. She closed the door, leaned against the wall, and slid down to sit on the floor with a strong urge to cry and covered her face with both hands as Romeo came over to see what was happening to her. She took him in her arms and heard the cell phone vibrating insistently on the kitchen counter. She pulled herself together and got up to answer it because at that hour, it could only be an emergency. She picked it up and heard a girl crying.

"Juliet."

"What's going on? Who are you?"

"It's Ellie. I've lost my cell phone. I want to leave New York. Help me, please. Juliet, help me."

"Ellie, what happened? Where are you?"

"In this fucking shitty hotel. Frank kicked me out of the shoot. He said, 'Go throw up a little bit.' That's what the bastard said to me, knowing my problems with bulimia. That's harassment and emotional abuse. Get me out of here!"

"Okay, breathe. Where's June?"

"That crazy bitch sided with the director and the producer. I don't want anyone from the New York office. You are my agent and my friend. I want you to help me."

"Okay. It's almost two in the morning here, Ellie. I can't do anything until tomorrow. I'm going to call Frank and—"

"No, I don't want you to call him. I told him that my agent was going to come, she was going to eat him, and he was going to shit. You have to come. Please don't leave me here."

"I'm not leaving you. Let's talk. It's all right."

"Juliet, come to New York. I can't leave the shoot without you in front of me because if I do, she'll sue the shit out of all of us, you know that. You have to come and fix this. We're friends. I love you. Please, I'm begging you."

CHAPTER TWELVE

"Do you know how many times she's asked me what her character thinks and why she drinks her coffee sitting down and not standing up? Do you know, Juliet?"

Frank Davis, a young, award-winning film director, the promising future of American independent cinema, looked at her with his hands on his hips.

Juliet, jet-lagged but perfectly aware of what was going on, folded her arms and nodded. "She's scared. She says you scare her, Frank."

"Because I can't waste my time with her. She's a supporting actress, and I chose her in England because they have a reputation for being professional and not insufferably whimsical. Every time she stops a scene and intervenes for thirty seconds to ask a stupid question, she wastes my dough. Don't you understand? We talked about her character at length via video conference, and when she got here, we discussed it again. I can't keep having the fucking shoot stopped because she wants to know if her character is a Libra or a Scorpio."

"Okay, what do you want to do? Do you want to terminate the

contract? You can go sign it right now, and I'll take it back to London."

"No, I'm not going to look for another supporting actress. I want Ellie to do her damn job and not complicate my life any further."

"Are you going to apologize?"

"Apologize to you?"

"To her. The Stanley Kubrick or Lars Von Trier thing won't work with her, Frank. It won't work with any of my actors because I won't tolerate it. No more verbal abuse, no more disrespect, and maybe we'll all stop complicating our lives."

"Fuck, Juliet!"

"If you're willing to apologize to her for the bad tone and the vomit reference, I'll make her do her job. She has ten scenes left, and then you can forget about Ellie forever."

"She's very good, Juliet. We don't want her to leave or feel mistreated," the executive producer interjected.

Juliet nodded. "Of course she is good. She is excellent and very professional. The problem is that she reacts badly to stress and rudeness. We don't work like that in Great Britain."

"In Great Britain, you are the same. You just say it better."

"I'm not going to go on forever about this. Shall we terminate the contract or go ahead with the usual apologies?"

"If I let her leave, are you going to sue me?"

"Of course I'm going to sue you, and if you ever speak badly to her or offend her again, I'm going to sue you for that too."

"Fucking hell!"

Frank Davis, who was too deified to have made more than three films, started blaspheming in Aramaic. Juliet searched for her actress. Ellie, who had gone to pick her up at the airport in tears, smiled from behind the cameras and blew her a kiss. Juliet winked and felt the producer's hand on her shoulder.

"Juliet, we don't want any more conflicts. We will start from scratch, and everything will go smoothly."

"Are you sure?"

She looked at Frank and he nodded, so she motioned Ellie over and put her in front of the director, stroking her back. The guy took a step and clasped his hands together before speaking.

"Ellie, honey, you know I like you. I'm crazy about you. I insisted that you play Monica. You were my first choice from the beginning, you always have been, and I don't want you to leave. Juliet says I've offended you, and if so, excuse me, forgive me. I will not yell at you or disrespect you again. I give you my word of honor."

"Okay."

"We have to work differently. I can't stop shooting every five minutes. If you have any doubts, we'll send you to one of the scriptwriters, and you can consult outside shooting hours. Whatever you want. Do you agree?"

"All right."

"Great, so let's get back to work. Bye, Juliet. Ellie, see you at six."

Having settled the conflict, Juliet looked at the executive producer and said a polite but firm and very serious goodbye. She added that she would stay in New York for at least a week to monitor the progress of Ellie's work and to check that Frank was keeping his word.

"I'm always surprised to see you working, Juliet."

"Why?

"Because you're the fucking mistress when you stand up to those arrogant bastards."

"I learned from the best."

She dropped her suitcase on the floor of her room, which was on the same floor as Ellie's, and threw her backpack on the bed. She took off her coat and boots and took a deep breath, then walked to the windows to pull back the curtains and admire the breathtaking scenery of Midtown New York, one of the most recognizable sights in the world.

"Two o'clock in the afternoon, and we've got it fixed. Ellie, you can't complain."

"Thank you for coming running. Now I feel guilty."

Juliet went over and hugged her.

"Don't worry. I'll take advantage of the opportunity to resolve a few other matters on my mind. There's always something pending in New York. Shall we order something to eat?"

"Aren't you tired?"

"I'm fine. I'd like room service."

"Okay, let's order some salads."

"Frank has promised to behave himself and not to be a nuisance again, and now you have to promise me that you will do your best. He's no Shakespeare, you've already mastered the role, and we can't afford to—"

"I promised, and I will do it, but let's be clear that I'm doing it for you, not for him, who I think is a complete asshole."

"He may be a total asshole, but he's in fashion, and you'll be in his next movie. Hallelujah."

She called room service, ordered lunch, and looked at the time. It was quarter past two in the afternoon local time. She had left London at ten o'clock in the morning, after deciding with Iona that it was best to get to New York to take care of Ellie and other things they had going on in the city, and after having kissed Michiel Lezer in the middle of an obvious mental derangement.

She had barely been able to sleep after that because it had thrown her, yet at nine o'clock in the morning, she was at Heathrow going through airport security and making calls, putting everything necessary into motion as she left London. She couldn't get him out of her mind. It would take time to forget that wet, passionate kiss because it had been sublime. A small reward after a rather long drought, and she couldn't stop wondering what this guy would be like in bed because someone who kissed that well had to be a real stunner between the sheets.

An untouchable wonder since they had both decided to put

the brakes on in time. She felt quite proud to have used her head and not her heart in such an intense moment.

"I want to call Richard M. I've been told he's here. Do you know anything?"

"Huh?" She looked at Ellie and slumped into a very comfortable chair by the window. "He's here, but wasn't it you that didn't want to know about, and I quote, 'that Scottish son of a bitch?'"

"He's hot. Much hotter than when he was dating me, and on top of that, he's loaded. Do you know how much Marvel paid him for the movie?"

Juliet shook her head.

"Is it true that they've signed him for two hundred and fifty thousand pounds for each episode of the second season of his series?"

"I don't know, and even if I did, I wouldn't tell you. It's confidential information."

"Fuck."

"Do you want me to discuss your contracts with others?"

"No, but it's about my ex."

"Ask him."

"His ex-girlfriends should found a club. We used to fuck him and put up with him when he couldn't even afford to buy dinner at a nice restaurant, and now look. He makes more money in one movie than all of us put together in five years."

"It happens."

"Next time, Juliet, I'm going to wait to see if the guy succeeds before I let him abandon me."

"Don't talk nonsense."

"Did you fuck him?"

"Who, Richard M? No!"

"Too bad. He loved you. He always said so, and he tried to

invite you to dinner several times."

"We only shared working dinners. Are you crazy?"

"You have the gift, or maybe misfortune, of not knowing what's going on around you, Juliet Miller. If you paid more attention, you'd have the sexual schedule of a goddess."

"I don't have time for that."

"*Carpe diem*, Juliet."

"One moment. I have to answer my phone."

She got up to retrieve the phone from her backpack and answered because it was a British number, although she didn't know it. The person who greeted her sounded annoyed.

"Ms. Miller?"

"Who is this?"

"I'm Phillip Glenn. I just called your office, and your assistant gave me your cell phone number."

"Mr. Glenn, how are you? What a surprise! How is your mother?"

"That's why I'm calling you—because of my mother. She spent a very restless night thinking about Audrey, and today, while we were taking a walk, she remembered two details that you and your husband might be interested in."

"Tell me." She felt guilty for lying to those kind people about her and Michiel being married, but it was too late to take it back, so she kept quiet.

"She remembered that Audrey moved to Australia, to Victoria, and the last name they used was McCrory."

"Great, thank you very much for telling me about it. You don't know how much I appreciate it."

"If you want, you can talk to her again. It was very good for her to chat with you. She is very animated today."

"Of course, it will be a pleasure to come and see you another day. I'm in New York right now."

"New York? You were here yesterday."

"Yes, I traveled this morning, but I can ask Michiel to stop by your house."

"She'll want to talk to both of you. Call me when you get back to London."

"Very good, and thank you again for calling me."

"You are welcome. Goodbye."

As she hung up, Ellie opened the door for room service, and a server came in with a cart full of delicacies. She thought about calling Michiel to tell him the news. She looked at the time and then at the phone, but before she hit his number, a call from him was coming in. She smiled at the coincidence and answered happily.

"Hello! We are in sync. I was just about to call you."

"Did you really go to New York?"

"Yes, this job is like that. You don't know!"

"Are you all right? I stopped by your place after work to say hi to you and chat about what happened last night and a girl I didn't know opened up to me. It was very weird."

"She helps me with the house and stays with Romeo when I travel."

"Now I know. She told me everything in detail. She's very nice."

"She is. She's a sweetheart. Do you know who called me?"

"No."

"Phillip Glenn, to tell me that his mother has remembered two fundamental facts. The first, Audrey went to live in Victoria, Australia, and the second, the supposed incognito surname is McCrory."

"Okay, great. We'll go that way."

"She also says we can go visit her again."

"Are you staying in New York for many days?"

"At least a week, and I'll take advantage by going to St. Mark's. I'll also snoop around a bit about the Stuyvesants. Since I'm on their turf, I can't pass that up."

"Okay."

"How are you doing?"

"I was a little puzzled by your sudden disappearance, but now that I've located you, I'm more at ease."

Juliet was surprised by the comment but said nothing.

"I can ask my colleague at the Dutch embassy to put you in touch with his friend at the New York Historical Society, so you can talk to him personally."

"That would be great."

"I'm quite envious that you're in New York."

"I'll look into it for both of us, my dear Watson. I'll keep you posted. I haven't much time to spare either, but I'll do what I can."

"Are we still friends?"

"Of course. Why do you ask that?"

"Last night, I kissed you. I just wanted to check that today everything is still good between us."

"You didn't kiss me. It was a shared thing. Don't worry about that. I've already forgotten about it," she lied. She could imagine that he was smiling. "I didn't sleep much on the flight, so I was able to write a lot."

"I'm glad to hear that."

"I have developed the plot of the script. Characters, lines of action, etc. I think it looks good. I'm going to send it to you so you can take a look at it."

"Great, Juliet. I'll love to read it."

"As soon as you read it and put your spin on it, I'll register it and start developing it. Then I'll find someone to help me with the technical script, and we'll put it in the right hands."

"That sounds very professional."

"I'm not an expert, but I have access to people who are and will be able to help us in the process."

"Juliet, come eat!" Ellie shouted.

"Michiel, I have to go. Let's talk, and check your email. I'll send you the script as soon as I hang up."

"Okay, and enjoy New York. Goodbye."

CHAPTER THIRTEEN

"Juliet, nice to meet you, and don't worry, you're only five minutes late. Shall we go in?"

"Of course, and thank you very much for meeting me so quickly."

"Herman says he is helping a Dutch friend with a dissertation on Governor Stuyvesant and the Dutch in New Amsterdam."

"Yes. I started helping him because a very dear neighbor was married to a Stuyvesant, and Michiel told me about New Amsterdam and the New Netherlands."

"You might know that St. Mark's, originally consecrated by the Dutch Reformed Church, was built by Petros "Peter" Stuyvesant, then-governor of New Amsterdam and director of the Dutch West India Company in the New Netherlands, in 1660," he said, not paying attention to what she'd said. He gestured at the building. "It was built as a family chapel within their farm, Great Bouwerie, which occupied almost the entire southern part of Manhattan. It is the oldest continuous place of worship in New York City."

Juliet nodded, remembering those very words in Michiel's mouth. She suddenly missed him. She walked into the church,

111

which, for someone raised in Europe, was not as impressive as New Yorkers thought it was but was very nice.

"The present church dates from 1799."

"Has it undergone many changes since 1660?"

"Yes. At first, it was in the Georgian style in fieldstone. In 1793, Peter Stuyvesant's grandson sold it to the Episcopal Church, which, in 1799, enlarged, completed, and consecrated it, making it the first Episcopal parish independent of Trinity Church, another historic church in the Episcopal Diocese of New York."

She followed Tompkins down the central hallway and noted how austere it was. At the same time, it seemed cozy. She touched one of the gleaming wooden benches, on which, at that midday hour, there was no one.

Her guide caught her eye by pointing at the ceiling. "In 1828, the famous steeple was erected, the design of which is attributed to Martin Euclid Thompson and Ithiel Town. It gave the church its definitive Greek Revival style. Further changes occurred in 1835 when the stone parish hall was built. In 1836 the interior was renovated, replacing the original square pillars with thinner ones in the Egyptian Renaissance style. A wrought iron fence was added in 1838, and at the same time, a second floor was fitted out for the parish school. In 1858, the exterior cast iron portico was added, the design of which is attributed to James Bogardus, and in the early twentieth century, prominent architect Ernest Flagg built the rectory."

"Where is Peter Stuyvesant buried?"

"In the vault under the chapel."

They went there to look, and Juliet attempted to take a picture, but John Tompkins stopped her.

"I have brought you a gift, a detailed and very complete book with beautiful pictures, which speaks about the church and the sealed vault of Peter Stuyvesant. We had better not disturb their rest by taking pictures."

"Of course. Sorry, I was just thinking about Michiel."

"I was thinking about the ghost of Governor Stuyvesant, who is one of the most famous specters in Manhattan." At last, the circumspect man smiled, and Juliet relaxed her shoulders.

"Don't leave me hanging. Tell me about the ghost, please."

"Many claim that the spirit of Peter Stuyvesant walks the corridors of St. Mark's, tapping his wooden leg, the famous prosthesis he wore after 1644, when a Spanish cannonball took off his right leg."

"Spanish cannonball?"

"In April 1644, Stuyvesant landed on the island of St. Martin in the Caribbean, which was recovered by the Spanish in the middle of the Thirty Years' War. It had been purchased from the United Provinces of the Netherlands in good faith. However, a Dutch fleet attempted to recover it. They arrived at the island, which had been claimed by Christopher Columbus for the Kingdom of Spain in 1493, determined to invade it, but Spanish captain Diego Guajardo Fajardo did not allow them to do so. There was a scuffle, and Peter Stuyvesant lost his leg.

"Incidentally, his life changed thanks to this tragedy. In May 1645, the Dutch West Indies Company chose him to replace William Kieft as director general in the New Netherlands, and he arrived in New Amsterdam on May 11, 1647 to become governor."

"It's especially interesting to hear that because I'm half-Spanish."

"Spanish?"

"My mother is from Cádiz, my father is English, and I was born in Gibraltar."

He continued telling her about the church and the great personalities besides the well-known Peter Stuyvesant who were buried there, such as the mayor of New York, Philip Hone, politician Miriam Friedlander, and the most notable, the former governor of New York, Supreme Court Justice and sixth vice-president of the United States, Daniel D. Tompkins who, he told her, was his relative.

"Even today," he continued, "almost every Dutch celebrity who visits New York comes to see St. Mark's. It is an undeniable Dutch landmark, a symbol of the Dutch presence in this city and also an example of support for the community, the arts, and the underprivileged."

"It's a beautiful place. Thank you very much for a very thorough visit, Mr. Tompkins. If you have a few minutes, I'd like to ask you a few questions about the Stuyvesant family."

"What do you want to know?"

"Can I buy you a coffee?"

"I would never say no to such a beautiful young woman."

Juliet ignored the comment because the man was old enough to be her father. She pointed at a coffee shop just across the street. Tompkins took her by the elbow and escorted her into the place, and they found a quiet table by a window.

"Do you know anyone in the Stuyvesant family? The current one, I mean?" She got straight to the point.

He blinked. "It is a very large family."

"I am talking about the direct descendants of Peter Stuyvesant. Do you know anything about Peter Gregory Stuyvesant III? He was born in Manhattan in 1928 and was a pilot in the United States Air Force."

"Why?"

"He was married to my friend, the neighbor I told you about, and I would like to know if he is the same Peter Gregory Stuyvesant III who is listed as a descendant of the governor of New Amsterdam."

"To what end? Doesn't your friend know?"

"I guess she knows, but she disappeared more than three months ago, and we don't know where she is. We would like to locate her possible in-laws."

"So, the dissertation does not exist?"

"Yes, it exists, but we also have a personal interest in the subject. We want to locate our friend, Audrey Stuyvesant, who married Peter Gregory Stuyvesant III on April 10, 1956 in London and check that she is still well."

John Tompkins frowned and turned pale, and Juliet Miller, who had fought thousands of battles with countless bigwigs in the film and television industry, knew she had just won him over to her cause. He leaned his back against the back of the chair and took off his beret.

"Your source of information is Mrs. Audrey Stuyvesant?"

"No, the truth is that we found this data thanks to Michiel Lezer, the holder of the dissertation. Herman's Dutch friend, who is a first-rate researcher."

"Lezer. Is he Jewish?"

"I don't know. He is Dutch. Can you provide me with any information about Peter Gregory Stuyvesant III?"

"Peter Gregory Stuyvesant III was the firstborn son of Peter Gregory II and Candance Stuyvesant. He appears on the family tree I gave Herman for his Dutch friend."

"We know, but his footprint disappears from the genealogical tree in 1956, precisely when our Gregory married my friend Audrey in London. There is no record of his death."

"Is he dead?" he asked, and Juliet nodded.

"Audrey's husband died in January 2019 at age ninety-one."

"Do you know your friend's maiden name?"

"Glenn. Audrey Rose Glenn."

Tompkins blinked imperceptibly, took a sip of coffee, and looked at St. Mark's Church before speaking again. "The heir of Peter Gregory II and Candance Stuyvesant was Charles, their fourth son, who died four months ago in the Hamptons. He was the second son of the marriage, and they named him universal heir when they repudiated the husband of your friend precisely for marrying her and not complying with the express wish of his parents."

"That's him!" she exclaimed and regretted not having Michiel at hand.

"The heir to one of the world's greatest fortunes defied his parents by becoming a pilot, but they overlooked it because he was young and at least he was honorably serving his country. When he showed up in Manhattan with a seventeen-year-old girl named Audrey Glenn, poor and so vulgar that Candance Stuyvesant almost had a heart attack, they invited him to come to his senses and warned him that if he continued with her, he would be disinherited.

"He not only showed her around New York, but he also returned to London and married her, breaking a tradition of over a hundred years of advantageous marriages arranged by his family."

"Audrey was neither poor nor vulgar. She was the daughter of a prestigious London printer," was the first thing that came out of her mouth, and he smiled at her.

"I don't doubt it, my dear, but to the Stuyvesants, everyone else is poor and vulgar. I'm sure your friend Audrey was a lovely lady."

"I hope she still is. She has disappeared, but we are hoping she is still alive. That's why we are following her trail."

"When did you say she disappeared?"

"Just over three months ago, from one day to the next, and she is not in the UK. Her family has told us that she emigrated with her husband to Australia shortly after they got married and that they even changed their surname."

"That is quite plausible. According to the records of the time, the offended Peter Gregory II not only disinherited his firstborn but also forced him to renounce his surname. Do you happen to know what they were called?"

"A sister-in-law of Audrey's told me that it was McCrory, but Audrey, at least when Michiel and I met her, used Stuyvesant. On all her official documentation, medical and social, she is listed as Stuyvesant."

"Maybe they recovered the family name over the years."

"I don't know. We are looking at all options, including a possible trip to Australia."

"Another option is that the Stuyvesants in Manhattan know her whereabouts."

"After what you have told me, I doubt it very much, but yes, it was one of the options we were considering, and that is why I wanted to take advantage of being in town."

"Mrs. Stuyvesant must be very special for you and your colleague Michiel to have come so far in your inquiries. I am very surprised that you have found so much information because even family biographers like me encounter a wall of silence around the disowned Peter Gregory III."

"Are you a biographer of the Stuyvesants?"

"Among other things."

"I didn't know that. Herman just told us that you were a member of the New York Historical Society."

"He told me that you were a tourist, the friend of a compatriot who was doing a dissertation on New Amsterdam. He never mentioned Peter Gregory III, much less his English wife."

"Sorry."

"What do you plan to do now, Juliet?"

"I don't know. We'll keep looking."

"I can dig into the hermetic Stuyvesant environment. Maybe someone has heard something about your friend. I don't think so because they haven't mentioned the wayward heir out loud for sixty-five years, but let's try it."

"I would appreciate it very much, Mr. Tompkins. You would be doing us an enormous favor."

"Please call me John so I can call you Juliet. You're the same age as my daughter. How long are you staying in New York?"

"It depends on the job, but I can extend the trip if necessary."

"Can I use the data you have given me about Australia, the McCrory surname, and the death of Peter Gregory III?"

"Of course, but there are still a lot of things to be verified."

"I hope to do my part to verify them," he told her. "I'll get to work. Now, I should be going."

"Thank you very much, John. You don't know how much you have helped me. It has been very revealing, and thank you very much for the visit to St. Mark's. I enjoyed it very much."

"It was a pleasure to meet you, Juliet. We'll keep in touch."

"Goodbye."

They walked out into the street, and she waved and turned to walk back to Midtown. At this point, she was incapable of getting into a cab because her adrenaline was pumping and she was excited, so she pulled out her cell phone to call Michiel. It was already four in the afternoon, nine in the evening in London, and she assumed he would be at home or out for dinner, but she didn't stop to think too much and dialed his number while walking.

"What's up, Sherlock? I haven't heard from you in two days," he answered on the first ring.

She smiled. "Michiel, sit down. What I'm about to tell you will blow your mind."

After ten days in Manhattan and away from her London office, she was growing impatient. She could not leave New York without giving one last chance to Mr. Tompkins, who had sworn on the phone that he was about to get her a personal interview with a member of the Stuyvesant family. The possibility was too tempting to let slip away, so here she was, stranded in the United States, working and busy, fortunately. However, time was running out, and so was her patience.

She walked into the Shaughnessy & McCameron New York

offices, thinking about what Michiel had told her about time in the real world when everything was running at a breakneck pace and thought that he was right and she should stay calm. She should also set a deadline to get home and back to work and, surely, that deadline could only extend a couple of days more. No longer, because she also had a lot of things to do in London and a lot of people counting on her to do them.

"Miss Miller, how are you?" someone said to her in Spanish with a terrible accent. She turned to see who it was. She smiled when a lovely, handsome, and very affectionate guy came over and hugged her.

"Richard M! How are you? What are you doing here?"

"What are *you* doing here? Still dealing with Ellie?"

"I'm not dealing with Ellie. I have other stories to close in New York."

"That's not what I've been told." He gestured eloquently at Jennifer Davies' office and Juliet snorted, swallowing her anger.

"Gossip at work, very nice."

"You know how it is. How are you? Lily says you didn't go to her birthday party alone."

"Seriously, you guys are a bunch of gossips."

"Nolan called me." He winked and changed the subject.

"Have you read the script?"

"Yes. I gave it an eight out of ten, and it's Nolan. I wouldn't hesitate."

"Okay. When are you coming back to London?"

"In a couple of days. What about you? What are you doing here? Do you need anything?"

"I don't need anything, thank you. I came to sign a contract, we had a videoconference with Iona, and everything is already closed."

"They didn't tell me anything. Since I was here, you could have warned me. I..."

"I didn't mean to make you get up early. Remember Helen?" He turned and waved at his last assistant.

"Sure, we met at the BAFTAs. What's up, Helen?"

"Hi, Juliet. Everything's fine, and you?"

"Great, thank you. Looking forward to going home."

"We're going to Los Angeles now, but I'll be in London in a week. I'll call you, and we'll have dinner, okay?" Richard whispered with that sexy accent and batted those blue eyes, and Juliet nodded.

"Sure, call me. I don't think I'll be here much longer."

"Juliet Miller, always a hoarder."

Jennifer Davies approached them with her feline gait, hugged her actor around the waist in an unprofessional manner, and kissed him on the cheek while giving her a suspicious look.

"Don't worry, honey. I'm not going to steal him from you. He's still yours."

"He will belong to whomever he wants to."

"He's already pissed me off. I don't know where he gets that sense of humor everyone talks about. He certainly never brings it out with me."

"Juliet is the best, and I'm still hers and her London office's," Richard M joked and turned away from her. He looked at Helen and then at Juliet, pretending to leave, but out of nowhere, the director appeared and stopped them all with his strong New York accent.

"Are you still here? Hi, Juliet. It's good to see you."

"Hi, Jack. Same to you."

"You're going to the meeting? We have a meeting in five minutes."

"I don't think Juliet should meet with us, Jack. She's just passing through, and we'll be dealing with issues from this office, not England," interjected Jennifer tensely, unable to contain herself. Juliet shared a glance with Richard M, who stepped forward and kissed her on the cheek.

"Bye, Juliet. I'll call you one of these days. Goodbye to the others, and thank you very much."

Everyone said goodbye to him and he left, followed by his assistant. Juliet did not move, but she did look Jack in the eye. He smiled very kindly at her.

"Stay, Juliet. I'm sure Iona would want you to participate in our weekly meeting. Don't listen to Jennifer."

"I don't listen to Jennifer, who, by the way, we always welcome politely in our offices and at our meetings when she comes to London. It's not about that. It's because I have other commitments and I can't stay. I just came by to drop off some documents, but thank you very much for inviting me."

"As you wish. You know this is your home. See you later," he said, stroking her arm. Juliet smiled at him and looked at Jennifer Davies, who was watching her with a tense jaw and so much hatred in her eyes that she felt a chill.

She stepped back without opening her mouth and spun like a furious diva, turned her back on them, and vanished without saying goodbye. Juliet realized she had stopped breathing for a few seconds, but she pulled herself together because her cell phone began to vibrate with a call from her sister.

"Sarah?"

"Juliet, Juliet, *Juliet!*"

She was screaming her head off, laughing and crying, and Juliet couldn't understand her, so she left the lobby and went to the office that was reserved for her when she came to New York. She stepped into the dim cubicle and tried to get her sister to calm down, but she blurted out the big news.

"Jonathan just asked me to marry him! Ayyyyyyyy! Here, in the middle of the officers' club. You're the first to know."

"Oh, my goodness! I'm so glad, honey. Congratulations to both of you." Tears came to her eyes, and she wiped them away with the sleeve of her blouse. "That's wonderful. I'm so happy for you."

"The ring is beautiful. It was his grandmother's. I'll send you pictures now. Our colleagues have recorded everything on video. I almost fainted, but it was just as I had dreamed it."

"I know, honey. Congratulations."

"I can only think of the Stella McCartney wedding dress we saw in Knightsbridge."

"It's yours if you want it. It will be my gift."

"I love you, sis. I called you first. I'm hanging up because I'm going to call Mum and Dad and then Jamie."

"Of course. I love you very much. Congratulations again!"

She hung up, as excited as Sarah was, thinking about what her parents were going to say, then sat back in her chair, wiping her tears. It was wonderful news because the boy was charming, and Sarah adored him, and without wanting to, she thought about the wedding planner they could hire and everything that had to be done. When her cell rang, she answered it without looking. When she heard LOML's voice, her joy vanished.

"Hello, missing."

"I'm not missing, Caden. Why do you always say I'm missing?"

"I don't know. Because you don't call, send a message, or follow me on social networks. You didn't even go to the presentation of my book. Have you read it?"

"I'm in New York and working. What do you need?"

"New York, what luck."

"What do you want, Caden?"

She waited for him to get upset for once in his life and confront her, giving her a chance to blurt out a few things, but, in his usual vein, he passed on the bellicose tone and went on.

"I am selling the paintings through several specialized Internet pages. I just wanted to give you the details and see if you can give me a like and follow me. I need to add followers, and if you could get just one of your famous friends to follow me, then..."

"Mother," she mumbled and took a deep breath. "*Email* them to me. I have to go. Bye, Caden."

She hung up on him, wanting to kill him, with that feeling of frustration and impotence that he always caused in her. It was the result of his indifference and his total and absolute passivity and lack of shame. The phone vibrated again.

She grabbed it in a very bad temper and barked, "Hello!"

"Juliet? This is John Tompkins. I'm calling you from my home, not my cell phone, so you won't recognize my number."

"John, how are you? I didn't even look at it. I was busy."

"Can you meet someone in an hour?"

"Who?"

"Victoria Stuyvesant is the daughter-in-law of Charles, the brother of Peter Gregory III. The one who just died in the Hamptons."

"Wow!" She jumped to her feet.

"She is married to Mark, Charles' youngest son, and is the sister-in-law of the current head of the family. I know her because she is a wonderful multidisciplinary artist."

"God, what luck! Thank you very much."

"She only agreed to talk to you because you are half-Spanish."

"Excuse me?"

"She is Spanish. Her maiden name was Victoria Ortiz de Guzman."

"The model?"

"Exactly. Can you go see her?"

"Of course. I'm on my way. Send me the address. Did you tell her any of the—"

"A little, but I'd rather you explain it to her. Make a note of the address, and good luck."

CHAPTER FOURTEEN

"I am here in front of the building."

"Okay, let's see if we can't have a three-way conversation."

"I'll try."

She interrupted herself by looking at the building on Park Avenue where Victoria Stuyvesant had summoned her. She recognized it because it had appeared in the remake of *The Perfect Crime*, the 1998 film directed by Andrew Davis that had starred Gwyneth Paltrow, Michael Douglas, and Viggo Mortensen. She thought it was the only movie by that director that was worthwhile and remembered that he'd had to call Gwyneth to talk to her about a solidarity issue that had been proposed to him. She took a step back, glancing at the doorman and the security guy guarding the gate, and finally turned toward the park to say goodbye to Michiel.

"You can't see the building in front of me. It may be the most expensive in the world."

"Upper East Side! God! I'll leave you. I'm going in."

"No, don't hang up. Keep talking to me."

"I don't think I can. I'm sure they have frequency inhibitors."

"You stay on your cell phone, and I'll stay here."

"When I see her, I'll ask her if I can call you, and the three of us can talk. For now, I think it's best to hang up."

"No."

"How tiresome you are, my dear Watson. I'm going in. Don't move."

He did not hang up, but she took the phone away from her ear and advanced toward the entrance, thanking God for having dressed well that morning. She stepped onto the carpeted rectangle in front of the gate, and the concierge, accompanied by the security person, cut her off.

"May I help you, miss?"

"I'm on my way to see Mrs. Victoria Stuyvesant. My name is Juliet Miller. She is expecting me."

"One moment, please."

"Of course."

He stepped aside to call on an internal phone and she smiled at the security guy, who was about four meters tall in a black suit with an earpiece in his ear.

"Go in, Ms. Miller, but please first hand over your cell phone and any electronic devices you are carrying."

"No, I'm not going to give you my phone. I can turn it off, but I'm not going to leave it here. You can keep my laptop if you want."

She took the computer out of her bag and handed it to him.

"One moment, please."

"Mother of God." She snorted as he called someone back and calmly waited for them to answer.

"All right, you can keep your phone, but turn it off. Not silent, off. Do you understand?"

"Perfectly. I'll call you back, Michiel," she said before hanging up and turning off the phone in front of those two characters, who looked like something out of *Peaky Blinders*. Then she entered the gigantic portal, where they passed a metal detector over her and searched her bag, and finally, she got into a special elevator.

The guy with the earpiece did not say a single word to her the whole way to the penthouse of the building.

"Good morning, Miss Miller." When the gilded doors opened, a butler, British and dressed to the nines, greeted her very kindly before pointing her down a beautiful luminous white hallway that led into the spectacular property. *It must be meters longer than Buckingham Palace*, she thought, taking a glance as they traveled along a shiny wooden floor at a good pace. They finally reached an equally white and luminous living room that opened to a dreamy terrace with views of Central Park.

"Juliet, welcome. I've heard so much about you," Victoria Stuyvesant exclaimed in Spanish and approached her to kiss her on each cheek. Juliet smiled, recognizing the spectacular woman she had seen hundreds of times in magazines and on TV when she was a little girl because she was a well-known supermodel who had burned up the catwalks in the late nineties.

"Thank you very much for seeing me, Victoria."

"Oh, how funny the Cádiz accent." She laughed, clapping her hands like a child, then took Juliet by the hand to lead her out onto the terrace. "Are you very cold? It's a bit chilly, but there's no wind, and it's lovely here. Would you like some tea?"

"Of course, thank you very much. What a view." She approached the balustrade that surrounded the perimeter of the building and looked at the priceless view of the park beneath her feet. "Is this the penthouse from the movie *The Perfect Crime*?"

"Yes. We bought and renovated it in 2010."

"It is beautiful."

"Thank you." Victoria stood next to her and looked her up and down. "So, you're an actors' agent? You work at Shaughnessy

& McCameron, don't you? What an exciting job! You must know a lot of people. I'm an actress too, you know."

"Oh, is that so?" she replied, puzzled because she didn't remember telling John what she did for a living. Victoria Stuyvesant, noticing her surprise, burst out laughing again.

"Don't worry, Juliet. I know all about you. To let you come up to my house, they've even investigated your early years in Gibraltar. It's a security protocol, and it applies to everyone. You understand that, don't you?"

"What a hassle."

"I once interviewed at your agency. I was looking for reps, and they told me that Shaughnessy & McCameron was the best in the world. They got the best auditions and signed the best contracts. I said to myself, 'Vicky, if you want to make it in the movies, you have to hire these people.'"

"What happened?"

"They threw me to the lions. They put Jennifer Davies in front of me. Do you know her?" Juliet nodded. "She took me in, gave me an hour and a half of bitching, and then told me that I was no good, that they only worked with real actors, not supermodels with starlet pretensions."

"Wow, I'm sorry."

"Anyway, as soon as I saw her, I knew what was going to happen. Do you know why?"

"No."

"Because she had dated a boyfriend of mine, theater director Joe Ostenberguer. He left her for me. That was about fifteen years ago, but she doesn't forget. She's a twisted bitch."

"You haven't kept up the acting?" Juliet played along because she didn't want to seem rude, even though she wasn't interested in talking about Jennifer.

"Yes, of course. I've done a lot of things. I still dream of having an agent like Shaughnessy & McCameron, you know? Although to tell the truth, I barely have time. I also paint and design clothes. I'm an interior designer and a full-time mother as well."

"Ah." She looked around, and Victoria opened her arms.

"Yes, you're not wrong. I decorated this house. Could you look at the audiovisual work I've done? I assure you I'm a very good actress."

"Sure, I'd love to see your stuff."

"Now that we're friends, you can plug me in."

"I can't promise anything because it's not up to me alone, but maybe we can do something."

"Don't say you don't play a role. Don't be so modest. When I found out what you did for a living, I made some calls. Everyone told me that you are one of the big shots in London and Iona McCameron's right-hand woman."

"Hm." Juliet picked up her tea, then sat down across from her, ready to cut the polite chit-chat short. Victoria seemed very nice, but she was more long-winded than her mother, so she touched the cell phone in her pocket.

"Can I turn on the phone? Do you think we could make a video call with my friend Michiel who is in London? Both he and I..."

"No, that is impossible. Safety measures." She made a circle with her finger, rolling her eyes as if to tell her that they were surrounded by cameras, then smiled at her.

"Do you want to talk about your business?"

"Yes, please."

"Shoot. I'm all ears."

"I suppose John told you that Michiel and I are looking for our friend, Mrs. Audrey Stuyvesant. Audrey is our neighbor in the Barbican Estate in central London. We shared a lot of time with her during the confinement, and she suddenly disappeared about four months ago."

"Suddenly?"

"Yes. She didn't say goodbye to either of us or anyone. She missed her appointments with her doctor and with Social Services, who sent her the home help she had been asking about for months. She left overnight, leaving her house untouched, by the way. We began to investigate, concerned about her whereabouts, and finally, here I am."

She smiled. "After much research, we discovered that her late husband, Gregory, was a member of your family. I know they haven't spoken to him in sixty-five years. John Tompkins confirmed this for me, but since I'm in New York on business and John offered to put us in touch, I just wanted to ask if, by any chance, you have any news of Audrey."

"Of course, we have news of Aunt Audrey. She's family."

"Excuse me?"

Her heart skipped a beat, and she gripped the edge of the chair to keep from falling to the floor. Victoria stretched theatrically, looking up at the clear Manhattan sky, then let out a laugh.

"It's amazing how legends continue to be created around this family, and we don't feed any of them."

"I'm sorry. I'm just shocked because we've been looking for her for three months. We've moved heaven and earth. Do you know where she is? How is she?"

"Perfect, she looks great. I think Uncle Gregory called her his "Rose of England," and rightly so since she is precious and unique."

"'Rose of England?'" Precious and unique? Juliet had never heard that before, and it sounded very farfetched, not credible. Very much like something out of a fifth-rate movie. She hid it well and took a deep breath, trying not to look disbelieving.

"Why have you moved heaven and earth? Is your friendship with Aunt Audrey so important?"

"We became very close and, to tell the truth, that a lady eighty-three years old, almost like my grandmother, would leave without warning or saying goodbye seemed very strange to us. It worried us a little. We could not let it go."

"She was very lucky to have people like you who loved her and took care of her during the confinement. When she became a widow, she was very lonely."

"Yes, she was very lonely. She always said she had no family and no one to count on. It's reassuring to know that she is well. Do you know where she is?"

"She is here in New York. When the family heard of her situation in London in that dreary little flat downtown, alone and pining for Uncle Gregory, God rest his soul," she crossed herself, closing her eyes, then sighed, "they decided to look for her. She now lives in the main house, that of my in-laws and my eldest brother-in-law, Charles."

"How nice. Do you think I could visit her before I go back to London? I know she would be glad to see me."

"Of course. This week? When is it convenient for you?"

"Whenever you tell me. I'll stay here until I've seen her."

"Let's see. It's Thursday, so the weekend for sure. Count on it. I'll call you. One more thing..." She looked at the time and stood up. "Don't believe that 'sixty-five years' without talking to Uncle Gregory. His father was indeed very angry with him when he did not marry the fiancée he had here and practically eloped with an English girl of seventeen, but, after a while, they saw each other again and treated each other well. Everything else is part of the legend. Believe me."

"Very good."

"The truth is that my husband and my brothers-in-law were heartbroken to learn that she was half-abandoned in London, asking for home help from Social Services, and they took action. Maybe it was hasty, and she didn't have time to say goodbye to you, but don't hold it against her. She was so excited about coming to New York that she forgot about everything else."

"It's all right. The important thing is that she is well."

"She is. Come on; I'll walk you to the door."

"Thank you so much for everything, Victoria. You have taken a huge weight off my shoulders."

"I'm glad to hear that. Now you can go on about your business," she said matter-of-factly. Juliet again felt that this was very strange, but she put it down to her usual paranoia and reached the front door of the house, where the butler was waiting for her with the elevator ready.

"Thank you very much."

"Thank you, Juliet. It was nice to meet you."

"You can send the material from your work to my email, and we'll see what I can do about it."

"Great! Thank you, love, and thank you for loving our Rose of England so much."

"You're welcome." She forced a smile. "I'll wait to go see Audrey. I won't move from Manhattan until I can visit her. In the meantime, please send her a kiss from Michiel and me."

She leaned over to give her two kisses, and Juliet saw a very peculiar guy appear from behind her—the so-called real estate agent, Jack Lynch, who had surprised them inside Audrey's apartment at the beginning of their research.

He was dressed in a black suit, just like in Barbican. He gave her a sidelong glance and disappeared immediately, but he had set off her alarms. She looked back at Victoria and insisted on visiting Audrey. Then she said goodbye, rode the elevator down to the lobby alone, got out without looking at anyone, and crossed to the park. She turned on the phone, so excited that she could barely press the buttons.

"Michiel!"

"Thank God! I haven't breathed for an hour. Are you all right? How did it go?"

"Audrey is in New York."

"*What?*"

"Victoria, who is a very peculiar person, I'll tell you, has confirmed that 'Aunt Audrey' lives in the main family house. Who knows what that is or where she is, but Audrey lives there, and she has assured me that she is perfect and lush, like a rose of England.

"A rose of England?"

"She says that's what Gregory called her."

"I've never heard that."

"Me either. Listen, this is important." She looked for a bench and sat down. "On the way out of the house, I caught a glimpse of that guy Jack Lynch. The real estate agent."

"Are you sure?"

"I swear to God."

"Fuck, Juliet! When are you coming back to London? This is giving me a really bad feeling, and it's getting weirder."

"It's weird, but it's not that weird. Maybe he's family security personnel or something. I can think of a thousand scenarios, but the important thing is that I'm going to be able to visit Audrey. Victoria has assured me, and I will not move from here until I see her with my own eyes."

"Are you going to the main house?"

"She told me the weekend. If she doesn't call me by Sunday, I'll ask again."

"Okay, fine, but you can't go alone."

"It is not Dracula's castle."

"I don't know, but it's wiser for you to be accompanied, Juliet."

"I don't think they'll eat me. It's the Stuyvesant residence in Manhattan, but if you insist. I can ask a colleague from the office to come with me, or one of my actors who are here, or John Tompkins."

"Not John Tompkins or anyone like him. I'm going to get a ticket, and I'll be in New York tomorrow."

"What? Are you crazy?"

"It's the mid-term vacation week. Daniel is going skiing with his mother in Switzerland tomorrow, and I can fly to New York. I don't know why I didn't think of that before."

"I am not a damsel in distress, my dear Watson."

"I know, but I also want to see Audrey with my own eyes, and I'll watch your back while I'm at it. That's always been my job, Sherlock."

———

"*Madre del amor hermoso,*" she mumbled in Spanish as she saw him get out of the cab and turned to see if anyone had heard her. Happily, no one had, and she returned her gaze to Michiel, who was arriving at the hotel from Kennedy Airport.

For some reason, his face, his appearance, had blurred in twelve days, and seeing him again in mortal flesh impressed her greatly. It reminded her of the kiss they had shared in the foyer of her house. She had to admit that it had been very good and that she had been very clumsy. Very rational, yes, but very clumsy to cut short a roll between friends that could have turned into something interesting.

"Hey!" he exclaimed when he saw her at the hotel door. He dropped the suitcase, reached out, and pulled her close to squeeze her against his chest. Juliet returned the embrace with her eyes closed and stayed there, smelling his aftershave and enjoying the feel of his shirt for a few comforting seconds until he pulled her away and looked her up and down.

"A thousand thanks for sending me a car."

"It's from the company, don't worry." She smiled at him, losing herself in those blue eyes that were so dark in the daylight that they were breathtaking. She cleared her throat to try to focus on what was important.

"How was the flight? I have news."

"The flight went very well. What's the news?"

"First, let's check you in." She took him to the reception desk and greeted one of the receptionists. "Brittany, this is my guest, Mr. Michiel Lezer. I believe Andrea made the reservation yesterday."

"Of course. You have a reservation with no departure date. I need your passport, please, Mr. Lezer."

"Thank you, Brittany." Juliet looked at him and gestured for him to hand over the passport.

"What's up?"

"Are you going to pay for my hotel, too?"

"I'm not paying for anything." She took the passport from him, put it on the table, and pushed it aside to talk to him quietly. "Shaughnessy & McCameron has an annual agreement with this hotel. We pay them a fortune every month to keep several suites available for us, even if we don't use them, and right now, they're all free. No problem. I can dispose of them as I wish, and you're my guest. Okay?"

"Sometimes I wonder how powerful you are, Sherlock. You're a little scary."

"It's okay to be afraid of me."

He picked up the card key and his passport and went to the elevators. Juliet followed.

"Victoria called me three hours ago to tell me that we can see Audrey today at four o'clock."

"So soon?"

"Yes. I don't know what happened, but today seemed to suit her, so I said yes."

"Of course, although I was planning to stay at least a week in Manhattan on the excuse of waiting."

"You can stay as long as you want, but for now, go upstairs and leave the suitcase. I'll wait for you here. We have an hour to get to their mansion."

"I'll take a quick shower and change. Won't you come up with me?" he asked as he stood outside the elevator.

"No, I have to settle something at work. I'll wait for you in the café. Take it easy, but don't be too long."

"One second. I have something for you."

He rummaged through his backpack, pulled out a folder the size of half a sheet of paper with transparent covers and the typical plastic binding, and handed it to her.

"I printed out your script. I don't object to it, and I have jotted down some notes of my own."

"Wow, what a nice guy! Thank you very much."

"I have two copies. Keep this one."

"I love it. Thank you very much. This is worth gold in my business, you know?"

"A little folder made in the teachers' lounge at my school?"

"No, what is priceless is an original idea." She kissed him on the cheek and hugged him. "I'll take the opportunity to show it to Audrey. I'd like her blessing before we get into the technical script and everything else."

"I'm sure she'll love it."

"I hope. Now go upstairs. I'll wait for you in the café at the entrance."

He waved at her, thinking she was amazing and adorable.

She went to the café to have a drink and called one of her actors, who was in the midst of an existential crisis, overwhelmed by the avalanche of projects on his plate.

It was curious because ninety-nine percent of actors spent their lives working and struggling to be famous, recognized, and claimed by all the producers and directors in the world, but some of them, as soon as fame came to them, especially if it was sudden, were alarmed and could not stand the pressure. Iona used to say that they were not star material or good professionals, and they would end up throwing away the great opportunity of a lifetime. Therefore, they made her waste time and money, and she got rid of them at the first opportunity.

She was implacable about that. However, Juliet preferred to

give them a chance, and that's what she was doing with Regé, her fashionable guy. A wonderful actor who, after eight years in the business, had become a bombshell, the most sought-after actor and the most besieged heartthrob. The poor guy had had to digest the great success overnight without expecting it and was on the verge of an anxiety attack and worse, of throwing in the towel. She wouldn't allow it. She wanted to offer him an emotional lifeline, so she called him and listened to him and comforted him until Michiel Lezer appeared at her table with wet hair, dressed to the nines.

"Reggie, I have to leave you, honey, but call me whenever you want. The time change works in our favor," she said, standing up. "Now I have an unavoidable commitment, but later, if you can't sleep, call me, and we'll continue chatting. Take care, bye."

"Did I take too long?" Michiel asked, fixing his hair with his fingers.

She shook her head. "I didn't notice because I've been on the phone for half an hour. You look very handsome, my dear Watson."

"I'm just trying to get to your level."

"Oh, how cute you are."

She looked carefully at her navy blue pants, her white shirt, and her fashionable black anorak and took her bag. She had also taken great care with her attire because she was aware that they were going to a very exclusive place and it was better to make a good impression. She clung to his arm, thanking God that he was there because she would not have been as happy to visit Audrey in the famous Stuyvesant residence alone.

"Welcome." A butler in a frock coat opened the glass door of an impressive mansion in the heart of the Upper East Side, a stone's throw from MoMA.

The two smiled at him, trying to conceal their surprise at finding such a palace in the heart of the city. "Juliet Miller and Michiel Lezer. They're expecting us," said Michiel.

The man stepped away from the door and let them into an equally impressive foyer. "I think they're only expecting you, Miss Miller."

"No, I..."

"Juliet, my friend!" a female voice exclaimed, and she saw Victoria Stuyvesant coming up to hug her. She was wearing a quirky hippie dress and a very strong perfume that made Juliet blink, but she returned the hug and pointed at Michiel.

"Victoria, this is my friend Michiel Lezer, and he doesn't speak Spanish, so if you don't mind?"

"We switch to English. Hello, Michiel Lezer. A little bird told me a lot about you, but it was an understatement because you are much more handsome than I was informed."

"Hello. Nice to meet you."

He was intimidated by the blatant scrutiny, and Victoria clapped her hands like a little girl before she gave orders to the butler about the winter garden and preparing a tea service. "Let's go to the solarium. Aunt Audrey is there with her nurse. It's freezing cold in Manhattan, but it's always *primavera* there. Come with me."

"Nurse?" they asked each other silently, looking into each other's eyes, then followed Victoria through the corridors of that house. It looked like a mausoleum. Everything was huge and filled with marble, paintings, gilding, and clocks, and it was silent.

Neither opened their mouth until Victoria turned as if she'd read their minds and smiled at them. "There is no one else in the house. The family spends the weekends in the Hamptons. There is only the nurse, Aunt Audrey, and me. She is very nervous about the visit, so be patient."

"Does she know that we are coming?"

"Yes, yes. We explained it to her."

As they reached the end of a corridor, Victoria pointed at a brightly lit area that appeared to be open to the outdoors but was glassed in like a greenhouse and invited them in. Juliet smelled roses, grass, and wet earth and heard water falling in several fountains. It was an enveloping sound, and without meaning to, she calculated that it must have cost a fortune.

"Aunt Audrey, look who has finally arrived."

"Oh, my God! I can't believe it," Audrey Stuyvesant exclaimed when she saw them. She stood up and opened her arms to them. They came up to her and hugged her in unison, which caused her to burst out laughing. They pulled away to look at her carefully. She looked gorgeous, with her hair professionally done, nice clothes, and a bit of makeup.

Juliet realized she was crying from the sheer relief of seeing her safe and sound and hugged her again.

"Don't cry, Juliet honey. How come you're in New York, and more importantly, how come you're here together?"

Michiel replied, "I've just arrived from London. I wanted to come with her to see you. We were very worried when we found out that you had left without warning, and we started to look for you together."

"It was his idea," Juliet told her. "He asked me about you one day, and we got to talking and decided to track you down to make sure you were doing okay. I'm happy to see that you're doing so well and looking so beautiful. Do you like New York?"

"I love New York, and being with my Gregory's family is priceless. They are so good to me."

"Because you're family, Aunt Audrey. How are we going to behave? We all love you," Victoria commented. "I'm going to check on the tea. I'll be right back."

"Sit down, you two. Have you fallen in love already?" Audrey let them go and returned to her chair, and they frowned at her. "Ever since I've known you, I've wanted to pair you up. I always told Michiel, 'Talk to the girl next door. She's adorable, she's smart, she's got a good job, and she's beautiful.' You're made for each other. Don't they make a wonderful couple, Fran?"

"Yes, Mrs. Stuyvesant," replied the nurse.

"She still won't let herself fall for me," Michiel joked, "but give me time, Audrey."

"Very funny." Juliet looked at the two of them, then sat down across from her. "Are you sure you're okay? Are they treating you well? Are you comfortable here? Don't you miss London?"

"I'm very comfortable. Don't you see that, honey?"

"How is your health? Are you continuing with your usual treatments?" Michiel asked.

The nurse answered. "Of course, sir. Mrs. Stuyvesant has the best doctors in the United States at her disposal. Her health is perfect; she is much better now than when she came from London. We take daily walks, go out to the theater, to dinner, and to the ballet. She enjoys whatever she pleases. The family has given strict orders that her every whim be indulged. Isn't that right, Mrs. Stuyvesant?"

"It's true."

"Do you live here or in the Hamptons?"

"We live here, miss. The humid climate of the Hamptons doesn't help her rheumatism."

"Manhattan is as humid as the Hamptons," Juliet rebutted, but Audrey interrupted her.

"Where are you staying?"

"At the Room Mate Grace Hotel. It's not far from here. Maybe we can come back tomorrow to take you to lunch."

"I'm going to Florida tomorrow. They say I'll love the weather."

"Really?"

"Really, Michiel. What about you guys? How's Romeo, Juliet, and Rocío? How's your son, Michiel? How are your families?"

"Everyone is well. We were with your sister-in-law, your

older brother's wife, and her son Phillip in Hampstead," Juliet told her, but she didn't seem surprised. "We had trouble finding them. It was lucky, and they were delighted to hear about you. Your sister-in-law is waiting for you to write or contact her."

"Rosamund is gossipy and envious. Why did you talk to her?"

"We were just trying to reach you."

"I hate Hampstead. My parents kicked me out of there, and I never went back. It brings back very bad memories."

"We didn't know you were on bad terms with your family, just as we didn't know you had emigrated to Australia with Gregory," Michiel interjected, and she squinted at him.

"Bah, what nonsense. I'm sure Rosamund told you that. Gregory and I spent our honeymoon there and stayed there for over a year, but then we moved back to London. We lived for many years in South Kensington, where we were very happy, and eventually, we bought the apartment on the Barbican Estate because I was mad to live in a modern, more secluded apartment.

"Ah."

"So, no hidden identities and false surnames?" Juliet asked directly, and Audrey started to get angry.

"No, but what lies are these? Pay no attention to what my family tells you, let alone what Rosamund might tell you. I'd like some tea, please. Fran, tell my niece to hurry up."

"Of course, Mrs. Stuyvesant."

The nurse stepped a couple of feet away to call on an internal phone. Juliet looked at Michiel in surprise because she had never seen sweet Mrs. Stuyvesant so upset, and he motioned for her to stay calm.

"We don't want you to be angry, Audrey. Juliet and I have come a long way to see that you are so happy and so comfortable. She has only asked you about the doubts that have arisen along the way, such as a supposed life in Australia and even a supposed change of surname. It is normal that we ask questions. We love you, and we are interested in you."

"All those things are lies."

"Very good, perfect. This garden is beautiful," commented Michiel, changing the subject.

Audrey's face changed from anger to satisfaction. "Yes, it's over a hundred and fifty years old. My Gregory used to play among these plants when he was a little boy, you know, and now the gardener lets me give him a hand. I love spending the day here."

"It is spectacular."

"Juliet, how's work? Are you writing any novels? She writes, you know." She looked at Michiel. "She's very talented, though she doesn't believe it."

"Work is as stressful as ever, and yes, I am writing something. I would love to write about your love story with Gregory because I think it's beautiful."

"Are you serious?"

"Of course. How you met in London, how you lived for each other. It was many years together."

"The unusual love story of an English box-office girl married to a rich American heir, isn't it?" she asked, and Juliet nodded. "Write it down. It's a movie, and I'd love people to know about it."

"That's great, thank you." She reached out and patted Audrey's hand. "I will consider myself authorized. We've gathered a lot of information about you and this family, and—"

"No, not about this family. Change the names, or they will come after you."

"What do you mean, they'll come after me?"

"They're bringing the tea, Mrs. Stuyvesant. They just wanted to give you some time alone," the nurse interrupted, and Juliet turned her attention to her.

"Excuse me, Fran. Where are you from?"

"Puerto Rico, why?"

"I am half-Spanish," she replied in Spanish, "and you have a slight accent. So, the lady is very well off here?"

"Yes, miss," she answered in Spanish. "They have her wrapped in cotton wool, although she lives with me. She hardly has contact with the family."

"Wow."

"Hi, guys! How's it going?" Victoria appeared out of nowhere and sat very close to them. "Pour the tea, Fran. Have you caught up yet?"

"Yes, we see that she is very well."

"I told you, she's like a rose from England."

"Have they brought all your things back from London yet, Audrey?"

"I don't need anything here, Juliet, and when I go back to Barbican on vacation, I can have the apartment just as I left it."

"Didn't you put it up for sale?"

Michiel looked at Juliet, stretched out his hand, and placed it on her knee. She raised her eyes and saw in the glass behind Audrey the reflection of that guy, the famous Jack Lynch, following the conversation attentively. She almost jumped, but before she could do anything, the guy came up to greet them politely.

"Good afternoon."

"Jack, come in. Have some tea," Victoria invited him, and he gave a small bow.

"No, thank you, Vicky. I was just stopping by to say hello."

"You know Juliet and Michiel. They have come all the way from London to greet Aunt Audrey. Guys, this is Jack Lynch, head of security for the Stuyvesant family. I think you've met him."

"Yes, but on that occasion, he told us he was a real estate agent," Michiel commented, and Victoria laughed.

"I'm sure I misspoke," Lynch said in a perfect American accent and gave them another nod. "Glad to greet you. Victoria, the car will pick you up in fifteen minutes."

"We'll be ready, won't we, Aunt Audrey?"

"Of course. I am already prepared. Victoria invited me to the opera, you know?" Audrey answered excitedly, and they looked at each other and left the teacups on the table.

"Yes, *Turandot* at Lincoln Center."

"I'm so happy to have seen you, my loves, but we have to go. We'll see each other another time, okay?"

"When are you coming back to London?"

"Soon."

"Then later. Greetings to all at home. Come, give me a hug."

Everyone stood up with her, and Juliet hugged her tightly, reminding her to let them know if she needed anything. She handed Audrey a card with their phone numbers, email, and all their details and stepped aside to let Michiel say goodbye. The butler, not Victoria, escorted them to the front door, left them on the stairs leading to the street, and closed the door gently and politely but forcefully.

"What do you think?" she asked Michiel as she zipped up her coat. He took a deep breath, looked at the cloudy sky, and put an arm around her shoulders to walk back to the hotel.

"I don't know, but I need a drink."

"She looks perfect, radiant, but she only gives us an hour of her time when we have crossed half the planet to see her? It's not like her. Something's wrong. She didn't even thank us. She's going to Florida tomorrow?"

"It's unusual. She was kind of abducted by her new family. Older people are sometimes like children."

"When I spoke to the nurse in Spanish, she told me that she lives alone with her and she has little contact with the family."

"That thing about changing the names, or they will come after you?"

"Very strong. I'm freaking out. Everything is so weird."

"It's all very strange. However, our objective was to find her, see her, and check that she was well, and we have achieved that. We should celebrate."

"You are right."

"Do you know of a place to get drunk, Sherlock?"

"I know a great hotel bar that is so trendy, it has a waiting list to get in. On top of that, you can get a bite to eat, and I'm starving."

"Great. Let's get wild."

CHAPTER FIFTEEN

"Iceland alone? Why?" Michiel asked, relaxed and a bit disheveled, from a sofa in the cozy and beautiful bar of their hotel where they had stopped after the visit to Audrey.

Juliet nodded with a wink. "What do you mean, why?"

"No one goes hiking in Iceland alone. It's a bore, Sherlock."

"It's not boring; it's quite the opposite. On top of that, I was not alone all the time. I met other hikers in the refuges or at refreshment points."

"You're a *rara avis,* Juliet. Why were you traveling alone?"

"I'm not that rare. I know many people who prefer to travel solo. It was the best decision I've ever made."

"Why?"

"First, because if I have to wait for someone to want to travel where I want to go and on the dates I can, I wouldn't ever do anything, and second and more importantly, because travel destroys a lot of friendships."

"That's not true. It's important to choose the right company."

"I must be a terrible choice because my travels have often become real torture. My best friend since kindergarten hasn't spoken to me since our last trip to Greece. She behaved terribly with me, and I must have behaved terribly with her because I haven't seen her since we parted at the airport. We traveled together other times, but this last time she was insufferable. She went too far with me. I ended up reproaching her, and she was not used to me confronting her. She stopped talking to me."

"When was that?"

"Two years ago, when I turned thirty. From that moment on, I decided I would travel alone for my own well-being and that of others because I must be a bloody nuisance."

"You know what? You have a very pessimistic view of people and a very unfair view of yourself, Juliet. You're an amazing, funny, and very interesting woman. You could never be a fucking nuisance."

"You're very nice, my dear Watson. Have a drink. It's on me."

"Will you let me take you to Amsterdam?"

"I've been there many times, but I'm up for going with a native."

"Thank you very much. I promise I will get you to trust in the human race again."

"I think that ship has sailed. My goodness!"

She sat up when she saw a group from her office enter the bar, including Jennifer Davies. She snorted because they had been sitting there for several hours, chatting about everything and reviewing the visit to Audrey, and she felt terrible that they might be invaded with greetings and idle chatter. She looked at Michiel, and he smiled at her.

"It's ten o'clock at night. Maybe it's time to go to bed. I'm a little bit loopy."

"Are you going to go upstairs to sleep at ten o'clock at night?"

"I'm jet-lagged."

"I know, but..."

"*Carpe diem*, Juliet."

"It can't be! That's the second time I've caught you with him, Juliet Miller. You're a very naughty girl," Jennifer exclaimed. She came closer, looking heart-stopping, and gazed at the two of them with her hands on her hips, then took a step toward Michiel and collapsed on his couch, very close to him.

Juliet followed the movement as if it happened in slow motion and wanted to strangle her, but she didn't do it and glanced at her with all the calmness in the world.

"How are you doing, Jennifer?"

"How about you two hotties? What are you doing drinking here instead of fucking in your room?"

"We were in the mood for a quiet dinner." She looked at Michiel, who was laughing his head off.

"We're all going to Leo DiCaprio's party. Did he invite you?"

"Yes, but I don't feel like going all the way to Brooklyn for that."

"Of course not." She winked, reached out, and placed her hand on Michiel's thigh. "If I were you, I wouldn't leave the hotel either."

"Don't bother him. Just for touching him like that, he could sue you for harassment, you know?" she whispered to Jennifer, wanting to pull her away by the hair. Before she could get up, her phone vibrated insistently, and she had to look at it to check that it was nothing important. Unfortunately, it was, and she greeted Regé, who had already left her a couple of voice messages.

"Reggie, how are you? Isn't it a little early for you?"

"They pick me up at five in the morning to go to the shoot. Listen, can we talk? Your press people have sent me press releases that I neither asked for nor understand."

"Okay." She turned to look at the couch where she had left Michiel and saw with horror that Jennifer was saying something in his ear while he was laughing loudly, not moving an inch away from her. She took a deep breath and stopped watching them. "Wait a second. I'm in a public place. Give me five minutes, and I'll call you back, okay?"

"Okay."

She hung up and retraced her steps to the couple. Michiel, seeing her face, jumped up. "Is everything all right?"

"No. One of my actors is in the middle of a crisis and needs to talk and have me explain some issues."

"At this hour?"

"Crises don't know about schedules. I'm going up to my room to talk to him, okay?"

"Okay. I'll come up with you."

"It's not necessary. The night is young. Have something else to drink, and if I can, I'll come down in a little while."

"Don't you want me to come up with you? You sure? I don't mind waiting for you to finish with your actor."

She gazed into his blue eyes. "It can take forever." Juliet thought about it, considered what Reggie was like, and shook her head.

"Don't you want to have a last drink with me in your room?" he insisted.

Juliet took a deep breath. "Shall I call you when I'm free?"

"If you don't want to, don't worry about me."

"Okay." She dialed Reggie's number and ran until she reached the lobby. The concierge stopped her. She approached the counter, and he handed her a large, thick, heavy envelope.

"This was delivered for you an hour ago, Miss Miller."

"Thank you very much."

She went up in the elevator, chatting, reassuring, and explaining to Regé the press releases Shaughnessy & McCameron wanted to issue to clarify his situation regarding the work that had made him famous and to which he did not want to return. She went into her room in her bare feet and sat on the bed with the phone and the envelope, assuming it was a courtesy gift or something related to her work.

"Are you calmer?"

"Yes, but I know that if I talk, they'll be all over me."

"That's why we will do it on your behalf. For the time being, the best thing to do is to forget about social networks."

He looked at the time and saw that it was midnight for her. "Okay, Juliet, and thanks for the support. I love you."

"That's what I'm here for."

"We'll talk. I've just arrived at the studio."

"Great. Have a good shoot."

She hung up on him, feeling immense exhaustion, then turned on the TV and collapsed on the pillow. She thought about calling Michiel to apologize for disappearing and remembered the envelope. She opened it, turned it over on the comforter, and saw that it contained four very mangled notebooks and a handwritten note.

My dear Juliet,

I am sending Fran with my diaries, the ones I brought with me from London that tell my love story with Gregory from the time we met until we left Australia to return to England. You can use all the information you want. I only ask you to change the names for security and out of respect for the Stuyvesant family. I give you my wholehearted permission to write a book or that screenplay you were always talking about, or both.

I knew I would have to give you a lot of explanations and tell you a lot of things. You and Michiel are the only friends I have had in years, so I hope these diaries will clear up all your questions.

Thank you for looking for me, for caring about me, and for visiting me.

I will love you always.

Audrey Stuyvesant

When she finished reading the note, she realized it was raining and called Michiel, but he didn't answer. She put on her shoes and went out into the hallway to look for him in his room, but he didn't answer either, so she went back to bed, put on her pajamas and glasses, and read the diaries. They told the passionate love story between Audrey Glenn and Peter Gregory Stuyvesant III in great detail.

Everything was dated and explained. There were even a couple of photos, and when she got to the Australian part, she discovered with astonishment that they had not made a mistake and the Glenns had not lied to them. It was true that Audrey and Gregory had emigrated to Victoria, where they had lived for more than twenty years until the death of Gregory's father, using the McCrory surname.

Audrey had denied it, but her diaries confirmed it, and now those diaries were in Julia's hands. She devoured them until it was late enough that she closed her eyes and fell asleep.

"I'm going to have breakfast, Mum. I'll call you later. I'm glad you are well."

"I'll see if you come in time to order the wedding dress. You have to give an astronomical deposit, but if you can't, I'll cover it until you come back."

"Okay. Thank you very much."

At ten o'clock, she got off the elevator and walked down the hall to the café, intending to have breakfast. After taking two steps, she saw Michiel Lezer kissing Jennifer Davies at the main entrance of the hotel.

It was like a cold shower hit her, leaving her frozen in place like an idiot, unable to take her eyes off them and feeling an absurd embarrassment that made her blush. She moved to the side and noticed without much astonishment that they were both dressed in the clothes from the day before, which made it abundantly clear that they had spent the night together.

"Mum, I have to hang up."

"Something's wrong. Your voice has changed."

"Nothing. It's just that I've seen something a little bad."

"What's a little bit bad don't scare me."

"No, it has nothing to do with me."

She turned slowly, determined to go back to her room and not leave until that horrendous discomfort was gone, but before she could do so, she heard Jennifer's shrill voice calling to her. She had no choice but to stop and look at her, hiding as best she could the internal revolution that was attacking her from within.

"Hi, Jennifer. Hi, Michiel."

"You missed an amazing party, and in the end, I ended up enjoying this handsome gentleman." She hugged Michiel and kissed his neck. "But I brought him back to you safe and sound."

"I'm glad. I am going to..."

She pointed at the elevators and started to walk to them but froze when she saw Jennifer pull the little black-edged booklet containing her script out of her purse. Her heart stopped, and she looked at Michiel with wide eyes.

"Michiel told me about your original idea. It will be a pleasure to hear about the script. You know that with my contacts..."

"How could you?"

She ignored Jennifer, and Michiel blinked, startled. He let go of Jennifer and approached her. Juliet stepped back, and when she was far enough away from Jennifer Davies, she stopped and pushed him in the chest.

"Why the hell did you give her my original idea? How dare you give her my work!"

"Calm down, Juliet. She's—"

"You fuck her, and now you betray me?"

"Betray you? She's your colleague. You told me she's very good and very efficient."

"I also told you that she spends her life trying to annoy me. Are you aware of what you've just done to me?"

"No. Come on. You know I would never hurt you. Juliet, listen..."

"Go fuck off with your new girlfriend and leave me alone."

She pressed the button to call the elevator, but he stayed beside her.

"Juliet, I only wanted to collaborate so..."

"You, like all the guys I know, fuck a hot chick and forget about everything else—friends, loyalties, common sense. You're just like everyone else, kid. Unfortunately, you just fucked up so bad that you'd better not say a word to me again in your fucking life. Is that clear to you?"

"No!"

"When did you tell her about my idea? When? When you were fucking her, or right after?" She looked him in the eye and he snorted, then put his hands on his hips. "You have no right to talk about me or my business with anyone. With *anyone*, much less with a bitch like her, who in bed may be a goddess, but in real life is a real horse's ass, especially to me."

"Juliet."

"Fuck you."

She entered the elevator, didn't let him in, and pressed the button for her floor while looking at her cell phone. Her pulse was racing, but not so much that she couldn't find her boss's number and dial it. She waited for two rings and heard Iona's voice.

"What is it, Juliet?"

"I need a favor."

"What's wrong? Are you all right?"

"I've never asked you for a personal favor, but now I need one."

"Relax, honey. What's going on? Are you still in New York?"

"Yes, but not for long. Listen." She swallowed as she reached her floor and walked to her suite. "I have an original idea, the script of a true story that could also be turned into a book. I have authorization from the protagonist to write it. I have developed the plot, the characters, and the lines of action, but due to a tactical failure, it has just fallen into the hands of Jennifer Davies.

I need you to endorse me and protect me against her. You know what happened with Shonda Rhimes. She claimed my idea, though she hadn't even read the books, and laughed at me to my face."

"I know."

"I'm going to send you the original idea in writing in five minutes and also to Bill so the legal department can register it in my name, okay?"

"Okay, but take a breath."

"Thank you." She went straight to get her suitcase. "This time, it's not an adapted script. It's an original script, all mine. I've worked very hard on it, and I'm not going to let that bitch steal from me again."

"Of course. One thing, Juliet."

"What?" She put the suitcase on the bed and opened the laptop.

"How did it fall into her hands?"

"The person who helped me document it slept with her."

"Fuck."

"I know. I don't know why I still trust people."

"Okay, don't torture yourself. We'll get on with it, and if Jennifer calls me to talk to me about it, I'll set her up."

"Thank you very much, Iona. I just sent you the document, and it goes with a copy to Bill. I need him to register it first thing Monday morning."

"I will take care of it personally."

"Thank you very much. As soon as I hang up, I'm off to the airport."

"Great, because we need you here. Goodbye, and take it easy, honey."

She said goodbye, still trembling, between pissed off, shattered, and desolated. Feeling like she was dying, she looked at the flights to London that were leaving that morning, then grabbed her credit card. The door echoed with several sharp knocks. She thought about not opening it since she didn't want to see anyone, but they were so insistent that she finally walked over, took a deep breath, and opened the door to find Michiel Lezer with a funeral face in the hallway.

"Juliet, I'm so sorry. It's clear that all the blame is mine, but I did it with good intentions. We're friends, and we're partners in this. How could I want to hurt you? You know me a little. You know I would never… Juliet?" He looked at her with wet eyes, but she didn't speak or move. "Okay, here's the script. Jennifer gave it back to me."

He held it out to her and she took it, and in the same motion, she slammed the door in his face without a word. She had nothing to say.

She backed up to the bed, hearing him repeat her name a few times, fortunately without knocking again. She opened the suitcase and took her clothes out of the closet. She packed quietly, picked up the computer, put it in the backpack, and then sat down for a while to catch her breath and compose herself. When she was calmer, she stood up, grabbed her luggage, and left.

PART II

MICHIEL

CHAPTER SIXTEEN

His name was Michiel, not Michel. He spent his life correcting people, and when he was much younger, he had even accepted Michel as correct to avoid explaining it over and over. Michiel was a name of Hebrew origin widely used in the Netherlands whose meaning is "Who is like God?" Michiel Lezer bore it for two reasons; first, because it was the name of his grandfather, the first Michiel Lezer in the family, and second, because of his Jewish origins.

Born into a modern and progressive Dutch Jewish family, he had grown up in Amsterdam with considerable freedom. His father, a musician by profession, and his mother, a psychiatrist, had instilled in him and his siblings a love of culture, travel, art, and humanity. From an early age, he had been surrounded by people and had never had any problems relating to them, much less with the opposite sex, to which he had devoted himself since adolescence.

Thus, when he arrived at the university, his experience in that field was already proven. He had no gaps to fill, no longing to fill in that part of his life. He did not subscribe to the idea of romantic love, nor did he aspire to achieve a movie romance. All that concerned him little. He had decided to move away from stable relationships to free and uncommitted sex. Open relationships provided him with well-being and comfort, serenity, and above all, independence.

When he reached thirty-one, one of his best friends proposed that he become the biological father of her child, and he accepted in exchange for letting him participate fully in the child's life. His universe had changed. Everything had become more stable, but he had still not considered a monogamous relationship with anyone.

The only stable and permanent thing in his life was his son Daniel, for whom he lived in London and with whom he maintained a continuous and unbreakable bond. At the age of forty, he was still living on his own, alone or combining passing affection with free and autonomous women with whom he did not maintain even the slightest hint of commitment. For that reason, too, his friends considered him a lucky guy.

He lived alone in an apartment in central London that he shared every other weekend with his son, he had a job that fulfilled him in many ways, and he had a family in Amsterdam that he adored. In short, he had a rich and well-organized existence that, for some inexplicable reason, was beginning to change. Something was moving around him; he couldn't explain it, but he could sense it. Something was about to happen, and as always in these cases, he knew there was nothing he could do to prevent it.

He got out of the shower and saw that it was three o'clock in the afternoon. With any luck, Juliet would be over her annoyance, and he could talk to her. With any luck, he could invite her for a walk in Central Park and then dinner. With any luck, he could make amends and make peace with her, he hoped, because otherwise, he wouldn't know how to handle it.

He got dressed while looking at the spectacular view from the window of his hotel, which was located in the heart of

Manhattan, Midtown. He could not help thinking about her angry and disappointed face, her harsh words, and the impetus with which she used to speak and which fascinated him in other circumstances. He felt terrible because she had every right to be furious, to not want to speak to him, because he had screwed up big time. It had lacked ill intent. He left his suite and headed straight for hers. They were only a few feet apart. When he arrived, he found the cleaning cart in the doorway and the door open. He poked his head in and saw two people cleaning the room.

"Do you need anything, sir?" one asked, approaching him with a pillow in her hands.

He flinched and shrugged. "Nothing, thank you. I'm in room 202. I was just coming to pick up my friend Juliet to go for a walk."

"There's no one in this suite anymore, sir. Miss Miller left the hotel this morning."

"She's gone?"

"Yes, sir."

He thanked her and walked toward the elevators but was unable to wait and decided to take the stairs down. He found the emergency exit and ran down to the lobby, walked briskly up to the reception desk, and greeted that girl, Brittany, whom Juliet was familiar with.

"Hello, good afternoon."

"Good afternoon, Mr. Lezer. How can I help you?

"I just wanted to check one thing. The housekeepers told me that my friend, Juliet Miller, checked out of the hotel this morning."

"Yes, she left around eleven-thirty this morning."

"It can't be."

"Excuse me?"

"It can't be. I just got here yesterday."

"You may stay as long as you see fit, Mr. Lezer. You are in one of the suites reserved by Shaughnessy & McCameron, and I have not been given orders to change your room."

"Are you sure she's left New York?"

"One of our cars took her to the airport. Do you need help?"

"No, no. Thank you very much." He took a deep breath, calibrating the situation, then spoke with conviction. "I'm leaving too. I'll be checking out in half an hour. Thank you."

"As you wish."

"Thank you."

He walked back to the elevators to go upstairs, pack his suitcase, and leave the hotel that Juliet's company paid for. He dialed her phone number, but it was turned off or out of coverage, and he didn't hesitate to leave her a voice message.

"Hi, Juliet. I guess you are on your way to London. I'm very sorry you left like that, without talking to me because I repeat. If I made a mistake by talking about your script to Jennifer, it was not with bad intentions. On the contrary. We will talk again."

He hung up feeling worse because it was true. He was a real jerk for talking to Jennifer Davies, her "nemesis," as Juliet had called her, about her original idea for a screenplay, but he had done it with the best of intentions.

He had spent a crazy night with Jennifer after proposing to Juliet three times to come up to her room and enjoy the rest of the night together—proposals that she had flatly rejected. Jennifer had told him with much regret about the bad personal relationship she had with Juliet, who was one of the most relevant people in her company and someone she admired and appreciated.

According to Jennifer, it was Juliet who was avoiding her and had never given her a chance to get close. According to her, they had gotten off on the wrong foot from minute one, and according to her, she was willing to do anything to remedy that frosty relationship.

Michiel had spent half the night skirting the subject. He had expressly asked her not to talk about Juliet, but she had insisted and insisted, and in the end, when she had asked him directly about what they were up to in Manhattan, he had given up and told her about the Audrey case. She had shown great interest in what they had achieved by searching together for an eighty-three-year-old neighbor. In the early hours of the morning, when they were in her apartment having the last glasses of champagne of the night, Jennifer had assured him that they had wonderful material to make a film and that she wanted to put herself at his disposal to help them with whatever was necessary.

"You should write a script about this story, Michiel."

"Juliet is already on it."

"Of course, she's a wonderful writer. You studied English Philology, didn't you?"

"Yes."

"Have you already started it? Is there any first draft?"

"Yes, she has developed the plot, the characters, and the lines of action. She has worked hard, but there is still a lot to do."

Perhaps out of pride and to show off Juliet's work, or because he was half-drunk, or because he was an idiot, it was not very clear, he had taken out of the pocket of his anorak the little notebook with the script and shown it to her. Jennifer had read it very carefully and then stood up, astonished.

"This is pure gold. Do you have more copies?"

"Juliet has another one."

"Great. Leave this one with me, and I'll take care of the technical script. I know the best in the industry, and having it produced in the US will drive Netflix or HBO crazy. We'll get to work right away."

"Juliet is already working on it."

"Yes, but she'll be very busy. It's better if she just works on developing the script, and I'll take care of everything else. Please, let me earn some points with her. Let me help. Maybe it's just what we need to get to know each other better and bring us closer together."

Like a jerk, he had agreed, and that was going to cost him one of the coolest friendships he had ever had in his entire life.

"Hello," he answered the phone as he finished closing his suitcase. He was greeted in Dutch.

"Michiel, it's Herman. What's up, man?"

"Herman! I was going to call you."

"Yeah, don't worry. I guess you're busy. How's everything going?"

"I'll let you know."

"Have you seen Mrs. Stuyvesant?"

"Yes, we spent an hour with her yesterday."

"Incredible, Michiel. You should think about starting a detective agency. You're great at it."

"Huh."

"Shall we meet for dinner? I want to introduce you to Andy so I can meet Juliet in person."

"Juliet is on her way to London, but I'd love to have dinner with you."

"She's gone to London? That's too bad. She told me we'd see each other before she left."

"It must have been an emergency because she didn't say goodbye to me either."

"What hotel are you in?"

"None now. I'm going to leave the hotel Juliet had reserved for me. Since she's gone, I'm afraid to stay here on her company's account."

"Come to my home. I have a lot of space, and we can catch up."

"I don't know."

"Uncle! I haven't seen you for two years. Come home, and we'll have dinner here. Andy is a chef. I'm sure he'll prepare some irresistible treat for us."

"Michiel Lezer?"

"Yes, it's me. Who is it?"

He came out of the Underground and took Daniel's hand to cross the street. It was raining heavily in London, typical late November freezing rain, and it was almost dark at that time of the afternoon, so they raced to get to the Barbican Estate, and he didn't bother to be nice to a woman who was calling him with a hidden number.

"Michiel, I'm Andrea, Juliet Miller's assistant. We met at..."

"Yes, yes, of course. Hello, Andrea," he replied, surprised she had his phone number. He looked at his son out of the corner of his eye. "Is everything all right?"

"Are you still in New York?"

"No, I arrived last night. Why?"

"I have sent you several emails, and you have not responded."

"I haven't seen them. What's wrong? Is there a problem?"

"No, don't worry. It's just that we would like you to sign some intellectual property registration papers."

"Intellectual property registration? Why?"

"It's for Juliet's script. We registered it a week ago, but there is an addendum that includes you as a collaborator, and we need to register it as soon as possible. I need your ID or passport number to complete the paperwork. Then I'll send it all to you by courier. You sign it and send it back to me."

"Excuse me?"

Arriving at his building, he let Daniel run up to the floor and stopped to pay more attention to this girl he had seen only once in his life and who was now telling him something he had absolutely no idea about.

"Juliet is giving you, in the case of the sale of the script, a percentage of the royalties for your help with the documentation and all that. If you don't agree with our terms, we can review them."

"I don't care about copyright. Where is Juliet? Why doesn't she call me? I've been trying to reach her for days."

"Juliet is working. I'm taking care of these arrangements, and the truth is that I'm in a bit of a hurry. Tell me when I can send you a messenger."

"Andrea." He walked up the stairs and through his door, handed Daniel the keys, and let him into the house while he walked to Juliet's apartment. "I've been trying to talk to her for a week, but she won't pick up the phone, and this story has me totally off my game. I'll tell you up front that I'm not interested in benefiting from her script. Tell her that for me, and also tell her, please, that it would be nice if she called me and we could discuss it in person. We are not twelve years old."

"She's been busy for a few days, but I'll give her your message."

"Don't talk to me like I'm a customer. This is personal, but thank you."

"You're welcome. I'll send you the papers."

"I repeat, I'm not interested. Do not include me in any of these arrangements. Goodbye, and thank you, Andrea."

He hung up, rang Juliet's doorbell, and waited patiently, but no one opened the door despite the hour. He rapped with his knuckles and got no answer either, then looked at the phone and dialed her number. He was upset, but he couldn't control himself and left her one more message—the nineteenth since she had left Manhattan without saying goodbye.

"Juliet, if you want to talk to me like an adult, you call me, and we'll talk about it. If you don't want to, I won't insist anymore. This seems puerile to me. Thank you, but don't include me in your copyrights. I'm not interested in them."

He hung up, shaking his head because he didn't like to get angry about idiocies. He turned, intending to enter his apartment, but Juliet's door opened, and someone spoke to him from behind.

"Michiel, sorry. I was in the shower."

"Rocío, what's up? Sorry, I thought Juliet..."

"She's not here. She left this morning on a trip," answered the guy who was always so nice, closing his bathrobe. "She has a very important shoot in Prague, with ten of her actors involved. She traveled with them, and I came over to stay with Romeo."

"I'm sorry I dragged you out of the shower."

"When did you arrive from New York?"

"Last night."

"You stayed many days."

"Eight. I was looking forward to enjoying New York and a few days off. I'm back at work today. I need to talk to Juliet. It's important. Do you know when she's coming back?"

"Dad!" Daniel called to him, peeking into the hallway. "Should we order pizza for dinner?"

"Yes, of course. Go ahead and order it."

"What happened to you in New York?" asked Rocío directly, and Michiel frowned. "I know something big must have happened because my girl came back quieter and more taciturn than usual."

"There was a misunderstanding. I've been calling all week, trying to get her to pick up the phone."

"A misunderstanding? I'm sorry. How did you find Mrs. Stuyvesant? Juliet says she wasn't very calm after seeing her, although she seemed delighted with life."

"Yes, she looks very comfortable and seems to be in perfect health, but I don't know. Something strange was in the air, and it's true that Juliet and I..."

He thought about Audrey and how he had practically forgotten about her during his stay in Manhattan because of Juliet, who had left him a wreck. He looked at Rocío, smiling.

Rocío said, "I assume Audrey is well and where she wants to

be. What she is most looking forward to is living near her Gregory's family. For Juliet, it is not so clear."

"We can't intervene or do anything. It was enough to find her and get to talk to her."

"Yes, what a success. You guys are the bomb."

"Yes, we were very lucky. I'll leave you alone. I'm going to see what Dani is doing."

"Michiel." Rocío stopped him again, and Michiel returned his attention to him.

"Juliet is the best. I don't know anyone like her, and although she is sometimes hypersensitive and too rigid in her behavior, she has a very good sense of humor. She's doing this because she has not had much luck with the people who approach her."

"I..."

"I'm not blaming you for anything, God forbid, my soul, but I had to tell you because I love her very much. She's always been great to me, and she's my friend."

"She is also my friend."

"All this talk of finding Audrey had her super happy and excited. She seemed different. She even worked less and enjoyed everything more, but the other day when I saw her after she got back from New York, she was between pissed off and sad. Super quiet. I got anxious. I only hope that this 'misunderstanding' that you say you had will be cleared up soon and you will be like before because your friendship was very good for her."

"It did me a lot of good too, which is why I've been calling her for eight days and leaving messages to try to fix it."

"Okay. I'm sure it will be water under the bridge in no time. She has a short fuse, and she gets angry quickly, but she also lets it go."

"I'll keep that in mind. Good night."

"See you later, handsome."

She blew him a kiss and went back inside the apartment. He

stood there thinking for a few seconds about how "Juliet hasn't had much luck with people getting close to her."

He already knew from Juliet that she had had huge disappointments with her famous Caden and with other people, but he did not fall into that category of exploitive sons of bitches. He was opposed to that kind of behavior and what pissed him off was that now, on top of that, she was including him in that package to end up labeling him as a "disappointment" when all he had done was commit an error. A regrettable error, it was true, but unintentional and without malice.

He entered his house, getting angrier, and took off his coat and boots. Daniel had turned on the television, which was forbidden during the week, but he was unable to prevent it. For one day, the world was not going to end. He passed him and stroked his hair. Daniel told him he had ordered a family pizza and went into the kitchen to set the table.

His best defense on the subject of screenwriting and Jennifer Davies, he thought while emptying the dishwasher, was that he didn't belong in that world. In the universe of actors, agents, producers, and technical scripts. He didn't know what kind of infighting these people were up to. Juliet had told him that Jennifer was her nemesis, but in the same conversation, she had also acknowledged that she respected her and would rather have her on her team than on the other one. That was what he had been left with, and neither the sex nor the drinks nor the revelry had overridden his understanding, as Juliet had wanted to imply. He had simply seen a good opportunity and accepted it. There were no more dramas, no more conspiracies, and he would not tolerate any more questioning.

"Hello," he answered the phone. It was Laura, and she insulted him as soon as she greeted him.

"You bastard, Michiel! Why didn't you tell me you were going to New York?"

"I'm with Daniel, and we're going to dinner if you don't mind talking tomorrow."

"You have your child on a Monday, why?"

"Because we haven't seen each other for many days, and his mother didn't mind."

"Fuck!" she interrupted him. "I'm ten meters from your house."

"You should have called earlier. I'm sorry, but I can't meet today."

"What if you let me know when he falls asleep?"

"No, we'll talk tomorrow. I have to hang up."

"Why did you go to New York? I had to find out from Gwen McMillan."

"It was a last-minute decision."

"Is everything all right? Gwen says you were going to do something important."

"In short, yes. Juliet and I found Audrey Stuyvesant in Manhattan."

"Juliet?" she interrupted, and he didn't answer. "You went to New York with your fifteen-year-old neighbor?"

"She is not fifteen years old."

"I'm kidding, but you can't deny that she looks like a child."

"The pizza is coming. I have to go."

"Okay, see you tomorrow."

"Goodbye."

He hung up, looked at the phone, and turned it off. He left it on the counter and went out the door to pay for the pizza, ready to disconnect, forget about the world, and enjoy a quiet evening with Daniel.

***

"There are only three weeks left until the Christmas gala, and we have to keep rehearsing a lot, okay?"

"Yes, Mr. Lezer!"

"All right. A little time at home every day, and then we'll go over it in class. See you tomorrow, have a good rest, and enjoy yourselves."

"See you tomorrow, Mr. Lezer!" shouted the twenty-five students in his first-grade class. He dismissed them at the classroom door, watching them leave in perfect order with Jason, his assistant, on their way to the playground, where their parents were waiting for them.

They were all very excited about the school Christmas gala. He thought about sending an email to the families to summon them and do a general review of the wardrobe a week before the big day, or they would be wrong, as usual. He went back to his desk with that idea, tidied the desk a bit, and sat down at the computer. He logged into the school's email to send the message, then he opened his account and discovered the latest documents John Tompkins had sent him.

John, who was the unofficial biographer of the Stuyvesant family, was an extraordinary guy. He had been delighted to meet him. They had become very good friends and had spent hours exploring New York. Many hours passed in chats about Peter Stuyvesant and New Amsterdam, and Michiel was glad that John was sending him more material about it.

He went through his whole inbox before reading John's documents and saw several messages with the domain Shaughnessy & McCameron. For a second, he thought it was Juliet, but no; Andrea Carpenter was writing to him. He opened and read them. Andrea signed herself as *Assistant to Juliet Miller, Executive responsible for Europe and UK*, about the script issue and all that copyright bullshit.

He didn't bother to answer because he had already told her he wasn't interested. He moved on to other family and friends and finally went back to John, who sent him more references, some articles of his own, and a report from the *New York Times* that he recommended he read immediately.

He clicked on the link, and the article made him frown.

The distribution of the billion-dollar Stuyvesant inheritance continues to be paralyzed by the demands of the executors. The core of the family rejects outright the universal heir designated by Charles Stuyvesant, who died in the Hamptons six months ago, and is blocking the signature of all the heirs.

He continued reading about astronomical values that the direct heirs of Charles, Gregory Stuyvesant's younger brother, were protecting with a huge team of lawyers. He reached the part where they talked about the "supposed" universal heir, a direct relative of Peter Gregory III, the legitimate heir of Peter Gregory II, who had been removed from the family and disowned by his father in 1956.

Without meaning to, he stood up and smoothed back his hair, thinking about Audrey. It couldn't be anyone else, and he reached for the phone to call Juliet, the only one who would care as much as he did about the news. He reached for her number with his thumb but remembered that she was no longer answering his calls, which was extremely frustrating.

He took a deep breath and sat down again, feeling a gaping hole open in the center of his chest.

"Dad?"

"Huh?"

He looked up to find Daniel and his mother entering the classroom with great determination. He looked at the time on the clock on the wall and wondered if he had forgotten something, but before he could ask, Fiona stood in front of him with a big smile.

"It's all right. I just came to tell you that we're rushing off to piano class."

"Ah, okay."

"I'm pregnant. *In vitro* finally worked."

"Great! Congratulations."

He reached over to hug her and out of the corner of his eye, he saw Daniel's sad face. He pulled away from Fiona, who was beaming, and reached out to ruffle his hair.

"Congratulations, Dani! You'll finally be a big brother."

"Yeah. Can we go? I don't want to be late, or Mrs. Hughes will get on my nerves."

"You have plenty of time, son. Don't worry."

"How are you feeling, Fi? How far along are you?"

"I just hit fourteen weeks. We didn't want to say anything until I passed the three-month mark. I'm forty-six years old, and the obstetrician keeps reminding me that I'm high risk, blah, blah, and not to get my hopes up."

"I'm sure everything will be fine."

"I hope so because Robert couldn't go through another disappointment, and I don't think I could either."

"Don't stress. The important thing is that you are calm."

"Yes. Anyway, we're leaving now. Say goodbye to Daddy, Daniel. I'll wait for you in the car. Bye, Michiel."

"If you need anything, let me know, and take care of yourself, Fi. Daniel, come here for a second." The little boy approached him as his mother went out into the hallway, and he hugged him. "For Mum and Robert, this is very important. Let's see if you can show a little more interest, okay?"

"They don't talk about anything else. They bore me to tears."

"Yes, because they are very excited, and you should be too. You are going to have a brother or a sister."

"Okay, bye," he said, shaking his head, then hurried out of the classroom. Michiel watched him until he lost sight of him, deciding on the fly that it was going to be necessary to talk to him at length about the subject of pregnancy. Suddenly, Laura appeared in his field of vision.

"Hello, stranger."

"Hello. Have you finished?"

"Yes. Today has been a quiet day in administration. Are you coming to McAllis? They're expecting us. It's Gwen's birthday."

"Wow, that's right. Yes, let's go."

He turned off the laptop, put it in his backpack, grabbed his coat, and went out with it on his way to the pub where they were celebrating the birthday of Gwen, a colleague he appreciated a lot. He had promised to stop by the pub to have a pint with them.

At the moment, he didn't feel like a five o'clock celebration with his colleagues because he had other more interesting things to do, but ten minutes later, he was in the mood to go to the party.

At McAllis, Michiel forgot about the Stuyvesants, Audrey, John, and even Juliet, and began to enjoy a very happy and relaxed Thursday evening talking about the vacations, soccer, and politics until, at eight in the evening, they said goodbye to go home. Laura joined him, determined to go with him, and he accepted the plan willingly because it suited him to end the evening together like before Juliet Miller came into his life and turned everything upside-down.

"Isn't that your little neighbor, Juliet?" asked Laura as they entered the hallway in his building. He looked up to see Juliet wrapped in one of those fancy coats of hers and talking on the phone as she walked straight toward them. He was overjoyed to find her, and his stomach contracted because he hadn't seen her for over two weeks. This could be a perfect opportunity to approach her, talk to her, and tell her the news about Audrey. He waited for her by the staircase, grinning from ear to ear.

He stood still, observing her steady gait in sexy boots, her flowing brown hair, and her look of an efficient, focused woman talking on the phone. As she got closer, he took a step toward her to greet her. She dodged him, briefly raised her black eyes, and told him and Laura "Good evening" without letting go of the cell phone in a neutral tone, without a smile.

In fifteen seconds, she had left them behind. He could feel his soul opening up while Laura hugged him and laughed.

"Fuck, what have you done to her? She used to be so attentive to you. You're a very bad boy, Michiel."

"Please," he snapped indignantly, then brushed her aside without much gentleness and walked out after Juliet. She was lost in the darkness of the Barbican Estate, a tangle of dimly lit concrete corridors with several exits to the street.

It was a guess which way she had gone, but he didn't care and kept looking for her, determined to take her fucking cell phone away and force her to talk to him.

They had not become good friends and shared so many experiences to end up as bloody strangers. That was beyond the bounds of common sense, even politeness, and he would not tolerate it. They were not fifteen years old, and no one would take his words away from him, least of all her.

He ran to the widest street in the neighborhood and saw her only a few yards away, but she was getting into one of those fancy cars that picked her up, and he raised his hand to her, but it was no use because the big black car accelerated and immediately got lost in the London traffic.

CHAPTER SEVENTEEN

Seeing the Shaughnessy & McCameron offices helped people to understand two things. First, these people were among the elite, and second, they were number one because no one else could afford such luxury in the heart of Mayfair.

He looked at the room in which the receptionist had told him to relax and marveled at the furniture, the natural wood floor, the beige walls, the immaculate curtains, the lamps, the paintings, and the carpets. He did not sit down so he could better observe everything and also because he was restless since he had shown up at Juliet's work to force her to talk to him.

The evening before had ruined his mood, his dinner, and his evening. In the end, he'd argued with Laura and asked her to leave because he had been unable to digest the persistent and absurd presence of Juliet, whom he considered an important friend. He felt the need to win her back, even if it meant chasing her and invading her workspace. He would never have thought of doing that in his life if she'd had the courtesy to greet him and treat him like a normal human being.

He was sure that he had gotten to know her well in the short time they had shared, and for that reason, he was also sure that it would not be easy for her to maintain that bellicose and uncompromising position much longer either since she was not like that. Juliet was an intelligent, tolerant, sweet, and kind girl. She was a real charmer. They had laughed together and shared talks, confidences, and the most important adventure of their lives. Because of the unique complicity they shared, he knew it was worth being in the elegant offices of Shaughnessy & McCameron, taking a gamble, and going beyond his limits to try to redirect their history, apologize again, ask for a second chance, and make it easy for her to end once and for all the misunderstanding.

"Michiel? I can't believe you're here."

Andrea entered the room with a folder in her hand and looked at him in surprise. He approached her and gave her the best of his smiles.

"Good afternoon. I was in the neighborhood, and I thought I'd come up."

"Sure, come in. Did you bring your documents? I'll make you a copy while you read."

"First I need to talk to Juliet. Rocío told me she is in London."

"Juliet is meeting with Iona, the boss. I don't know what time they'll be done."

"It's okay. I'll wait."

"I don't think that's a good idea, Michiel. As soon as she's done, she's off to an event at the Royal Albert Hall."

"I only need five minutes of her valuable time. Where can I wait for her?"

"Come to her office, please, and while you wait, you could read the copyright documents. Since you've come, let's see if you'll sign the papers for me."

My goodness, what a persistent girl, he thought, following her down the carpeted corridors to Juliet's brightly lit minimalist office. A lovely space with a foyer and a desk that he assumed was Andrea's and, to the right, an office that was currently closed must be that of Juliet Miller, executive manager for Europe and the UK.

He looked at the white sofas that perfectly matched the carpets and curtains, walked over to a huge glass vase filled with white roses, smelled them, and then turned to Andrea.

"Are these her favorite flowers?"

"Juliet's? No. Well, yes. Those were sent to her as a gift this morning. People send her a lot of flowers. She doesn't have a favorite, but if you want her to like them, make sure they're white. It's her favorite color."

"I noticed." He nodded and sat down on one of the couches next to the windows overlooking the exclusive streets of Mayfair and thought of the color white, which was present in almost all of Juliet's clothes. She had exquisite taste.

He had always marveled at the way she dressed, even before he spoke to her, when to him, she was just a pretty young neighbor passing like a whirlwind through the corridors of the Barbican Estate. Even then, he had stopped to admire her style because she had so much of it. Always fashionable, of course, but very simple, with nothing to clash and nothing to make her stand out.

Clothes, shoes, bags, suitcases—everything about her was sober and discreet. Even her perfume was almost imperceptible.

She always looked superb, and he had been fascinated by that from the very beginning. From the moment he had moved into Barbican Estates and seen her for the first time until the night before when she had passed him in her elegant black coat without paying the slightest attention to him.

"Here are the documents. Please read them," Andrea said, passing him a folder. He shook his head.

"First I need to talk to Juliet. Didn't you tell her to call me to discuss this matter?"

"Yes, Michiel. Of course, I told her to call you, but she's been very busy, and I take care of this kind of business. She doesn't usually call anyone."

"We've been talking to each other every day for months."

"Consider yourself lucky. You can't imagine how many people would kill for the chance to talk to her for just five minutes."

"Okay."

"Look, I think their meeting is over," she told him, pointing down a hallway. He saw Juliet, in black dress pants and a white blouse, coming down a flight of stairs, talking animatedly with a super-familiar actor. He knew because he had just seen him in a Netflix series playing a Dutch diplomat, not because he usually recognized the actors, and he stood up to greet them.

"Michiel?" she asked with wide eyes when she saw him in her office. He came out to intercept her before she fled in panic. "What are you doing here?"

"I need to talk to you. How are you? Michiel Lezer," he told her companion, extending his hand.

He was greeted very kindly. "Billy Howle. Pleased to meet you."

"I'm Iona McCameron," greeted a tall, mature, and very elegant woman, appearing from behind Howle's back with narrowed eyes and a very warm smile. He knew at once that this was Juliet's famous boss.

"Michiel Lezer, are you Jewish? Because I'm also Jewish on my mother's side. Where are you from?"

Michiel shrugged. "Yes, I'm Jewish from both sides, and I'm from the Netherlands. From Amsterdam."

"Of course, like Michiel Huisman. You have a very familiar look."

"I adore Michiel. He's charming. You're not related to him?"

Michiel chuckled. "No, I am not."

"Michiel is a neighbor of mine, Iona," Juliet interjected. "And he's not an actor."

"What a pity. With that charm and that look, we could have done wonders. What do you do for a living, Michiel?"

"I am a teacher."

"Blimey, in my day, there was no teacher like you," she joked, then grabbed Billy Howle and kissed him on the cheek. "Goodbye, love. You'd better get down, or the driver will kill us. This is Mayfair, not the M25, and you can't park." The lad hugged Juliet, said goodbye to everyone, and shot off toward the front door, where a young man in a suit was waiting for him. Michiel looked at Juliet, and she grabbed him by the arm and pulled him into her office, waving goodbye to Iona.

"What are you doing here?" she asked very seriously, closing the door.

"What do you think, Juliet? You haven't answered my calls for two weeks, you haven't spoken to me, and last night—"

"Last night?"

"You walked by me as if you didn't know me."

"I greeted you and your girlfriend. What else did you want me to do? I don't feel like talking to you at all."

"How long will this last? Because it's very uncomfortable."

"I'm sorry, Michiel, but when I get angry, I prefer to keep my distance. It's better than ending up saying things I might regret later."

"Don't worry about me. You can say anything to me, and I won't be offended. It's better for you to insult me and let me know how you feel than for you to disappear and leave me hanging."

"I said all I had to say in Manhattan, and I don't intend to say it again."

She rounded her desk and sat down in her elegant leather armchair, putting on her glasses. He was silent for a few seconds, then walked over, leaned on the desk with his fists, and searched her black eyes as she narrowed them.

"I'm sorry, Juliet. I'm so sorry. I'm sorry for everything that happened. I'm sorry I didn't see more clearly what was going on between you and Jennifer. I'm sorry I didn't read the situation because I had only understood that you were professional rivals but that, deep down, you admired her and preferred to have her on your side. I do not know your world, your way of working, or your personal quarrels. I did not know anything about that because you had not explained them to me. I only know that she told me that she needed to ingratiate herself with you and that she wanted to help with whatever we were working on."

"She registered the original idea in her name that morning. Since it was Sunday, she couldn't register it in person until Monday, which gave us time to register it in London. Thanks to Iona and our legal team flying in to give me a hand, I saved the day, but don't be surprised when a movie or series starts shooting in the US shortly that looks an awful lot like my script."

"I can't believe it."

"That's the way things work in this competitive universe, Michiel. Logically, you didn't know that, but it would have been enough to shut up in front of your flirt. I didn't let my brother talk about it because he's a journalist and you objected, but you didn't mind blurting it out to a complete stranger in the middle of a fuck."

"You're absolutely right."

"Anyway, she already got what she wanted, and it's too late for regrets."

"Fuck!" he exclaimed, feeling idiotic. He turned his back to walk around the office. "When she gave me back the script, she told me that it was forgotten and buried, not to worry about it."

"Yeah, I can imagine. Then she ran off to hire a scriptwriter to develop the idea at full speed."

"Shit, Juliet! I'm so sorry. I'm really sorry."

"These maneuvers happen all the time. The public doesn't know about it, but ideas are copied and repeated tirelessly. I guess Jennifer did what anyone would have done. Not me, of course, but she's a ruthless shark, and she's had it in for me, so you gave it to her on a platter. That's why it hurts so much, and I'm still so angry. Do you understand? Perfect. Now, if you don't mind, I have to work."

"I do mind. I'm not leaving until we fix this."

"Do what you want, but have a seat. I'm leaving in fifteen minutes.

"Okay." He sighed and decided to change his strategy. "John Tompkins wrote to me. He sent me an article from the *New York Times* about the universal heir appointed by Charles Stuyvesant, Gregory's younger brother."

"I know. I read it this morning."

"It's Audrey, don't you think?"

"I don't know."

"But..."

"In any case, Jennifer will be all over it. Ask her."

"I never told her about the Stuyvesant family, and in your script, you didn't give their names either. I don't think she can relate."

"Look, good news. From now on, however, when you're with her, try not to go off the deep end."

He stood still, watching her tense chin and her bright eyes. For a second, he saw it very clearly. He saw that this went far beyond the purely professional and that the damage on a personal level was irreparable. He felt terrible, so much so that he backed off and decided to leave and not press her any further.

"Okay, I'll let you work."

"Goodbye."

"Juliet."

"What?" She raised her head and stared into his eyes, taking off her glasses.

"This is not going to stay like this. I'm leaving now, but I'm not leaving without a fight. I don't give a shit about Jennifer. We haven't even exchanged an email since that awful morning in

New York. However, I do care about you. I care about our friendship, and I care a lot about what we achieved together. I care about having you in my life, and I will do whatever it takes to get you to trust me again."

Celebrating the last weekend of Chanukah at his parents' house was an impossible tradition to avoid since it was hard enough for them that he was not in Amsterdam for the lighting of the first candle of the menorah nor during the eight days with their respective nights of dinners and family celebrations. Not only for him but especially for Daniel, their only male grandson, who was growing up under the protection of Jewish tradition despite his mother being an agnostic by conviction and a Protestant by birth.

He did not consider himself religious, and neither was his family, but they respected their traditions, their origins, their blood, and the memory of their ancestors. Especially those of their paternal grandparents, Esther and Michiel, who had married in Tel Aviv in 1950 after having miraculously survived the Nazi Holocaust during World War II, and who had fought until the end of their days to keep their family within the precepts of the people of Israel.

Three-quarters of the Dutch Hebrew population had been annihilated during the war. His family, like most, had lost immediate family members, distant relatives, friends, and neighbors.

For that reason and many others, even though they were not religious, they did not usually go to synagogue, but they complied with certain precepts. They accepted their culture, respected it, and lived it in the best possible way, especially since there were children.

He turned to look for Daniel, who at that moment was at the piano, practicing a Mozart piece with his grandfather. Michiel smiled to see him so focused and happy and speaking Yiddish, which he spoke less in England, and enjoying a typical Chanukah afternoon with his family while it was raining and cold outside.

He took a deep breath and approached one of the living room windows to admire the beautiful landscape in front of his parents' house, which was located in the traditional neighborhood of Jordaan in the heart of Amsterdam. He touched the frosted glass and observed the Prinsengracht or Prince's Canal, the longest in the city center, which was full of people sailing in their little boats despite the bad weather. Without wanting to, his mind flew to the last thing John Tompkins had told him.

The day before, as soon as he set foot in the airport from London, he had read with surprise the latest articles that the American press was publishing about the famous "Stuyvesant Inheritance." Within a week of the first public mention of the subject, there had been a proliferation of information and articles on the matter. According to John, nobody talked about anything else in Manhattan, and it was becoming increasingly clear that the center of the conflict was Audrey Stuyvesant, the widow of Peter Gregory III, whom the family was keeping isolated in a secret and inaccessible place.

Contemplating the possibility that Audrey might be living estranged from her in-laws made him uneasy, and he couldn't get it out of his mind. It was no longer his business, but he couldn't help thinking of her isolated somewhere, alone and far away from her country, from her apartment on the Barbican Estate, where everything was still intact. At least, it seemed so from the outside. He hadn't been able to go back inside to check.

After that day when he and Juliet had entered the apartment with Romeo and been surprised by Jack Lynch, someone had changed the locks. Now not even the manager, who claimed to have a lot of people interested in buying or renting the property, had access. There it remained, alone and silent like a mausoleum or like the Great Wall of China, separating his house from Juliet's, whom he had not seen since he had treacherously appeared in her office.

"So, Fiona is going to be a mother again?" asked his brother, patting him on the back. He jumped up.

"Eh, yes, and according to Daniel, it's going to be a multiple birth."

"What does Daniel know about these things?"

"Fiona and Robert told him yesterday."

"How is he doing?"

"Not so good since his friends with younger siblings have told him that babies are the worst thing that could happen to him."

"Mother of God." David snorted, then burst out laughing, and Michiel shook his head.

"We are working on it before he decides to run away from his mother's house."

"Couldn't he live with you?"

"Yes, but this issue is non-negotiable. He will adapt like everyone else."

"If he lives with you, you could both come back to Amsterdam, and everyone would be happy." David shot a thumbs-up toward their parents, and Michiel shook his head.

"No. I would like to, but he is only eight years old. He needs his mother, and my agreement with her does not include stirring up that kind of drama."

"I know. It was just an idea."

"What are you talking about?" their mother interrupted very attentively.

"Fiona's future baby, which seems to worry Dani a bit," David replied.

"He told me this morning that he doesn't feel like sharing a house with a couple of crying babies. I've explained to him that family is important and that this is the only chance he'll have to enjoy siblings, so he'd better get used to the idea."

"That's it, Mum? You're throwing in the towel with Michiel?"

"Of course. Given his lifestyle and with his fortieth birthday in November, I guess he threw in the towel a long time ago."

She stared at him and he nodded, accepting that she was right because, as far as children were concerned, it was clear to him that, unfortunately, that chapter had closed with Daniel's birth.

"Your father and I are still amazed that our wayward firstborn gave us a grandson. It is a true miracle, and we are content."

"Wayward?" He looked her in the eye and laughed. "I've always been a saint."

"Not with women, but I'm not going to say any more because it's Chanukah. Would you like some punch?"

"Yes, thank you. Hold on a second." He felt the phone vibrate in his jeans pocket, and when he saw it was his friend Lucy, he stepped aside to answer.

"Hallo, schoonheid."

"Hi. I'm glad you still call me beautiful, Michiel."

"How are you?"

"How about you? The rumor has it that you're in Amsterdam, and I've dropped my panties just imagining it."

"Mother of God!" He burst out laughing and left the room.

"What time are you coming home? We can enjoy the night in perfect and passionate harmony."

"I'd love to, but I don't know if I'll be able to get away. I'm here with Daniel for Chanukah. This is the last weekend."

"Happy Chanukah!"

"Happy Chanukah. Thank you very much."

"We'll be here. You know I'll be waiting for you with open arms and panties on the floor."

"A perfect plan. Let's see what I can do."

"Great. *Kusjes* and love."

"Kisses."

He said goodbye, thinking seriously about sneaking away to spend some quality time with Lucy, who was a great friend, fun, and who he appreciated a lot. He looked at the time, calculating the margin he could count on until the phone vibrated again. When he saw who was calling, his heart skipped a beat.

"Juliet?" he answered immediately. She greeted him seriously, but she greeted him, and that made him smile.

"Hello, Michiel. Sorry to call you on a Saturday and at this hour. Are you at home? I'm in Willesden at my parents' house, but I'm getting an Uber now, and I'll be at Barbican in about twenty minutes. I'd like to talk to you."

"Shit," he mumbled, rubbing his face with his free hand.

"Excuse me?"

"I'd love to be home to talk to you, but I'm in Holland. It's the last weekend of Chanukah, and I've come with Daniel to see my parents."

"I'm so sorry. I didn't know. Happy Chanukah."

"Thank you very much. I'm going back to London tomorrow. I'll be home around nine o'clock in the evening."

"Don't worry. I'll tell you over the phone if you have five minutes."

"For you, I have all the time in the world."

"I just got a call from Victoria Stuyvesant. She's arriving in London on Monday on a professional matter and wants to see me because she's interested in us taking over her acting career. That's not important. The important thing is that when I asked her about Audrey, she told me that she doesn't know anything about her. That she doesn't see her because she's separated from her husband, and she hasn't had access to anyone in the family for the last six months."

"How long has it been? A month ago, I was in Manhattan with Audrey."

"I asked her the same question, and she confessed that the family asked her to put on a show and arrange our visit so that we would stop snooping and forget about Aunt Audrey."

"*What?*"

"John Tompkins coming to her and telling her our story and

our concern for Audrey set off all the alarms, and she was asked to meet me. She says it was a mistake to tell her husband but that she did it because she was trying to ingratiate herself with him."

"Why did they want you to supervise the meeting?"

"Because they have been trying for months to isolate Audrey from outside interference. They took her to Manhattan to keep her under control, or so Victoria assures me, and for us to show up asking questions..."

"So, can we take for granted the hypothesis that Audrey is the universal heir?"

"It would be a compelling reason to take her to New York and isolate her from the world."

"Fuck, this smells awful. Poor Audrey. I hope they are taking good care of her despite everything."

"I don't know. I feel terrible hearing all this. I'm going to see Victoria in person on Monday and find out more, but in the meantime, I'm going to talk to my agency's legal department to see if we can get Audrey some legal assistance because I think what they're doing to her, a vulnerable person, may be illegal."

"Daniel's mother, Fiona's husband, is a marriage and inheritance lawyer and all that kind of stuff. I'll check with him."

"That's much better. Better someone specialized. Anyway, it was just that I—"

"Thank you so much for calling and telling me, Juliet. I haven't been able to get Audrey out of my mind. At least now we know why they decided to take her away overnight and without warning."

"If we take Victoria's word for it, yes."

"I don't think she needs to lie."

"She lied to us in Manhattan while playing the role of her life. I prefer to keep her version quarantined until I talk to her."

"You are right. If possible, I would also like to talk to her face to face."

Juliet was silent. "Okay, I'll let you know when I have a

concrete date. Goodbye and happy Chanukah. Give Daniel a kiss for me."

"Juliet."

"What?

"This call is the best Chanukah gift I could receive."

"Goodbye."

She hung up on him, but he overlooked it because at least she had called him. He smiled, feeling great relief, and went back to the living room to celebrate.

CHAPTER EIGHTEEN

ichiel was at Shaughnessy & McCameron again, but this time, he had arrived with an invitation and a compelling reason to be there: to meet with Victoria Stuyvesant.

He left his shoulder bag on a chair in the elegant boardroom overlooking Grosvenor Square, where Andrea had installed him, and looked at the art and film books that were strategically placed around the room. Everything seemed simple, but it was an illusion because the hand of professionals could be seen every-where. Nothing was randomly placed or tampered with; every-thing was perfect and smelled wonderful.

He approached one of the windows to look out over the park, and the door opened. Juliet came in with some folders in her hand, talking on the phone. She greeted him with a smile and put the papers down on the glass table while still chatting in Spanish.

She looked very pretty in a short black dress, black stockings, and sexy high-heeled boots. She wore her brown hair loose, long, and wavy, as was usual for her, and had added a silver chain that went down to her navel.

He blinked in awe and watched her sit down in a chair without paying any attention to him.

"Okay, bye." She hung up.

"I'm sorry, Michiel. I had to take that. Sit down, please."

"Thank you." He found a chair near her and sat down. "How are you doing?"

"How was Amsterdam? How was Chanukah?"

"We were only there for two days, but Daniel loves being with the grandparents."

"I can imagine."

"I've brought you a Dutch edition of *Romeo and Juliet*."

"Thank you very much. You're very kind," she said. "We are meeting here, in my office because Victoria wanted it to be like a professional meeting. She's a little paranoid."

She watched him for a few seconds, surely wondering the same thing he was. Why were they talking as if they were in an elevator or didn't know each other? She attempted to break the ice and move on to personal topics, but she couldn't because the door opened again. Andrea entered, followed by Victoria Stuyvesant.

Juliet and Michiel stood up politely. "Victoria, welcome. How are you? Do you remember Michiel?"

"Of course. How are you? Good afternoon."

"Come in, sit down. Andrea, please, can you bring tea and coffee for everyone?"

"Sure, I'll be right back."

"We sat down, didn't we?" asked the tall, elegant woman, who seemed more insecure and less glamorous than she had been when he had met her in Manhattan. He smiled at her and sat next to Juliet and across from her, thinking about how human beings could transform depending on the circumstances.

In New York, she had seemed like a relaxed diva who controlled her surroundings perfectly, but in London, she seemed like someone else. He felt a little sorry for her, so he let Juliet open the meeting and take control of the conversation.

"Where are you staying, Victoria?"

"I'm staying with friends in Surrey. This is a very nice place." She looked around the room and then touched the natural stone necklace she was wearing. "I don't want to keep you. I think Mark's henchmen follow me everywhere, and if they know I've come to talk to you..."

"You are supposed to want to work with the agency. It is normal for you to come to see us. No one knows that Michiel and I are here with you."

"They know everything, honey. What did you want to ask me? And for the record, I'm talking to you because you promised to squeeze me in and get me some jobs, Juliet."

"Of course. Don't worry about it."

"Why are your husband's 'henchmen' following you?" Michiel asked, very surprised by the term.

Mrs. Stuyvesant laughed. "I can tell you don't have a family like this, fortunately for you. They control each of their members, especially if they try to get you to stop screwing around and disappear."

"You mean the divorce?"

"Of course I'm talking about the divorce. We are separated, but I don't want a divorce. I have two children, and I don't want to get out of the way because my hubby has taken a fancy to a twenty-year-old brat. If he wants to fuck her, let him do it, but don't touch my children and me."

"Tea." Andrea entered with a uniformed waiter and a tea service worthy of the Ritz. Victoria was silent until they were alone again.

"Mark kicked me out of the house to get his little whore into my bed. Nobody knows about it, not even my family, and because of a draconian confidentiality agreement he made me sign before he married me, I can't talk about it. If he insists on divorcing me, I'll speak up and fuck up their lives, you know? They are like a mafia. You have to swallow whatever they decide, and if they get tired of you, get the fuck out."

"I am very sorry."

"They will do the same to your friend Audrey."

"What do you mean?"

"You'll see. She'll get her ass kicked any day now."

"Why did they take her to New York?" Michiel asked.

She shrugged. "Because my father-in-law decided to leave everything to his older brother, Peter Gregory III, Audrey's husband. According to him, he wanted to restore what his father had unjustly taken from him six decades ago when he disinherited him and cut him off from the family. At first, he wanted to do it during his lifetime, but it was impossible because old Peter Gregory II had left everything tied up tightly so that his disowned cousin would never touch a penny of his fortune. He wouldn't even let him use his last name, you know?"

"We know."

"He never forgave Gregory. He even put in writing that he was not to be allowed to appear at his funeral, and when Charles made the first attempt to make amends in the family drama, the lawyers came down on him and prevented him from doing so. He finally turned to an outside team of lawyers and independent executors and named him his universal heir. His children learned of the move at the reading of his will."

"Wow."

"Chuck, his eldest son, had a heart attack during the reading of the last will and testament. A huge scandal ensued, and the plan to usurp Peter Gregory Stuyvesant III's legitimate rights began."

"They didn't know he had died, of course."

"They didn't, but within hours, their network of henchmen had placed Gregory in London, dated his death, and stumbled upon his sweet widow in her early eighties. She had no idea, but the lawyers and executors needed to solve the problem. They were very lucky that she was alone and didn't have children capable of standing up to them."

"Did it not occur to them to give her some money and leave her in London?"

"The fact is that this type of family, which is like a large company, has many control filters, including executors, boards of directors, lawyers, advisors, etc. It was necessary to take Audrey to New York so that she could first accept the inheritance and in a reasonable time, pass it on to her nieces and nephews. It seems that this was the simplest and cleanest way to settle the succession."

"I imagine all this was without giving you proper legal advice."

"Yes, Michiel, because the legal advice came from his lawyers. Therefore, according to some friends of mine, there was a conflict of interest, and the whole process could be annulled. She, of course, will refuse to contest anything because she is delighted with her nephews, whom she has met twice, but whom, inexplicably, she adores."

"She loves everyone. She's very lonely and gets attached to anyone who gives her a little attention," Juliet commented, shaking her head.

"Did they at least offer you good financial compensation?"

"Money is not the problem. They don't care about money. What matters to them is power, prestige, and all the crap associated with their heritage. I'm sure they have given her a lot of money, don't worry about that."

"She's not interested in money either. It's terrible that they're using an eighty-three-year-old in this way," said Juliet.

"I know, but Stuyvesant was a real piece of work. When they found out she had no one, they came quietly to London, showed up at her house, bent her ear, and took her away to "vacation" in New York. It was a piece of cake."

"What a horror."

"The priority was to avoid outside interference, and they succeeded. They isolated her there and maneuvered her as they pleased. They pushed her to do exactly what they wanted her to do, and she said yes to everything without complaint."

"From every point of view, this looks like it's illegal. We should try to get someone to review it, Michiel. Maybe it can be challenged."

"At her age, why does she want a multi-million-dollar inheritance and all the problems that go with it? They have committed an illegality or, at least, an outrage, I agree, but what matters now is what they will do with Audrey when they no longer need her."

"I suppose they'll forget her in one of their properties under the care of a nurse," Victoria opined. "They don't care about her at all. I saw her in person for the first time the day you went to the Upper East Side house. I only showed up a few minutes before you arrived."

"You didn't feel sorry for her? You could have said something to us and not kept up the happy family lie," Juliet whispered. "We do care about her, and we could have brought her back home."

"I felt sorry for her, yes, but the fact is that there were cameras and microphones, and I had been asked to supervise the visit so you wouldn't make Audrey frightened or nervous. They see everyone as the enemy, and I did it for her and for you. It would have been worse not to collaborate so that you could see her."

"Cameras and microphones?"

"They wanted to check that you weren't after her dough or trying to get information out of her or mess with her head. It's the usual *modus operandi*."

"I hope it was worth it, Victoria."

"Don't judge me, Juliet. My husband has taken custody of my two children, he's put me out on the street, and when he asks me to go and supervise his aunt's fucking date with some nosy neighbors in London, I go and do it because I'll do anything to get in good with him. He's a twisted son of a bitch who likes to be paid homage. Do you understand?"

"We understand," Michiel interjected, touching Juliet's forearm. "We understand, and we don't judge you, but you understand how it feels for us to know this whole story. Audrey is our friend, and we care about her."

"She is no longer your friend. Forget about her. She now belongs to the Stuyvesant family, and they won't let you near her anymore."

"We'll see."

"Good luck. I'm leaving, I've already told you everything I know, and it's getting late."

She stood up, and Michiel stood with her. He looked at Juliet, who was mute and self-absorbed in her seat, and motioned for her to react, but she didn't.

"Victoria, thank you very much. I'll see you another time."

"I hope so since your girl owes me a debt."

"I'm not his girl, and don't worry." At last, Juliet stood up and fixed him with her dark eyes. "I don't lie or judge or break my word. We'll find you auditions in London and keep you informed."

"I hope so. Goodbye."

She turned like the runway model she had been and walked out of the meeting room with her chin up and her back straight. Michiel looked at Juliet and saw that her eyes were filled with tears.

"Juliet!"

"What a horror show! Once again, reality overcomes fiction."

"We will not stand for it. We must try to bring Audrey back."

"We will have to consult with the Ministry of Foreign Affairs or the British Embassy in the United States. *Something* can be done."

"You're going home. We can share a cab. It's raining hard."

"I don't know."

"You've been mad at me for three weeks. Will you never forgive me?"

"I have nothing to forgive, but that doesn't mean I don't feel like being friends with you anymore."

"Excuse me?"

"Did you know that your friend Jennifer sold 'her' story to Netflix? She's agreed to leave Shaughnessy & McCameron after what happened with me, but an hour ago, she sent me an email saying goodbye, telling me how much money she got out of this whole episode, and sending you lots of kisses. Forgive me if I'm not feeling very inclined right now to share a cab with you, no matter how hard it's raining."

"I don't think I've ever felt so guilty in my life. I am *so* sorry, Juliet."

"Fuck." She took a deep breath, put her hands on her hips, looked at the floor, and then raised her head to look him in the eyes. "I'm sorry. I'm not spiteful or a bad person, but this has gotten the better of me."

"It's okay. It's just that..."

"It's going to pass, but I'm having a hard time because it was so unfair. Don't apologize again. You don't have to. I know you didn't do it on purpose, nor were you in cahoots with her to screw up my life. I know you're a good guy, Michiel, and my head understands that Jennifer used you, but my heart..."

"That's good enough for me," he interrupted and bent down to pick up his coat and backpack. "We can share a cab without talking, or we can even talk about other things and relax a little."

"My brother and sister-in-law are putting a lot of pressure on me. I understand because they need to clarify the future of the twins, but..."

"What?"

He turned his attention to her, skirting the Thomas More Residents Garden next to the house, and Juliet stopped and looked at him with a shake of her head. She looked beautiful with her hair full of raindrops and a long classic coat, and he gawked at her until she nudged him on the shoulder to wake him up.

"What are you looking at?

"At you, Juliet. Who else am I going to look at?"

"Okay, the thing is that I love James and Harry. They are my nephews. How can I not love them?" she continued. "I don't know if I'm the best person to take care of children who, hypothetically, lose their parents. I don't have children, and I don't have a normal life. I spend my life traveling, I hardly see poor Romeo."

"Surely nothing will happen, and you will never have to take care of them."

"What if it happens?" She started up again and stopped a few steps away. "I shouldn't have had that shot of tequila, Michiel. I'm a little tipsy."

"It was just a shot."

"Two pints and almost without eating because I haven't had time for anything today. See? This doesn't happen to me in Spain. There, the tapas save your life."

"Tapas, what a delight."

"I'm telling you, drinking two pints and a shot with just a couple of peanuts should be forbidden."

"The walk will clear your head. Come on."

He offered her his arm, and they continued walking together toward the Barbican Estate. Two hours ago, they had caught a cab in Mayfair on their way to the Barbican and had decided to stay at London Wall for a drink in a pub. At that time of the evening, there was a lot of activity in the area, lots of people drinking after work, and as they were both still shaken by the talk with Victoria Stuyvesant, the first pint had come in handy, as had the second and the shots of tequila that the barman had given them after tirelessly trying to flirt with Juliet.

He had never noticed how annoying some guys could be. He knew, but he had never paid much attention to what some girls had to put up with. In the end, he had called the guy on it. The man had apologized by giving them the shots, which Juliet had accepted with all the normality in the world, but he had not. He had begun to wonder if he was getting old.

"Aren't you overwhelmed by the responsibility of being a father?" she asked him suddenly, and he blinked.

"Sure, sometimes, but most of the time, I take it for granted. I fought hard to be able to have that responsibility."

"What do you mean, you fought hard?"

"Fiona, one of my best friends, was thirty-seven years old when she proposed that I be the biological father of her child. She had been longing for several years to be a mother. I, after much consideration, decided that I would be the baby's father, but only if she let me participate one hundred percent in the child's life. She took her time and presented me with a thousand legal agreements, and in the end, we reached an agreement that suited us both. That was how Daniel was born."

"I had no idea."

"Nowadays, there are families and situations of all types. We form a peculiar one, but we can't complain. On the contrary, everything has gone very well because we are very good friends. We are only interested in Dani's well-being, and we respect each other's space."

"Does Daniel carry your last name or hers?

"Both. We made it a compound. Hers is Jansen."

"You Dutch have always struck me as a very civilized people." She shook her head, and he laughed. "I'm serious."

"Okay, if you say so."

"Have you always liked children?"

"I've always gotten along well with children. That's why I'm an elementary school teacher."

"How many siblings do you have?"

"Two younger than me, my sister Rachel and my brother David."

"What do they do? Do they live in the Netherlands?"

"Yes, they both live with their respective families in Holland. My sister is a violinist and works at the *Concertgebouw*, the Amsterdam Philharmonic, and my brother is an oncologist and works at the Antoni van Leeuwenhoek Hospital, a public hospital dedicated to the study and diagnosis of cancer."

"Wow, how interesting."

"They are both very nice and very interesting."

"What a blast to be a violinist in a philharmonic orchestra. Oncology is great, of course, but a professional musician? Wow!"

"My father is a professional musician too. He is an orchestra conductor."

"Really?" She stopped again.

"Yes. He retired from his artistic life, but he teaches at the Amsterdam Conservatory."

"Do you play an instrument?"

"The piano and the electric guitar, but I didn't inherit the family talent."

"I'm sure you did."

She held his gaze. He wanted to reach out and caress her face because she was gorgeous and they were so close, but he didn't dare and looked at the dark sky before nodding at their building.

"We're here. Let's go upstairs before it starts raining again."

"What does your mother do?"

"She is a psychiatrist."

"Your family is very interesting."

"Like all families. Come on."

"What do we do about Audrey?"

"I'll talk to Herman to see if he knows what can be done at the diplomatic level in New York, and we'll leave the legal stuff to him. We will also talk to Robert, Fiona's husband, who should be able to give us some insight and guidance."

"Perfect."

"How is the script coming along?"

"I have stopped writing the script."

"Why?"

"Why? For obvious reasons. It's not a good time to bring out a screenplay on the subject with Jennifer Davies starring on Netflix. I'll take it easy now that I know my dramatic knot goes beyond a simple mystery of repudiated children and hidden identities.

"You'll leave her with her ass in the air."

"I hope so. Besides, Iona had advised me to write the book first because it's much better when it comes to adapting a script, and since there's no hurry, I think that's what I'll do."

"It's a great idea."

"I didn't tell you, but Audrey sent her diaries to me at the hotel in Manhattan."

"What?"

"While you were banging Jennifer, I was reading Audrey's diaries."

Hearing her say that was like getting hit by a bucket of cold water. He let go of her arm and approached the door of his apartment, taking out the key. Anger blinded him, but he took a deep breath and, before entering the house, he turned to her and spoke to her as calmly as he could.

"I asked you three times if you wanted to go up to your suite together, Juliet, and you blew me off, so don't reproach me if, after being so openly rejected, I went with Jenifer. You can blame me for the rest of your life for everything that came after that, but you can't blame me for going up with her."

"Excuse me?"

"You heard me. Good night."

"Hey, I'm talking to you when I shouldn't even be talking to you. Don't turn your back on me."

"Have a cup of coffee, and then we'll talk."

"Are you calling me a drunk?"

"No, Juliet. I'm sending you home. Come on." He stood in the hallway waiting for her to go to her door, but she didn't move. "Juliet?"

"I'm not six years old. I'm not one of your students, you know?"

"Sometimes I question it."

"I'm still very angry with you. Don't provoke me."

"I don't care if you're still mad at me. I've blamed myself to infinity. What else do you want me to do, Juliet?"

"Juliet, Juliet! What a pain in the ass."

"Go home. We'll talk tomorrow."

"I don't want to." She pushed him and entered his house with determination. He smiled because he was very amused to see her tipsy, and he relaxed his shoulders, forgot his anger, and tried to look more understanding and less tense.

"Okay, shall I make you some coffee?"

"You know it broke me in two that you gave my original idea to that witch. That was a bitch, but it also really pissed me off that you slept with her. Weren't there a thousand other women in Manhattan that you could sleep with? Did it have to be her?"

"No, Juliet. It was supposed to be you, but you didn't listen to me."

She froze, not batting an eyelash. For a moment, he thought she was going to grab a book off the shelf and throw it at his head.

To his surprise, she simply looked at him for a long time with her big black eyes shining. Then she let go of the bag, crossed the distance that separated them, and grabbed him by his shirt to plant a kiss on his mouth.

At first, he held her by the wrists and made a pretense of pushing her away to behave like a gentleman, but she did not let him. She embraced him with her whole body and continued giving him those delicious kisses he had tasted once and not forgotten. Then a spark of lucidity went through his head and forced him to jump up with his hands in the air.

"I like you very much, Juliet. Much more than you can imagine, but you're in no condition."

"I am not drunk. I know what I am doing, my dear Watson."

She cornered him against the wall again and took off her coat. Michiel held her and caressed her cheeks and then her lips. She smiled, stood on tiptoe, and kissed him.

In a matter of seconds, he was pulling up her short dress and ripping her black stockings off as she took off her coat without stopping at the buttons. Everything flew into the air, but they didn't stop. He tried to take her to bed without any success, so he had no choice but to push her against the wall.

He slid both hands under her dress and caressed her breasts, soft and perfect, still kissing her, until she caught him by the hips with such dexterity that he had no trouble opening the buttons of his jeans and penetrating her with a dry stroke.

"Juliet."

She moaned, leaning her forehead against his. It was so intense that his knees weakened, and he ended up smiling like a satisfied child. He tried to calculate how long he had wanted this. Maybe all his life.

"I just lost a bet with Iona," she whispered after a few minutes of cuddling. He put her down on the floor and looked into her eyes, pushing her hair out of her face.

"I beg your pardon?"

"Iona bet me a hundred pounds that I'd end up making out with you."

"Oh, yeah?"

"Yes. After meeting you in the office, she told me I would fall, and here we are. I have to go now."

She bent down to pick up her torn stockings, coat, and purse, and he helped her by closing his pants. He was self-conscious. He didn't know why since he had a thousand encounters behind him, but there he was, nervous and confused. He only managed to smile.

"Would you still like some coffee?"

"No, thanks. Romeo is alone, and it's late."

"Sure. Wait, I'll come with you." He attempted to grab his coat, but she stopped him by opening the door.

"Don't go out. It's cold, and I'm next door."

"I'll walk you over."

"It's not necessary." She put a hand on his chest. "Michiel…"

"What?"

"This won't change anything between us, will it? If I have to choose between a friend and a sexual affair, I prefer the friend."

"It's not black and white, Juliet, but don't worry. It won't change anything between us."

"Okay, good night."

She smiled at him, and he walked over and gave her a fleeting kiss on the lips before letting her out into the cold hallway of the Barbican Estate. He stood at his door, more relaxed than he had been in years, and saw her reach her door, then waved goodbye. She did the same and disappeared.

CHAPTER NINETEEN

He sat down at the piano and looked at the time before starting the song. It was the tenth time he had looked at the time that afternoon. He had been like that all day, watching the clock and the phone like a teenager, waiting for Juliet to call him and accept the dinner invitation he had made that very morning. It was a day and a half after they had made love in the foyer of his house.

He wasn't the type to call girls after a furtive sexual encounter because it wasn't normal. The normal thing in a catch-and-release was not seeing each other again, but with Juliet, the issue was different, very different. She was his friend, his colleague, and his neighbor, and on top of that, he liked her very much.

He could still taste her mouth if he closed his eyes and the feel of that soft, warm skin of hers, her firm breasts and erect nipples against the palm of his hand. He moved uneasily. He was going crazy because he wanted her so badly. He couldn't stop thinking about her and wanted to see her, smell her, touch her, and take her to bed for a week. However, he knew he had to have patience and take care if he didn't want to mess up.

The important thing was to go slowly and not forget their

sincere friendship, trust, and companionship. She saw those as important, so he had let her breathe for a day. It was not in his plans to appear impatient, so he had only sent her a message explaining that he had consulted Robert about Audrey's inheritance, then asked her how she was and invited her to dinner. She immediately replied that everything was fine and she would call him later. Neither had mentioned their sublime fuck, but the electricity was sparking in the air, and that novelty had him fascinated.

"Bravo!" shouted the crowd, and it was back to reality. To school. To the assembly hall, to the piano, and to the dress rehearsal for the Christmas performance, which was only two days away.

He left the piano and stood up to applaud his class, who had done wonderfully, then busied himself getting the children off the stage with the help of Jason and one of the mothers. They removed their paper costumes and carefully stored them in a wicker trunk they had brought from their classroom. They were all very excited as he said goodbye to them, giving them final instructions for review at home.

"You've got it mastered, Michiel. Congratulations," the principal told him as Jason led the little ones out into the courtyard. He smiled at her.

"Can I leave the trunk here so that we don't have to carry it and then bring it back?"

"Of course, of course. The Chanukah song is beautiful."

"A little cultural diversity doesn't hurt."

"All parents agree with this choice, don't they?"

"Yes, we talked about it in the general tutoring at the beginning of the course. Don't worry about it."

"I'm not worried, but it pays to be safe because you know there's always a bigoted conservative who can ruin the gala for us."

"The third graders are going to dance to reggae. *That* could ruin the gala."

"The father of one of the children is an international reggae megastar, and we couldn't refuse. According to Silvie, he convinced the parents. He even threw a party at his house to woo them."

"Professor Lezer, Michiel, can I talk to you?"

Out of nowhere, one of the mothers appeared and stood in front of them, interrupting their conversation. Virginia said goodbye, and Michiel stopped what he was doing to pay attention to her.

"Tell me, Adele."

"I wanted to give you an invitation. It's for the New Year's Eve party I have every year at my house. A lot of famous people and friends are coming, and I'd love to see you there."

"Thank you very much." He accepted the invitation and put it on top of his backpack.

"Daniel told Iris that you are alone for Christmas, and it broke my heart. If you feel like coming by the house, you will be welcome. I will also be alone because of the divorce."

"Thank you, but I don't celebrate Christmas. I'm Jewish."

"Oh, right. Don't let me down on New Year's Eve."

"May I bring someone?"

"I beg your pardon?" Her face changed dramatically.

"If I can, we can drop by."

"Honestly, that wasn't the idea."

"Okay. Don't worry, and thank you very much."

She turned her back on him to go about her business, cutting short her improper attempts at flirting. She went away, mumbling something. He ignored her and looked at his phone, which was glowing on the piano. He reached over and, seeing that Juliet was calling him, answered it immediately. "Juliet."

"Hi, how are you? Sorry I haven't called sooner, but I've been working at Pinewood all day."

"Pinewood?"

"At the film studios. It's in Buckinghamshire, about forty minutes from London. I had a little problem with two actors. Anyway, I've just stepped into the office, and I've had another setback, so I can't meet for dinner. Sorry about that."

"It doesn't matter if you're late. I can cook something light, and we'll have dinner at home."

"No, it's impossible. Shall we talk tomorrow?"

He ruffled his hair, annoyed. "Sure, we'll talk tomorrow."

"Great, and thank you for the invitation."

She hung up on him without further explanation. He contemplated the idea that she was avoiding him, but he preferred not to make absurd conjectures. He gathered his things and got off the stage, intending to return home to review the latest papers John Tompkins had sent him about the now-famous Stuyvesant estate.

"Hello, Misha." Laura appeared like a ghost and startled him. "Did one of those she-wolves try to take you to the garden again?"

"Why do you call me Misha? Nobody calls me Misha."

"Stop. If you're angry, don't take it out on me."

"I just don't understand where you get it from."

"It's an affectionate nickname, honey. Don't be surly." She leaned closer and folded her arms. "The Greenwoods mother seems very offended. She was telling other mums in the lobby. You turned her down?"

"I have to go," was his reply as he put on his coat.

She winked at him. "I love it when you turn down all those rich women. I wish I could tell them you're going to bed with me."

He watched her for a few seconds, not knowing what to say. In the end, he said nothing. "Goodbye."

"Shall we go to dinner somewhere nice in your neighborhood? My treat."

"No, thanks. I have a thousand things to do."

"It's been a long time since we've been together. Ever since you started with the missing old lady mystery, you've been avoiding me. What the fuck is going on?"

"Excuse me?"

"Okay, I didn't mean that, but it's just…are you seeing someone important?"

"I don't have to explain myself to you, Laura. We've both been clear about that from the beginning."

"Yes, but seeing other women had never stopped you from seeing me. What's happening now?"

"I just don't feel like dating anymore."

"Are you leaving me?"

"Leaving you? What are you talking about? You and I have nothing permanent."

"It's her, isn't it? Your little friend Juliet, that bitch. Has she managed to cajole you at last?"

"I won't allow you to talk about her like that, and don't forget that I have no commitment to you, and you have no commitment to me. Let's leave it here and part in peace, okay? I'll see you later."

He left the school, still indignant, said goodbye to some parents at the main entrance, and started walking toward the Underground. It was unbelievable that people to whom you had made clear the rules from minute one then dared to demand or reproach. It was immature and stupid, and he regretted having embarked with a coworker on an absurd and superficial adventure that meant nothing to him and that, given what he had just seen, would end up bringing him a headache.

One of his sacred rules was not to go out with people from his work environment. He never did that unless they were lifelong friends, like old college classmates, but never new people. However, Laura, who was an administrative secretary at his school and, *a priori*, a liberal and modern woman of the world, had insisted on meeting, and in the end, he had agreed to see her outside the school after meeting her by chance at a swingers' party he had attended.

She had sworn to him at the time that she was used to open relationships and that she saw herself with a lifelong boyfriend and other friends. Theirs would just be another fling. The plain truth was that she had always demanded quite a bit of attention and companionship, which had caused their affair to go awry even before he first spoke to Juliet.

He arrived in his neighborhood and calculated how long they had been seeing each other. It had been about five months since he had returned from Amsterdam after spending part of the confinement with Daniel.

Before the pandemic, they had hooked up at that swingers' party and then seen each other once, but with the quarantine, they had stopped seeing each other, although she had FaceTimed him almost every day. He had not seen her again until late summer when he had returned to London to prepare for the start of the new school year.

"What are you doing here, Laura?"

An hour after setting foot in his house, the doorbell rang. He opened the door and found her standing there with an innocent face and a bag of takeout in her hand. He snorted, determined not to let her in, but she snuck down the hallway and didn't stop until she reached the living room.

"I'm so sorry. Really, Michiel, I'm sorry. I didn't mean to badmouth Audrey or make you angry or insult your neighbor Juliet. It's just that I'm exhausted. There's a lot of work before winter break, and I just wanted to spend some quality time with you."

"You'd better leave."

"I bought dinner at that place you like so much. Let's eat and chat. It's better to talk on a full stomach."

"I've already got dinner, and I've got a lot of things to…"

"You do what you have to do, and I'll eat quietly. What I don't want is for us to end up like this."

"There's nothing to finish," he said firmly, but before he could continue the argument, the doorbell rang again. He had no choice but to leave it there and go out to open the door. He walked down the hallway, looking at the time because he wasn't expecting anyone, opened the door, and found an agitated Juliet.

"Juliet?" he asked like an idiot and smiled at her, but she squinted and pointed inside the apartment.

"Is your girlfriend here? Ask her to come out, please."

"My what? What's wrong?"

"Your girlfriend. Tell Laura to come out."

"What the fuck?"

"Hey, you!" She pushed him away from the door and came in. She saw Laura coming from the living room, faced her, and pointed her finger at her. "You're not so brave in front of 'your man' anymore, right?"

"Look, Juliet—"

"'Look, Juliet,' my ass. I don't know how things are in your world, but in mine, if you dare to insult me and threaten me, you'll end up in court. You've been warned. The next time you insult me in public or in private, I'm going to report you, and I'm going to get a restraining order against you. You now know that. Goodbye."

"What happened?" Michiel cut her off, and she stopped.

"Your very jealous girlfriend cornered me in the takeout place to call me a whore. I will not allow it. You know that. Control your girl a little, or I'm going to put a cigar in her ass."

He turned to Laura angrily, and she shrugged and whined, "It's your fault, Michiel. Ever since she—"

"What!"

Juliet grimaced. "She told me that if I don't stay away from her man, she's going to send some Romanian guys to break my legs. I have witnesses, the whole damn place, so be careful. There are laws against that, and I'm going to use all of them."

"You're lying. I don't—"

"I'm lying. Is it also a lie that you're going to drag me by the hair for coming to your boyfriend with the story? Huh? I've already come to him with the story. Let's see what you do now." Juliet turned furiously toward the exit, and he followed her. She reached the hallway, and he saw that a tall, very handsome guy was waiting for her at her door with a bag of groceries in his hand.

"Juliet!" He grabbed her arm and she dodged him, but she stopped to look him in the face.

"You know she's not my girlfriend, and I have absolutely nothing to do with what she does or says."

"You've got a problem, kid, because *she* thinks she's your girlfriend. If she treated me like that, she'll do it to everyone."

"Fuck me!"

"Okay, breathe. I know you had nothing to do with this, but make sure she stays away from me."

"You'll never see her again, and neither will I."

"I'm not going to get involved in that. It's none of my business. It's enough for me if she leaves me alone."

"In any case, I am very sorry."

"I'm sorry for the outburst of madness too, but it's just that this drama gets on my nerves. I hate girls like that. They can be very dangerous, you know?" She pointed her thumb at the guy who was waiting for her. "If it wasn't for Caden, she would have beaten me up on the street."

"Caden?" He squinted and moved closer to her. "Really, Juliet?"

"You see to it that your friend never speaks to me again. Good evening."

She turned her back on him and walked quickly to her place, where that tall, blond, young, surfer-looking guy was waiting for her with calmness and an advert's smile on his face.

Michiel wanted to grab him by the neck and throw him off a

balcony, but he restrained himself and watched helplessly as he entered her house with all the naturalness in the world.

He suddenly remembered Laura, who was crouched in his living room.

He looked at his apartment, deciding whether he should call the police to report her, but before he could decide anything, he saw her open the door with the takeaway in one hand and the other showing him her middle finger.

"Fuck you both, assholes!" she shouted and disappeared.

An open relationship is consensual, ethical, and responsible non-monogamy, where love is open and free of jealousy. You can choose to have it as a single person or as a primary partner with other secondary partners. There can be a love triangle and other combinations. The point is to maintain your freedom without harming anyone.

The theory was simple, but in practice, you had to be made of special stuff to respect the rules and agreements. To live without guilt or envy and to enjoy that part of your life without making it the center of your existence. In short, to be consistent with your decisions and not end up screwing up people's lives.

He took a sip of his pint and surveyed the packed pub on December 22nd at six o'clock in the evening. The whole school seemed to be there, celebrating the successful Christmas gala. Out of the corner of his eye, he spotted Laura, who had turned up in his classroom after the little message she had given him to reassure him that she was in psychiatric treatment. She took a lot of pills and did not know what she was doing, but that it would not happen again.

He was more pissed off than he should have been. He had barked four sentences at her and demanded that she disappear from his life and especially from Juliet Miller's. If she dared to come within a hundred yards of Juliet, he would not be held accountable for his actions.

Damn it, he thought, running his hand over his face. He never spoke like that to anyone because for him, conflicts were resolved by talking calmly or even by letting them go. Apparently, Juliet had imbued him with her impetuous Mediterranean spirit, which fascinated him, and he had ended up exploding and saying direct and forceful things without caring what the other person felt. In this case, Laura, who deserved it after how she had behaved with them.

"With us," he whispered, thinking of Juliet, that beautiful woman who had him enraptured. He concluded that, given her character and her passion, she was the worst candidate to survive an open relationship. She would never understand consensual, ethical, and responsible non-monogamy. She had already made it clear to him once, and he loved it because, deep down, he knew that he couldn't share her with anyone either. Least of all with that guy, that Caden, who had left her house half an hour after the incident with Laura.

"Hi, handsome." Gwen touched his back and leaned next to him on the bar. "You're very quiet. Is everything all right?"

"Yeah. I was just thinking. How about you? Your group did great with the reading of *A Christmas Carol*. Congratulations."

"They're old enough to read Dickens. Paul!" she called to her husband, who was also a schoolteacher, and he came over to them.

"Would you like another round?"

"Not me, thank you. I'm going home. I'll be up early tomorrow.

"Michiel!"

"Seriously, Daniel is leaving early for Holland with Fiona, and I want to go and see him off."

"Aren't you going to Amsterdam, man?"

"Not this time. I spent a weekend for Chanukah and, before

that, eight days in New York. The time has come to take advantage of time off in London."

"Is it because of the doctorate? Virginia says she's convincing you to finish it here."

"We'll see. What do you guys do on vacation?"

"We will go to the Canary Islands for a week for the New Year."

"Enjoy it very much. See you in January."

He hugged them both, said goodbye to the rest of his companions, dodging protests and attempts to hold him back, and finally went out into the street, where it was freezing cold.

He stopped at the curb to wait for a cab and at that moment, he decided he could devote part of his vacation to resuming his doctoral proposal. Virginia, the school principal, had offered him funding and support to pursue his doctorate. He had been waiting since Daniel's birth when he had put everything on hold to take care of his son.

The subject had been on his mind for eight years. People like his parents continually reminded him of his honors degree in history and his thesis on the New Netherlands and Peter Stuyvesant, which had won awards and opened the door to a master's degree paid for by the Dutch government and the doctorate. Perhaps the time had come to take it up again. Maybe the Audrey case was pushing him to take up that unfinished business. Maybe not, but he would do it. Besides, he could give a new approach to the thesis with the help of experts like John Tompkins.

"Robert?" He got into a cab while answering a call from Fiona's husband. He informed him that he was driving but that he couldn't wait to tell Michiel what had just happened to him. "Man, I'm freaking out."

"Are you all right?"

"Yes, yes, everything is perfect. I just left Fi and Daniel at home, safe and sound. I am referring to the Stuyvesants of New York."

"What happened?"

"As soon as you asked me about the inheritance, I went on the Internet to have a look. Seeing that it was all conjecture, I called a colleague who works in our affiliate in Manhattan to see what he knew, and he told me that the matter was ironclad. It was being handled by a team of family lawyers, completely anonymous and bound by confidentiality agreements. He said he had no idea of the details but to assume that any move by these people had legal backing. He said the Stuyvesants in New York were not going to make a false move and that your neighbor, Mrs. Stuyvesant, would have no luck if she challenged the process because no American judge would entertain a claim against that family, so the healthiest thing to do was to forget about it."

"I don't want to contest anything."

"Yeah, I told him, but the guy got a little defensive, and I passed. Today, three days after that talk, I got a call on my cell phone from a Jack Lynch, head of security for the Stuyvesant family, asking me if I had any professional interest in the estate and if I represented anyone in particular in England."

"I can't believe it. I know exactly who this Jack Lynch is."

"He was exquisite in manner and treatment, but man, how did he find out that I had tried to inform myself about the process? Ralph, my colleague, swears he did not discuss my call with anyone, not even his wife. I assume that they have spies everywhere, which makes me think they are trying to hide something shady now that they are worried sick that someone from London, especially a lawyer, is snooping around."

"I guess what they're worried about is Audrey's family finding out about the inheritance and trying to get to her."

"Do you know about possible heirs?"

"As far as I know, he has nephews."

"Then I would try to keep the lady isolated and half-sequestered if I had made her give up hundreds of millions of dollars without providing her with independent legal counsel. If so, the screw-up is monumental, and no judge could dismiss a lawsuit."

"I assure you that Audrey is not interested in that, and neither is her family. She hasn't spoken to them for over sixty years."

"They have violated the rights of an octogenarian lady. They have isolated her and manipulated her in a country that is not hers. I can represent the family. The call from Lynch piqued my curiosity, and I would love to get my hands on a case of such proportions."

"The only thing we're concerned about right now is getting Audrey back and being left alone. The money and everything else is big for her, believe me, but if for some reason the family or she herself decides to go against the Stuyvesants, I will do my best to make the case yours."

"Done. I'll take your word for it. I'm getting horny, just thinking about a lawsuit against those people."

"Thanks for everything, Rob."

"It has been a pleasure. Keep me posted. Bye."

He got out of the cab at the Barbican and looked around, wondering if they were being watched in London. That was perfectly plausible, given the way the riffraff was behaving.

He ran up the stairs of the building, reached his floor, and passed Juliet's apartment first. He knocked on the door, but no one answered. He decided to call her, but she was out of range, so he went into his apartment, put his things down, and made himself a sandwich. He sat down and thought about the fuss they had unleashed just for asking a few questions and worrying about a neighbor they knew very slightly. It had all been worth it for Audrey and, especially, for Juliet.

"What are you doing out there in the dark?" Juliet asked an hour later. He was in the hallway, leaning on the banister and smoking a cigarette. He smiled and ran his eyes over her.

"I was waiting for you."

"Really?" She walked over and settled down next to him. "It's not too cold to smoke out here?"

"I don't like to smoke indoors."

"It's the first time I've seen you smoking. How are you?"

"I don't smoke much. Only when I'm on vacation."

"Oh, right, school vacations. Lucky you. Give me a puff."

She took the cigarette from him and took a quick puff before handing it back. "It feels bad, but it tastes good."

"Jack Lynch called Fiona's husband Robert to ask him why he was taking an interest in the Stuyvesant estate and whether he represented anyone in England."

"No! How strange."

"He had made a few inquiries about it on the Internet and in the New York branch of his law firm, and the guy goes and calls him on his cell phone. He identified himself as the head of security for the Stuyvesant family."

"My goodness! How did Robert take it?"

"Like the lawyer he is. He says there is a good chance of contesting the probate and has offered to represent Audrey or her family against the Stuyvesants."

"I don't think that's the case. Do you get along with him?"

"Of course. He's an excellent stepfather, and my son has lived with him since he was four years old. We get along very well. I get along with everyone, just like you do with your friend Caden."

"He needed a laptop to work. I had an unused one at home, so he came to get it, and I gave it to him. Nothing else happened. Well, not nothing. He saved me from the beating your friend Laura wanted to give me."

"Touché." He laughed, and she laughed with him. "I confess

that last night, I kept waiting for you to leave. I've developed a rather powerful protective instinct toward you, Sherlock."

"Were you spying on me?"

"No, I was smoking."

"Very funny."

"Come to bed with me," he whispered. He took her hand. She got up and stood in front of him.

"Tomorrow, I'm going to Spain with my family. I'm going to spend Christmas in Cádiz."

"All the more reason to sleep with me tonight." He pulled her close and kissed her, parting her soft lips with his tongue. After a minute, she put both hands on his chest, pushed him away, and smiled at him, combing his hair with her fingers.

"You have such beautiful hair. It's the first thing I noticed when I met you."

"Come to bed with me, Juliet. Don't make me beg."

"I'm never going to get into that bed with you." She indicated his apartment with her thumb, and he blinked.

"Why?"

"Would anyone get into the bed of a polyamorous, or polysexual, or whatever you call it? Not me. I'm repulsed."

"What?" He laughed, and she backed away.

"It makes me cringe just thinking about how many women have slept there, including your friend Laura."

"It hasn't been that many. Don't overdo it."

"Just in case, I will keep a safe distance from your bed. However, you can come to mine."

"No one has slept in your bed? Your little friend Caden, for example?"

"In my bed, only Romeo has slept, and he seems to like you, so I'm sure he'll give you a place."

"I like you, Juliet," he blurted without thinking. She smiled, took a deep breath, and offered him her hand.

"Are you coming, my dear Watson?"

PART III
JULIET AND MICHIEL

CHAPTER TWENTY

She was startled by a cell phone alarm and opened her eyes. She tried to get her bearings since sometimes she didn't know which country she was in. She saw that she was in London, at home, in her bed, and Michiel Lezer was hugging her with his whole body. The alarm was his cell phone since she didn't have to get up this early.

She didn't move, and he squeezed her before turning off the alarm. They lay there for a few seconds in silence. They had gone to bed late and slept little, he thought, looking at the time on the digital clock on his bedside table. It was six o'clock in the morning, but he had to get up early to go to the airport to pick up his parents, who were coming to London to attend a friend's birthday party.

She closed her eyes, intending to continue to sleep until half past seven, but she couldn't. She watched as Michiel sat on the edge of the bed with his hands resting on the mattress, staring at infinity. He had a spectacular back, shoulders, and neck and that beautifully disheveled hair. She felt the urge to kiss him, but she didn't because she couldn't keep him on the first day back to school after Christmas break.

Romeo climbed into bed and let him caress him for a few seconds, and she closed her eyes again since she was happy but exhausted and needed to regain her strength.

They had been cooped up at her house since December 30—almost four days—making love, chatting, and eating anything and everything while watching movies and series between one wild fuck and the next.

It had all started the day of the interview with Victoria Stuyvesant in Juliet's office when they had ended up succumbing to the inevitable—sex in the hallway of Barbican Estates. Since then, when they saw each other, they did not stop.

She would not have planned it this way, and although he had attracted her from the beginning, never in her wildest dreams would she have imagined taking the first step, overcoming her fears and insecurities, and throwing herself on his neck to unleash a roller coaster of passion and incredible enjoyment. Of complicity, of chemistry, and of eroticism. They also got along wonderfully under the sheets and on them, and in the bathtub, and on the sofa, or against a piece of kitchen furniture. Her experience in this "wild" terrain was null because she had always looked for love and butterflies in her stomach. She had never allowed herself to be with a man for pure and crystalline pleasure, and trying it with Michiel was the best decision she had ever made in her life. She felt full, feminine, sexy, and desired. He was an expert lover and sweet, adorable, and beastly at times. That had her fascinated and captivated.

She still felt like being with him even though they had been together for a couple of weeks, with several days between since she had spent Christmas in Spain and four days in Bulgaria for work before returning home.

On December 22nd, they had stayed up all night making love, stopping from time to time to catch their breath and talk about the Stuyvesants, Michiel's doctorate, and the novel she had finally started to write. Mainly, they had fucked like in the movies, as she had never done with anyone. She had left the next day to be with her parents, almost unable to walk and with shivers of pleasure ravaging her from time to time.

Wonderful, pure magic. That was why she had returned to London like a madwoman to kidnap him. They hadn't even contemplated going to one of the New Year's Eve parties they both had on the agenda. Nothing like that. Without talking or making any decisions, they went for a walk in the neighborhood, bought special food for dinner, and spent midnight in bed.

She had not even eaten the grapes, which would have killed her grandmother if she had known, and they had turned off their phones after talking to their respective families to dedicate themselves to just the two of them. To their usual quarrels. To be in silence, to touch each other, and to get to know each other. She had to learn a lot because she had been uninhibited as never before and had spent the best New Year's Eve of her life.

Carpe diem, *Juliet*, she thought all the time. She felt like the happiest and most satisfied woman to walk the earth.

"I'll call you later," he whispered in her ear before kissing her. Juliet came back from the world of sleep to smell the scent of shampoo and shower gel he was giving off. She nodded without moving and opened one eye to watch him pull a gray t-shirt over that perfect, warm torso and how he finger-combed his wet hair before leaving the bedroom.

Everyone who knew her knew she never let a guy sleep at her house, not even Caden because she was weird about her stuff and her privacy. However, Michiel Lezer coming in and out of her room, cooking in her kitchen, or showering in her bathroom turned her on, and the novelty made her smile. She hugged her pillow and fell asleep.

CHAPTER TWENTY-ONE

"He refuses outright. Says he has no intention of flying to the Caribbean to join a fifth-rate chorus and spout three bullshit sentences. Those are his actual words."

Rose, one of her co-workers, looked at Iona, who was chairing the first meeting of the year at Shaughnessy & McCameron, and shrugged.

"He hasn't worked since October."

"It's not all going to be *Downton Abbey* or *Game of Thrones*. We'll give him an ultimatum. If he doesn't accept the next project, we'll terminate the contract." Iona snorted, looking at the group. "I don't know what these people think. Everyone is doing *Crime in Paradise* on the beach. As if it's a vacation, for fuck's sake."

"They're only staying four days."

"I don't care. It's work, and actors kill for work. What's that thing about there being no such thing as a small part? Fuck it. I don't want to hear any more complaints about it, but Juliet, if you would talk to him, I'd appreciate it."

"Me?" Juliet, who had been listening to everyone for twenty minutes without getting involved because all she could think about was Michiel's big blue eyes and his tongue, which was super soft and super delicious, looked at the boss and shifted in her chair. "As you wish, but..."

"Warn him on my behalf what we have decided. We will only give him one more chance. If I call him, I'm going to make a mess, and that's not the plan."

"As you wish."

"Finally, I don't know if you know this, but Jennifer Davies has founded an acting agency in Brooklyn called Davies and Associates. The bitch took over half the New York office's portfolio over the Christmas holidays, so keep your eyes peeled. We will be sending a statement to all our clients thanking them for their loyalty and trust, affirming our confidence in them, and making them aware of it. The legal and press departments are in the process of finalizing it and will send it to you as well."

"That bitch," Juliet mumbled. She looked at Fabio, who couldn't take his eyes off her, and he shrugged.

"I hope you enjoyed your little Christmas vacations and came back with your batteries charged and that you sign lots of contracts for me. Happy New Year to all of you. Get back to work."

Juliet stood up, gathered her things, and calmly waited for everyone to leave the room. Fabio grabbed her by the arm and pulled her into the hall.

"Juliet Miller, you haven't hooked up with LOML again, have you?"

"With who?" LOML seemed like a hieroglyphic, but when it dawned on her that he meant Caden, she shook her head emphatically. "No, why?"

"Are you sure?"

"Of course."

"You've screwed someone and a lot because that face and that luminous complexion of yours are the results of a great lover."

"Shit. Let's get to work. There's a lot to do."

"I don't sleep with girls, but I watch them, and you've had great sex."

"Fabio!"

"On second thought, it's obvious that it's not Caden because that asshole didn't leave you like that. He left you empty and frustrated, and you're in glory. Who is he? Do I know him?"

"Leave it, will you?"

"Would it be Richard M?"

"How can it be Richard M? He's shooting in Los Angeles."

"He likes you a lot, and he is not in Los Angeles. He came to celebrate Hogmanay with his family in Scotland and has stayed a few more days in the UK. He has an awards show in London today."

"Oh, my goodness."

"Give me a name."

"Another day. Let's go."

"So, I'm not mistaken. You *have* a lover, Spanish princess. Who is he?"

"It's her Dutch friend, Michiel Huisman's double," Iona interjected, appearing from behind her. Juliet's eyes narrowed. "See, there's that look of satisfaction. She's finally shagging a real man, and for the record, I warned you as soon as I saw them together. You owe me a hundred quid, gorgeous."

Juliet widened her eyes. "Who do *you* sleep with?"

They both laughed, and she turned her back on them and locked herself in her office. It was obvious that she was more transparent than water. As her grandmother used to say, she could neither steal nor lie nor cheat because her face gave her away. At that precise moment in the morning, she didn't feel like providing away material for office gossip, so it was better for her to withdraw until the silly face she must be wearing went away.

"Juliet." Andrea peeked into her office, and she turned her attention to her. "I have several roles for that woman, Victoria

Stuyvesant. I emailed them to her, and she replied that the person who is to accompany her should pick her up in Surrey."

"Really? That's funny."

"Shall I write to her?"

"Yes. Please explain to her that we don't lead new actors by the hand to auditions and that she has to find her own way."

"It will be a pleasure. Don't forget that at three o'clock, you have the first fitting of Sarah's dress."

"Oh, of course. Thank you very much, Andrea."

She recalled the appointment, and her spirits were dampened because she'd planned to see Michiel before he had to go to dinner with his parents and Daniel and before she had to attend an engagement in Chelsea. She shook off the bad feeling because Sarah came first. More importantly, it was time to come back to reality, come to her senses, and master her lust, or she would go crazy.

"Hello, Richard," she answered the call from Richard M, her superstar, without taking her eyes off the computer screen.

He greeted her in his sexy, vibrant Scottish accent. "Hiya, Juliet. Happy New Year. Is it still possible to say Happy New Year?"

"I think so. Happy New Year to you too. How are you doing? Do you need anything?"

"I'm in London, and in November, you promised to have dinner with me."

"Huh?" She took off her glasses and paid attention to him.

"In New York, we said we were going to have dinner one day, and I don't get here much. Can you meet me tonight?"

"I'm going to a book launch in Chelsea. When are you leaving?"

"The Alexandra Collins book?"

"Yes."

"Great, I'm going too. I'll drop by after the awards show at the

Royal Albert Hall. See you there? Let's see if we can chat like old times, Juliet. I miss it so much."

"What times those were."

"Yeah. Anyway, I'll see you tonight?"

"Perfect. See you tonight."

She hung up on him, remembering the idle hours of shooting, rehearsals, script readings, and trips in which she had made so many friendships and received so much sincere appreciation and felt nostalgic. Now that she had more responsibility in the agency, she felt like she neglected her clients. She thought about getting a cup of coffee to cheer herself up, but the phone lit up again. This time, it was her beautiful Dutch lover.

"Hello."

"Good morning, miss," he said in Spanish, and she smiled.

"How are you?"

"I'm fine. How are you?"

"Well. How are your parents?"

"My parents are fine, thank you. I'm on a break and I'm not on the playground, so I decided to call you because I can't stop thinking about you."

"Oh, can't you?" She felt her panties metaphorically fall to the floor, and an electric spark went through her from north to south. She stood up. "What a coincidence. The same thing happens to me."

"Why don't you call me?"

"Because I don't know your schedule. I don't want to bother you."

"Tonight, I will give my schedule to you."

"You know what? Jennifer Davies has set up a representation agency in Brooklyn and has stolen half our portfolio of actors from Shaughnessy & McCameron, New York. You can tell she's into stealing stuff."

"What a nightmare."

"It is."

"How is your morning going?"

"Lots to do as usual, and at three o'clock, I have to go to Knightsbridge for the first fitting of my sister's wedding dress. I had completely forgotten. I'm sorry about that."

"So, we won't see each other?"

"Not until after dinner."

"Hello, Dani," he greeted his son, and she heard his voice.

"Didn't you bring me Grandma's cookies?"

"No, she has them. I forgot to ask her for them. She'll bring them to dinner tonight."

"Who are you talking to?"

"Juliet."

"Hello, Juliet. Say hello to Romeo!"

"Okay, go back to recess. See you later. Did you hear that?"

"Yes. How nice he is."

"I'm a little bit confused because I wanted to undress you and put you to bed at three o'clock in the afternoon, but if there's no other way, I'll just have to be patient."

"Same here."

"See you tonight, Juliet. Let me know when you get home."

"Of course. A kiss."

"A kiss, *Zissele.*"

"*Zissele*," she repeated, hearing him hang up, and went straight to Google to look up the word because he had said it to her many times over the weekend, and she hadn't dared ask what it meant.

She typed in variations of the phonetic until the search engine recognized the Yiddish and translated it, leaving her excited and a little shaky in front of the screen. It was an affectionate vocative meaning sweetness.

"Juliet?"

He opened the door to find her standing in the hallway,

gorgeous in a black cocktail dress with a wide skirt like the ones Audrey Hepburn wore. He smiled delightedly because they weren't supposed to see each other until later, and she pushed at his chest and pulled him into the foyer, throwing her purse and coat on the floor.

"I couldn't wait. I have about fifteen minutes, I'll be late, but I don't care."

She slid her hands under his shirt and stood on her tiptoes to bite his mouth. He responded to her kisses with the same eagerness, yet he tried to hold her by the wrists to get her attention.

"*Zissele*, wait a minute. Juliet?"

"What? Don't you feel like it? I'm not wearing underwear, you know."

"Of course I feel like it. I can't wait." He lowered his voice and grabbed her around the waist. "But I'm not alone."

"I beg your pardon?" She took a step back with a frown, and he grabbed her hand again.

"My parents are in the living room."

"I thought you were going to tell me you were with one of your girlfriends."

"Excuse me?"

"It's plausible. Don't be like that."

"Fuck me, Juliet. You're amazing, but we'll discuss that later. For now, come on in. They'd love to meet you."

"No. I'm sorry I came without calling. I'll leave you alone. I'll call you tomorrow, or tonight, as we agreed."

"No, miss. Don't you have about fifteen minutes?" He took her hand and dragged her into the living room, where his parents were having a glass of wine before leaving for Fiona's house to pick up Daniel.

"Mom, Dad, this is Juliet Miller. Juliet, these are my parents, Ruth and Michiel Lezer."

"How are you?"

"She's beautiful," her mother whispered in Yiddish, then

looked her in the eye and spoke to her in English. "How do you do, Juliet? Michiel and Daniel have told us so much about you."

"Oh, well…"

"How are you?" Her father offered her his hand, then pointed at the bottle of wine on the counter. "A small glass of wine? It's a Dutch Gewürztraminer. I don't know if you know it."

"I think so. It's sweet, isn't it? I've tasted it a few times in Amsterdam."

"Exactly. Have a drink."

"No, thank you."

"Come on, Juliet. It will only take a moment." He stroked her back and pointed at a couch. "Fifteen minutes, please."

"Okay. It's just that I have an engagement in Chelsea, and I don't want to be too late."

"We are leaving in a little while to pick up the grandson. We have made reservations at a restaurant near his mother's house."

"Which hotel are you staying at?"

"At Claridge's. We always come to Claridge's."

"I love it. It's very close to my work."

"Fascinating work, Michiel told us."

"I find *yours* fascinating."

"Don't you represent musicians?"

"Not specifically, but many of our actors and actresses have complete musical backgrounds. It's a common mix that enriches their value."

"Of course. Actors have always sung or played the piano or danced."

"Since the beginning of time." Michiel's father smiled. She looked up at him, and he came over to her, pulled up a chair, and sat down opposite her.

"Daniel says you have a beautiful and very good Russian blue."

"Yes, his name is Romeo. The truth is that he is very handsome and very quiet. He is four years old."

"Will you let us meet him? All of us Lezers love cats."

"Of course. How long are you staying in London?"

"We don't know. We came for three or four days, depending on what comes up, but we are not in a hurry to go back. This way, we can enjoy our son and grandson. Does your family live in London?"

"My parents and older brother live in the suburbs, in Willesden, and my younger sister lives in Scotland."

"She's in the army," Michiel commented, and his mother nodded.

"Your mother is Spanish, right? We love Spain. It drives us crazy. We have always thought about buying something small to spend the winters there, but we have never made up our minds."

"Because we also travel a lot in the winter to Israel," her father said. "Do you know Israel, Juliet?"

"No, not yet."

"You have to go with Michiel. He lived there for a year. He knows it very well, and we have a great apartment in Tel Aviv on Gordon Beach, in front of the sea."

"Did you live in Israel?" She searched Michiel's eyes, and he nodded.

"Like almost all young Jews from all corners of the world, he went to the motherland for a year of community service. He came back from there wanting to devote himself to teaching."

"Really? You didn't tell me about that, Michiel."

"He had just finished his degree in history in Amsterdam. He went to work for a year on a kibbutz and was assigned, among other things, to work in the school. As soon as he got a taste of that, he decided that he was going to work at educating young children," his mother explained proudly.

Although, when that happened twenty years ago, they had almost suffered a heart attack because since he had decided to study history and not medicine or architecture, he would end up working as a professor in some great university, not in an elementary school teaching six-year-olds. Without meaning to, he smiled but didn't open his mouth. He gazed at Juliet intently. He thought she was gorgeous, with her beautiful legs perfectly entwined, her signature heels, and so attentive to the talk, charming and polite, sitting just a few centimeters away.

He wanted to reach up under her black dress, stroke one of her thighs up to her groin, and check if it was true that she was not wearing underwear, but he just continued to listen to the conversation in silence until a very loud noise startled all four of them.

"What was that?" He stood and looked out onto the terrace. Juliet did the same with a questioning face. They waited in silence to see if it was repeated because it had been quite loud. When it was, they looked into each other's eyes.

"Audrey's apartment," they blurted in unison, and they spun around toward the door to rush into the hallway.

There were two movers standing by Audrey Stuyvesant's door, which was very strange because it was half past five in the afternoon. He looked at Juliet out of the corner of his eye and they approached, determined to see what was going on.

"I knew they'd show up eventually," commented Jack Lynch, who, as always, was there running the show. He watched them patiently and invited them to enter the apartment with a gesture. Several workers were busy packing Audrey's things into identical boxes.

"Good afternoon, Miss Miller, Mr. Lezer."

"Good afternoon. What's going on? Are you selling the apartment?" asked Juliet. "Audrey told us she would keep it intact for when she came on vacation."

"I'm afraid I can't give out the details of my bosses' plans, Miz Miller."

"Come on. You know perfectly well who we are. You saw us with Audrey in Manhattan. That's enough with the mysteries."

Lynch took a deep breath and indicated the terrace. "Please come with me."

"What's going on?"

"I am sorry to inform you," he whispered solemnly, "and I should not, because no one has given me official authorization, that Mrs. Audrey Stuyvesant passed away on Christmas Eve in New York."

"What?" Michiel exclaimed, then frowned. "How? We saw her six weeks ago, and she was perfect. Better than ever."

"I know, Mr. Lezer. The doctor certified the death as a stroke, which is very common in people of her age. She died in her sleep and in peace. I am very sorry for your loss."

"Michiel," Juliet mumbled with tears in her eyes. He pulled her close and hugged her against his chest.

"I know, *Zissele*. I know, and I'm so sorry." He kissed the top of her head, then looked Lynch in the face. "What have they done with Audrey's body? Has there been a funeral? She didn't want to be cremated. She wanted to be buried with Gregory in Kensal Green Cemetery here in London."

"I'm sure the family has made the best decision for her."

"What do they know? They barely knew her," Juliet said tearfully, and the guy shrugged.

"I'm afraid I can't comment on that, Miz Miller."

"Okay, perfect. Who can I talk to? We need to know the details of her death, what they have done with her, and where she is buried. Audrey was a very religious woman and had many acquaintances in St. Giles next door."

"I will pass on your inquiries to the family, and I will contact you to give you as much information as I can, miss."

"They couldn't have left her in New York. She wanted the little mausoleum she had bought with Gregory in Kensal Green. They wanted to be together here."

"I've already told you what I know. Now, if you don't mind, we have work to do, and these people charge by the hour." He gestured at the movers and made an attempt to go back into the apartment.

Juliet cut him off to force him to look at her. "They have no soul. It's unbelievable that they would do this. This was her home and her husband's home. There are thousands of mementos and objects of sentimental value that she adored. Can't they let us select what they can take?"

"That's enough. Who do you think you are? You're nobody. What do you want with so many questions and so many requests? Leave the damn thing alone!"

"Hey, man!" Michiel felt an ancestral fury rise in his body. He stepped in front of Juliet to pull her away from the gorilla in the suit. He pushed him back with his eyes because they were the same height, and when he had him against the wall, he pointed his finger at him, sincerely wishing he would get cocky and give him a good excuse to break his face. "Don't talk to her like that, Lynch. Don't you dare talk to her like that, or I swear to God I'll break you in two, is that clear? I've had it up to here with your mysteries and your Rambo bullshit. Juliet?"

"I'm fine." She grabbed his hand.

"Let's go."

CHAPTER TWENTY-TWO

No, Juliet. Don't start that bullshit. No true love, no Hollywood romance, no Jane Austen. Stop it. Enough is enough, she scolded herself, covering her face with both hands because she was starting to despair. Finally, she took a deep breath, leaned against the back of the chair, and looked out across the huge window at the Thames, the Millennium Bridge in all its splendor, and the beautiful, majestic, and impressive St. Paul's Cathedral. It was one of her favorite views of London.

A very kind server came over with the still water she had ordered and left her a mini cheese plate to nibble on. It was great because she was very hungry and her brother had warned her that he would be ten minutes late. Typical of him. She took a small piece of feta and a piece of toast and tried to remember that she was at that Greek restaurant to have lunch with James and give him the signed consent papers to become the twins' legal guardian, not to think about Michiel. Michiel Lezer, that brilliant, gorgeous, sexy, affectionate, and on top of that, brave guy who had stood up for her over Audrey's death two days earlier, so upsetting her life that he had been completely out of the game for those two days.

She didn't need saving. Juliet Miller was many things, but she had never been a damsel in distress. She knew she appeared fragile to many people and sometimes a little helpless, but she was just the opposite. She was a strong, resourceful, and fearless woman and had been from a very young age. Even though she was four years younger than James, she had often stood up for him, for Sarah and her friends, and for her actors, whom she defended tooth and nail against anyone.

She had a lot of character; she knew it, and those who knew her knew it. She was a whirlwind of energy, her grandmother said. That had made her go through life on her own without asking anyone for help, feeling self-sufficient and sometimes lonely. She did not perceive her life any other way because she had not met anyone who would take the reins and stand up for her, take care of her, and make her feel protected and safe. She had only experienced that sensation in her family environment, especially with her mother, and suddenly feeling it with someone she had only known for a short time but liked very much had made her cry with emotion and anguish. She knew that a feeling of such proportions could not be ignored and that it meant too many things.

The first thing was that she was Michiel Lezer's for good. If they had been sweethearts, she would have proposed to him on her knees that very night, married him the next day, and started having a bunch of blue-eyed children right away because a man like that, capable of those gestures, was what she had been waiting for all her life.

Unfortunately, that had not been possible since they were not starring in a romantic movie. They were not even on the same wavelength; he was light-years away from her. He had made that clear to her ten minutes after meeting her when he had explained to her about free relationships and his healthy lifestyle free from commitments. Therefore, he would vanish like a mirage at some point, probably with one or two other girls he liked more, and that hurt. It made her face a dilemma: keep seeing him until whatever they had was over, or do the right thing, get ahead of the drama, and cut off the affair once and for all.

"Julie, *miarma*, you look beautiful," her brother told her in his thickest Cádiz accent. She smiled and kissed him twice, admiring his spectacular looks. James was the best-looking of the three Miller siblings. He had inherited the best from his father and mother and had a great face and an Andalusian flair that contrasted with his appearance of being a British boy from a good family.

"Thanks, kiddo. Same to you."

"What's up? Have you got a boyfriend?"

"Why does everyone assume I've got a boyfriend when I look so much better? Do I usually look that bad?"

"You've got a boyfriend. Hello!" He switched to his long-winded English to greet the server and order the food, then looked at her with his green eyes. "Who is it, Bill Richardson from Willesden?"

"No, I haven't even met with him."

"Please don't tell me you're seeing the Aussie bastard again because I'm going to break his soul. Do you hear me? And this time, I'm serious."

"James!"

"What a pig the guy is."

"You woke up being very much from La Línea de la Concepción this morning."

"I just hung up the phone with Uncle Juan. I'm so relaxed speaking in Spanish. Doesn't it happen to you?"

"No, although I still prefer to swear in Spanish."

"Yeah, Siobhan too, and I don't know how to explain to her that she has a shitty accent."

"Oh, poor thing. She's trying so hard. Don't tell her anything."

"She's been learning Spanish for ten years and nothing, *pisha*. But come on, as long as Jamie and Harry speak it well, the rest doesn't worry me. Did you bring me the signed papers? Did your lawyer review them?"

"I told you I don't have a lawyer, but a colleague from the agency's legal department took a look at them and gave me her okay. Here they are. I'm sorry for taking so long, but I had to think it over."

"That's precisely why we want you as our children's guardian. You think everything through, and then you follow through, even if it costs you your life."

"It's an honor."

"The honor is all ours. You don't know how reassuring this is for Sio and me. Thank you very much."

"You're welcome. Do you remember Mrs. Stuyvesant, the one we were looking for and found in Manhattan?"

He nodded.

"The day before yesterday, we were told that she died on Christmas Eve."

"Oh my goodness! I'm so sorry."

"We spent so much time together during lockdown that she became like a surrogate grandmother. I don't know; I was very sad to hear that she died alone and far from London. They didn't even want to confirm if they are going to bring her here to bury her with her husband as she wanted."

"Who told you?"

"A guy who works for her in-laws. By chance, we caught him emptying her apartment, and he had no choice but to tell us. Neither Michiel nor I was very happy about it. It's very weird."

"Michiel your neighbor, the Dutch professor at the American School?"

"Yes, that Michiel."

"At Christmas, you told me that one day you were going to tell me the whole story about Audrey the neighbor."

"I will. As soon as we clear up every last detail of her death and we're calm, I'll tell you all about it."

"What do you mean, clarify every last detail of her death? What's going on? Is there a catch?"

"We don't know, but Michiel and I don't trust the American family, and we've been left with our heads in the sand. We will investigate a little more, and until we have everything tied up, we will not let it go."

"Michiel again."

"He's my Dr. Watson."

"Sherlock is sleeping with Dr. Watson?"

"James, seriously?"

"You should see your face."

"Siobhan told me Harry is starting piano lessons next Monday, but Jamie doesn't want to go."

"They've just turned four, and as soon as one of them sees the other playing the piano, he'll want to learn too. In concrete terms, you're not skimming. Have you got yourself a Dutch boyfriend who's a professor at the American School?" He put his fork in the air and looked at her with narrowed eyes.

"He is not my boyfriend."

"No way."

"He's not my boyfriend. That's unfeasible."

"Why is it unfeasible? Is he married?"

"No. On the contrary, he is in favor of polyamory. He is not into stable relationships."

"Does he sleep with you and others?"

"I hope not right now because we've only been seeing each other for a short time, but it's going to happen any minute."

"Maybe this is different and thrives."

"No, not at all. This is your uncle in his forties, with clear ideas and a free and open life that he loves. He told me about his polygamous choice as soon as we met. There's not much more to consider about it."

"Are you aware that adult people change their minds, their choices, and their lives all the time? Not everyone is as immovable and inflexible as you, my dear Juliet. I believe that, technically, it is not polygamy that you practice because to be a polygamist, you have to be married to several women."

"He also told me that he was not fond of polyamory because it was not about love but about sex, so I don't even know how to qualify it. It's none of my business either."

"It's none of your business. Don't you like him enough that it's your business?"

"Of course I like him. I like him very much. If I didn't like him, I would not be with him."

"Did you tell him?"

"What for, to make him run away?"

"You wouldn't dream of thinking that someone could fall in love with you, would you? Seriously, Juliet, that jerk from Australia hurt you a lot."

"Don't blame everything on Caden."

"You spent eight years, *eight* years, dancing with that Caden guy. That *guiri* of the balls just let you down, frustrated you, and used you without the slightest hint of shame. I understand that wear and tear made you feel very insecure, but listen to me. Thank God, not all the men around you are like Caden-fucking-Brown."

She looked at him for a few seconds with her eyes as wide as saucers, and he shrugged and raised his hand to order dessert. Juliet took a sip of water and sighed.

"I agree, but in this case, my friendship with Michiel is more important. I care about him, I need him in my life, and I don't intend to spoil it with sentimental or commitment considerations that don't fit into his universe."

"*Carpe diem,* Juliet."

"Why does everyone tell me *carpe diem?*"

"Because you are the queen of anti-*carpe diem.*"

"Excuse me?"

"You are organized and responsible, meticulous in everything.

You turn everything upside-down and backward, and that makes you an excellent professional and a stable and complete girl. But for your love life, that is disastrous, sister. You never let yourself go, and you never live in the moment. You immediately start to conjecture, foresee, suppose, or deduce. You don't let go, and you don't know how to give yourself. Just enjoy, Juliet. Live in the moment. Recognize what you feel and stop anticipating what may happen. Feelings are unpredictable."

"I wish I could."

"We all love you. Everyone who knows you adores you."

"Don't believe it. A lot of people don't like me," she interrupted him, but he remained very serious.

"You're going to be the legal guardian of my children because you're amazing. I'm sure that Michiel, if he's a little bit smart, already knows that."

She stroked his hand.

"What?"

"It is easier for those who found the love of their life at the age of twenty-four."

"I was lucky, but I also did my part." He looked at the time and put the napkin on the table. "You just give yourself permission. Listen to your big brother. I'm sorry, but I still have to go to the editorial office. Where are you going?"

"I have a meeting near San Pablo."

"Okay. I'll come with you and take the Underground from there."

They stepped out onto the street and crossed the Millennium Bridge in the middle of a considerable blizzard. It was very cold, and James hugged her shoulders. They had to get to the other side of the river and skirt the cathedral on their way to Cheapside, from which he could take the Underground, and she could look for the law office of Robert Hawksmoor, Fiona's husband, Daniel's stepfather, who had summoned them to his office to talk about Audrey.

She said goodbye to Jamie, promising to see him the following weekend, walked ten yards, and found Robert's building, which was in the heart of London's most famous law firm district. She climbed to the top floor, thinking about what her brother had told her, which had only added to the tangle in her heart and head. As soon as she entered Smithson, Hawksmoor, & Phillips Attorneys, a very friendly receptionist escorted her to a meeting room. Michiel and a very elegant black man who looked like Idris Elba were waiting for her. He approached her with an outstretched hand and an open smile to welcome her.

"Juliet, nice to finally meet you. I'm Rob Hawksmoor. Please sit down."

"Delighted. Wow, how beautiful it is here." She admired the view and then looked at Michiel, who had stood up to greet her. "Hi. I hope I'm not late."

"No, right on time. Would you like a coffee?"

"Yes, thank you very much."

"Great. Coffee for everyone, Miriam, please. Sit down, guys. I've been looking forward to meeting you, Juliet. Daniel showed us pictures of your now-famous cat."

"Romeo," Michiel interjected, sitting down and winking at her.

"We would love to adopt a cat, but with the arrival of the girls..."

"Girls?"

"Yes, Fiona and I are expecting twins in May."

"Congratulations. I am very happy for you."

"Yes, especially we who are of a certain age and don't have much time to increase the family. Anyway, I don't want to take up too much of your time. I printed out all the material we have been able to gather on the Stuyvesant estate and your friend Audrey's role in the whole plot, and we have also located the executor responsible for her English estate.

"We have discovered that there is a will, but the executor,

whom I know well as she is a colleague with whom we work often, says that she has not received a death certificate for the person she represents."

"Audrey never ceases to amaze us."

"Imagine her executor. She is perplexed by the whole American inheritance thing because no one has informed her of anything, even though since Gregory Stuyvesant's death, she is the sole administrator and legally responsible for his widow and all his assets. She's going through the roof."

"Wow!" Michiel's blue eyes glinted, and Juliet snorted.

"Will she see to it that Audrey's last wishes are carried out? To be buried next to her husband here in his mausoleum at Kensal Green?"

"Of course, Juliet, but first, we have to locate the Stuyvesant family, get access to them, ask for explanations, and demand the death certificate. If it hadn't been for you, we would not have found out what had happened."

"Which doesn't speak very well of her work," Michiel said. "Are you ready to take the reins from now on? Juliet and I can't do much more."

"She will do it, don't worry. We will be on top of it, and we will put all our resources at her disposal. She will do her job looking after the interests of her client while we will go against the Stuyvesant family."

"How?"

"Here before us is a lawsuit that any judge will entertain. There is irrefutable evidence that Mrs. Audrey Rose Stuyvesant was located and transferred to New York in a hasty and veiled manner without informing her legal representative to fulfill the succession aspirations of her in-laws, without her welfare or her best interests being considered."

"If she's dead, what good is that now?"

"The rights of an eighty-three-year-old British woman who was disowned by her in-laws in 1956 have been violated. She and her husband had to emigrate to Australia and change their surname because of the demands of that same family who, now, sixty-five years later, came to London, removed her from her home, and isolated her God knows where to coerce her to sign over an inheritance worth billions without the necessary legal advice. Any public prosecutor could act ex officio. The whole maneuver was executed in the shadows and protected by the unlimited power those people have in the United States."

"I suppose it's to do justice to Audrey," Michiel whispered, "but it's too late."

"For her, unfortunately, yes, but not for her family," Robert replied. "Her direct heirs have rights and can contest whatever they want. They may lose the lawsuit, but at least we will put the Stuyvesants on the ropes and make public what they are doing."

"Her family may be within their rights, but they didn't care for her for sixty-five years," Juliet replied. "In any case, I don't think this is our concern any longer."

"We got this far. We gave you the details about her nephew, Phillip Glenn. He and his mother live in Hampstead, Rob. Give them a call, and good luck."

"Great. Thank you, Michiel."

"Will you keep us informed about what her executor gets? I hope they manage to bring Audrey back to London. It was very important to her."

"I will keep you informed of all the details. Without you, we would not be here."

"Thank you very much. Who do we need to talk to about the expenses this has generated?"

"Juliet, don't worry about that. What we've done is just a preliminary investigation. You provided me with virtually all of it, and if the family decides to go after the Stuyvesants, the prestige and the money it will bring in will more than cover the effort."

"Very well, then. Thank you again."

They said goodbye to Robert, who was a man full of energy and confidence, the kind of person you wanted on your side. They rode down in the elevator in silence and without touching.

When they reached the street, Michiel took her hand to make her look him in the eye.

"Are you all right?"

"Yes. I don't know. It's like everything has suddenly gone haywire, hasn't it? We just wanted to locate our neighbor, and now there is talk of ex officio proceedings, challenges, and millionaire inheritances. I don't know."

"We have done what we could. Now let the others make their own decisions."

"You are right."

"How did it go with your brother?"

"Very good. He's very glad I finally signed the papers. Are you coming to the Barbican? We can walk there. I have work to do, but I think I'll do it from home."

"I..."

He looked at the sky with those stunning blue eyes, and Juliet saw how handsome he was with that two-day beard and the gorgeous hair. He lowered his head and looked at her.

"I'm meeting a friend in Covent Garden for coffee and then the theater. We've had the tickets for weeks."

"Ah." She realized that he was telling her he had a date and inadvertently cleared her throat. "Okay, enjoy yourselves."

"Shall I call you?

"No, don't worry. It's better another day."

She forced a false smile, and fortunately, her cell phone vibrated in her coat pocket before she dropped to the ground in disappointment. She pulled it out and, seeing that it was William Harrison, Iona's ex-husband, turned her back and waved goodbye.

"Hello, William. What a pleasant surprise."

"I had lunch with Iona, and she told me about your literary project."

"Wow, she can't keep quiet about anything."

"She is very proud of you, and I want to publish it."

"Publish it? I just started. I have a lot of material and documentation."

"Juliet, you've been with Iona for over ten years. I know how talented you are. You practically wrote her memoirs, and the little she has told me about what you have in hand fascinates me. Make me a synopsis, send it to me, then come see me and sign a contract. Is it true that you have written authorization from the protagonist to publish it?"

"Yes, and she gave me her diaries."

"Wonderful. Come and see me, and we'll sign whatever you ask me without a literary agent getting in the way. I hate agents."

"Something similar is said about us by film and television producers."

"I know. It's just that you're all so heavy. Will you come, and we'll close the deal?"

"William, I am very flattered by the confidence."

"You get your act together and send me that synopsis. Bye."

He hung up on her, and she shivered. Tears came to her eyes, and she remembered Michiel. She turned to see if he was still around, but he had already disappeared. He had an engagement and a busy night, and tickets to the theater with a friend from weeks ago.

She squared her shoulders, trying to cheer herself up and not sink into misery. She headed home, thinking the dilemma she'd had that morning would no longer exist because after her forced landing in reality, there was no room for doubt. She would do the right thing. She would get ahead of the drama and stop seeing him from that very moment.

CHAPTER TWENTY-THREE

"Wow," he whispered. He let out a whistle of admiration, and Juliet jumped up and turned with a frown.

She was spectacular in a low-cut black dress and high heels. Her hair was in a very elegant bun, her lips were painted red, and her dark eyes were perfectly made up. Gorgeous, sexy, and very stylish. He walked over to her with his mouth open. She closed her coat and fastened it with a wide belt.

"You can't smoke there in the shadows. One day someone will call the police."

"I don't think so. I'm just doing it to wait for you."

"I have to go. They're coming to pick me up in a couple of minutes."

She turned her back to him to lock the door, and he took a deep drag on his cigarette.

"Where are you going?"

"To a party."

"Did I miss something, Juliet?"

"What?" She looked at him seriously, and he shrugged his shoulders.

"You've been avoiding me for three weeks again."

"I've got a lot of work to do. Awards season is starting, and I've spent two weeks in Los Angeles. I thought I told you."

"Yes, you sent me a message."

"Well, that's..."

"Not even a call to a friend despite the awards season?"

"Look!"

He watched as she put her hands on her hips and lowered her head.

A gaping hole opened in her stomach. "I'm not going to justify myself. It's true that I've been avoiding you, and I'm sorry, but I needed to get away for a while. I don't want to go on with this thing we had set up. It doesn't suit me, and I didn't know how to tell you."

"Don't you want to sleep with me anymore?"

"Exactly."

"Why doesn't it suit you? I thought we were doing great."

"I would love to go back to December 22nd and just be research colleagues."

"I like you very much, Juliet."

"And three or four other women, and I'm not ready for that. Maybe in another life or a few years, but not now."

"Are you like my mother, who thinks that because I don't want a stable, committed relationship, I'm promiscuous?"

"I'm not saying that."

"Ah, aren't you?"

"No!"

"Do you think I go around like a sexual predator, harassing everyone?"

"I think you have great and healthy sexual freedom, but I'm not comfortable with it. I can't get it into my head to be with a man who, after getting into my bed, sees it as normal to go out with others. To go to the theater with others or go on dates with his special girlfriends."

"Is it because I went to the theater with a friend instead of coming home with you?"

"That was the straw that broke an already full glass of doubt, Michiel. I'm not into that. I seriously don't care what you do. I like you and I hope we remain friends, but nothing more. I'm not a masochist. I know very well what I want and need in my life, and it has nothing to do with this. I don't know how to handle it, and I don't want to learn."

"Being comfortable with someone doesn't mean you can't go to the theater with another person or share time with your friends."

"Of course not. Don't take umbrage. That's the least of it. I'm not jealous or selfish or possessive of the people I care about. Just ask Caden."

"I'm going to overlook you bringing that asshole into a conversation about us, but please, Juliet, don't compare me to him."

"I have to go. I've said what I should have said weeks ago. I'm sorry it took me so long, I'm sorry, but I was a bit overcome. I hope that from now on, everything will be back to square one. I would hate to lose a friendship like ours."

"I wouldn't like it either."

"Great." She smiled, brightening everything, and he sat up to get closer and look her in the eye.

"What do you need from me, Juliet?"

"Nothing. Why do you ask that?"

"Because while we're on the subject, I'd like to know."

"I don't need anything from you. You're great, and I love being with you, but friendship with the right to touch is not my thing. Maybe I'm too conservative, immature, or a very simple person; I don't know. I just know that I don't have the energy to repeat my feelings of insecurity and frustration."

She took a deep breath and looked at the sky. "I've been thinking a lot about *carpe diem* and letting go, but I can't fool myself. I'm not like that. This is not going to work, and the truth is that I don't want to feel like an 'option' ever again."

"Did I make you feel like a choice?"

"Juliet, what are you doing? I have the car in the second row."

Out of nowhere, a guy in a tuxedo straight out of a fashion magazine appeared. Michiel squinted when he approached her, grabbed her around the waist, and kissed her on the cheek, letting out a whistle of admiration.

"Oh, my goodness! What a beauty, honey!"

He was a very well-known actor. Michiel couldn't name him because he didn't watch the kinds of movies he starred in. He knew he was a famous actor because that was the only kind Juliet represented. He took a step back to get a better look at him, and the man smiled very kindly.

"Hello, good afternoon."

"Hello."

"Michiel," she whispered without introducing them. "Everything in order between us?"

"Of course, of course. Don't worry."

"Great, I'm glad. Bye. Give a kiss to Daniel."

She and her companion ran out to the main street. Michiel, with the cigarette still between his fingers burning out, leaned against the railing again with the icy wind whistling around him and wondered if his big mistake had been involving a young and different girl like Juliet Miller in a sexual adventure of his type without thinking about her needs or romantic aspirations, though they were light-years away from his vision of life.

Normally, he would have smiled at a confession like the one she had just made because she was naïve. In real life, everyone was an option for everyone else, and if you'd lived a little, you knew that all dating relationships caused some degree of insecurity and frustration. That was her bread and butter, and if she wasn't prepared for that, she wasn't prepared to cope with any intimate relationship. Not only with him but with most of the men she would meet in her lifetime.

However, he understood what she had wanted to explain. Among other things, because he knew that she had been in a toxic and destructive relationship for many years with an asshole who had treated her terribly and taken advantage of her and her generous and honest ways. He had disillusioned and deceived her by giving her glimpses of commitment and loyalty and all those things she valued so much from time to time, and he had shown her, although she was not yet able to realize it, that courtships or stable and monogamous relationships were no guarantee of anything.

He, in a few months, had been infinitely more loyal to her than her friend Caden had been for as long as she had known him. That Australian fucker had never played fair, but as long as she didn't see it that way, there was nothing he could do to convince her otherwise.

It was a shame since he loved her.

Juliet drove him crazy. He had no intention of denying it. She was the smartest girl he had ever met in his life, the funniest, the one with the best sense of humor. She possessed a unique energy, and she was a wonderful and luminous woman who shone everywhere. On top of that, she was beautiful, and sometimes he thought he would do anything for her. Anything except lie to her, deceive her, or create false illusions because, as much as he liked her, he still thought formal arrangements were not his thing, neither commitments nor fidelities sworn in front of an altar. His was a life without burdens or servitude, without ties, free, and he would not change that for anyone, not even her.

"End of story, Michiel," he told himself as he went home to have dinner and do some work on his thesis. He wanted them to remain friends, and they would because he considered her a colleague and could no longer conceive of his life without her. However, that was as far as it would go in this sweeping affair that had started as a spark and had nearly turned his life upside-down.

———

"John. What's up, buddy?" A couple of hours later, he answered a call from John Tompkins, realizing that he had been studying and working for a long time. That was just what he had needed to get Juliet, holding hands with the little boy who had come to pick her up, off his mind. He got up from the table and went to the kitchen to pour himself some tea.

"How are you, Michiel? How are you? How's Juliet?"

"I'm fine, thank you. Juliet is well, I spoke to her a little while ago after three weeks without seeing her, and she is doing fine."

"You still haven't asked her to marry you?"

"No."

He laughed because John, who was seventy years old and an old-fashioned ladies' man, was half-obsessed with her and praised how beautiful, elegant, and lovely she was whenever he could. He shook his head and put the water on to heat.

"If I was your age, I would."

"I don't doubt it. How are you doing?"

"You young people are not aware of what you have and how short life is. Anyway, I am calling to tell you two pieces of news. First, I have sent you a real treasure—a copy of a letter from Charles Irving Stuyvesant explaining to his executor and other close friends his reasons for naming his brother Gregory, not his eldest son, as the heir to his fortune."

"How did you get it?"

"I will not reveal the source, but it is real. We authenticated it with two experts. It is written in his handwriting and tells how he never wanted to go ahead of his dear brother in the succession matter. He was forced by his parents, coerced and threatened, and he had no choice but to obey because he was so young. The poor man lived with this burden and guilt all his life and wanted to make it up to Gregory in some way. Deep down, he just wanted to put things right again."

"Yeah, that's clear."

"I would add to this that his sons are self-interested scoundrels and the father couldn't stand them, but the altruism toward his brother and his sense of justice is much better."

"Can we use it? I mean in Juliet's book."

"Of course, but on that note, here's my second piece of news."

"What happened?"

"I have been expelled from the New York Historical Society."

"What? Why?"

"Officially, for a harmless screening of partners, renewing experts, etc., but the truth is that the Stuyvesant family expressly requested that I be barred."

"Can they do that?"

"They have been patrons of the New York Historical Society since its founding. They are on the board of trustees, they pay the bills, and they are pissed off about my relationship with you. They've gone so far as to say that I've revealed secrets and conspired with third parties to discredit the family."

"I'm so fucking sorry, John. I don't even know what to say."

"It's okay. It's about time I retired. I don't care. I wasn't even getting paid. Besides, they can't stop me from working from home, and my agent is rubbing his hands together because I'm coming out with a new biography next winter, including the Audrey Stuyvesant episode."

"I think it's a great idea."

"That's what my agent says, and I'm very excited, at my age, to stand up to that bunch. As far as I'm concerned, everything's fine. Now I'm worried about you two."

"Us?"

"These people take time, but they retaliate, my dear Lezer, and you and Juliet have removed the shitbox without anyone asking you to. You are in their crosshairs, and I think you should be careful. Maybe I'm exaggerating, but you work at the American College. Their tentacles are very long, and they can get you fired, for example. With Juliet, it's more complicated because she works in a private British company, but you never know. I'm sure they'll find a way to screw her up. I would be *very* careful."

"Oh, man!" He ran his hand through his hair, and John snorted.

"My daughters say I'm a catastrophist. Maybe they're right, and it's not worth worrying about, but I think it's my duty to warn you."

"Thank you very much, John. I'll talk it over with Juliet."

"Great. Now I'll let you rest. Give a kiss to Miss Miller for me. Bye-bye."

Michiel hung up, trying to digest the news. This was beginning to sound like a Scorsese movie. He thought about discussing it with Juliet the next day as he went back to the desk to continue working. The phone rang again; it was Robert.

"Rob, man. Is everything all right?"

"Fine. Sorry about the hour, but Audrey's executor just called me. The family has just responded to her requests and sent her a certificate stating that Mrs. Stuyvesant was cremated on December 26 at ten o'clock in the morning at Trinity Church Cemetery and Mausoleum in Manhattan."

"Incinerated?"

"The ashes will be brought to London for burial at your convenience, and a funeral will be held at St. Giles Church next week. I am sending you the details now."

"Did the Stuyvesant family organize it?"

"Everything down to the last detail. One of the nephews is coming personally to deliver the ashes and, by the way, to meet with the Glenns and me. I have half the office working on that right now."

"So, are the Glenns going to sue?"

"Yes, didn't I tell you? I'm sorry; we are very busy."

"No big deal. Another thing. I just got off the phone with a friend in New York, a historian and a biographer of the Stuyvesants, who was the first lead Juliet and I followed to find Audrey in Manhattan. He helped us tremendously at the time, and we have continued to keep in touch. Now he tells me that he has been expelled from the New York Historical Society, where he has worked for more than forty years. He is unofficially accused of revealing secrets and conspiring with third parties, i.e., with us, to discredit the family."

"Don't fuck with me. Tell him to talk to my office in New York. We will help him to solve it. Now I will send you the data."

"He is not worried about leaving the historical society. He is seventy years old and plans to concentrate on his new book. What worries him are the possible reprisals they may make against us."

"Of course. It will be one of the points we discuss with the Stuyvesant who comes to see us. We won't leave you hanging, Michiel, don't worry. We will try to protect you. It is my commitment to you and Juliet."

"So, you think they are capable of…"

"I've seen worse in my line of work. Please send me in writing what you have just told me, with concrete data such as the name of your friend, and I will put it in our priorities. Okay?"

"All right, and thank you."

"Thank you. Bye."

Michiel hung up, looked at the computer, and opened his email to download the letter from Charles Irving Stuyvesant that John had sent him. The doorbell interrupted him. He looked at the time, stood up, and went outside to open the door, tidying his clothes a bit.

"Juliet?" He caught her in the hallway with her arms crossed and blinked to convince himself he wasn't dreaming. "Is everything all right?"

"Did I wake you up? Are you alone?"

"It's not that late. I was working on my thesis, and I'm alone. Come in. I'm glad to see you because I have news."

"Thank you. I called you on your cell phone, but it wouldn't connect."

"I know. Are you all right?" he asked, letting her into the apartment. She leaned against the wall in the hallway and took a deep breath.

"I went to Iona's birthday party, and her ex-husband, William, who is a publisher and until yesterday was pressuring me to sign a pre-contract for my future book on the Audrey case, told me that he can't collaborate with me at the moment. That I'd better cancel my project and sit tight for a while."

"What?"

"In those words. One of his partners, who is an American, is a personal friend of the Stuyvesant family and leaked the details of the project to them, which resulted in an urgent warning of embargoes, lawsuits, and other such nonsense if they dared to publish me."

"I can't believe it."

"I explained again that I have written consent from Audrey authorizing me to write her story, but it doesn't matter. He says the Stuyvesants have set the coercion machinery in motion and that they are not willing to confront her."

"What a shitty publisher."

"I agree. You don't know how glad I am that I didn't sign a pre-contract with them, or they could have left me in the freezer for the rest of my life."

"John Tompkins has been expelled from the New York Historical Society."

"No! Really?"

"Yes, the Stuyvesants, who are patrons of the society, have accused him of revealing secrets and conspiring with third parties to discredit their family off the record."

"The third party is you and me?"

"Yes. I just told Robert about it, and he promised to discuss the matter with one of Audrey's nephews, who is coming next week to London to talk to him and the Glenns."

"So, the Glenns are going all-out?

"Yes. A funeral has also been arranged at St. Giles, after which the executor can bury Audrey's ashes wherever she sees fit."

"She was cremated? It's unbelievable."

"Yeah, it's really gotten out of hand."

"As it continues to get out of hand, I might decide to tell my brother about it so he can publish it in his newspaper."

"I think that's perfect."

"Tell me that nothing bad has happened to you, please."

"Except that the girl I like has given me the push, no."

"Very funny."

"It's not funny." He smiled at her, and she folded her arms.

"Where is your escort?"

"Edward? He stayed at the party."

"I'm glad." He held her gaze, and she started to get nervous. He didn't move and ran his eyes over her a couple of times until he was transfixed by her mouth. He took a deep breath, realizing he'd had a hard-on since he'd seen her at the door. He wanted to turn away and walk toward the living room but couldn't.

"No, don't do that, Michiel Lezer. Don't look at me like that."

"How?"

She pointed at him, and he smiled with an innocent look on his face. "I thought it was clear that..."

He stepped across the short distance that separated them, put his arms inside her open coat, pulled her close to his body, looked at her closely, leaned in, and kissed her.

"You can't imagine how much I've missed you, *Zissele*."

"Michiel."

"I can't give you up. I'm trying to convince myself that I can."

"You don't make it easy for me, you know?"

"I haven't been with anyone else since I've been with you, Juliet. I give you my word of honor. Nor with the friend I went to the theater with. I can only think of you, and I only want to be with you."

"You don't have to lead me on."

"I'm not trying to trick you. I'm telling the truth. I will never lie to you. Look at me." He held her face and forced her to look him in the eyes. "Whatever happens, I will be honest with you, as I know you will be with me. Okay?"

"All right."

He kissed her again, enjoying her feminine scent and the taste of her mouth. He was determined not to let her escape, and she, who suddenly seemed to have the same purpose, embraced him and returned his kisses between sighs. Then she stopped and looked him in the eyes.

"Let's go to my place, but know that this will be the last time."

***

He brushed her skin, and an electric shock knocked her out. She smelled his scent and wanted to die of pleasure. She wanted to devour him and never leave her body again because she could not separate from him. She did not want to stop feeling him inside her. She could not because she only dreamed of loving him again and again, and he would envelop her and fill her and fill her with that superhuman chemistry they shared.

She felt tingling in her legs and had to hold on to the wall so as not to fall to the floor. She raised her head and looked at her mother, who was watching her with a scolding face and a very bad temper. "She seems to read my mind," she said to herself, blushing up to her ears, but she pulled herself together, made an effort to stop thinking about Michiel Lezer and the last spectacular fuck they had shared in the shower that morning, and concentrated on Delilah, the real estate agent friend of her parents who had summoned her to South Kensington to show her a very nice apartment.

"According to your credit report, you can afford it, Juliet. It's beautiful, and you have the park so close. It's perfect for a single girl."

"With a cat," her mother remarked, inspecting the qualities of the American kitchen.

"Yes, it's very nice."

"Have you seen the bathroom? The bathtub is made of porcelain. The renovation alone cost a fortune. It is fortunate that it is now being sold in a hurry and for so little money."

"Not so little money," she mumbled, walking toward the dreamy bathroom that was almost as big as the only room in the apartment. She stroked the bathtub, imagining her and Michiel in there for hours, chatting, making love, and drinking wine, which was something they had done quite often in the past eight days since they had reconciled after her first serious attempt to get away from him.

She had left it all behind after realizing that he was still dating. He was probably still seeing his regulars, and his life was never going to fit in with hers. She had even left for Los Angeles without saying goodbye to him and had disappeared for three whole weeks, determined to put out the fire that was waking her up and clouding her common sense, but to little avail. The first night she had met him smoking in the hallway, she had lost control of her actions, and three hours later, she had left Iona's party and her companion, Edward Holcroft, to run home with an excuse to talk to him. A good excuse, but an excuse nonetheless.

All it had taken was for him to look at her the way he did, like he was caressing her or making love to her, lulling her with delicacy but at the same time with great intensity. With a delicious faith that she had never before perceived in anyone. She had instantly lost her way, and all her good intentions had gone to hell.

At Iona's party, she had done nothing but think of him. Of his eyes burning her as they calmly roamed over her. She had started to feel shivers down her spine, imagining his kisses and caresses until William had told her about his problem with the book. Then she had the perfect reason to run off to drown her sorrows with her beloved Watson, who was the only human being on the planet who understood her.

He had listened to her and comforted her. He had said the words she needed to hear. He had taken her side, and together, they had reconciled between the sheets. Since that night, they had not separated again except to go to work. Since that night, they'd had dinner together every night and slept together. They were enjoying an oasis of happiness and frenzy that contrasted greatly with everything going on around them.

In short, *Carpe diem*, Juliet.

"What do you think of the dressing room?" Delilah asked, pulling her out of her musings. She nodded, although she hadn't even noticed the bocote-wood shelves, the full-length mirrors, and the velvet-lined shoe racks she was pointing out.

"It's all very nice, Delilah."

"Don't say no. Take a couple of days before deciding. I doubt very much that we will find a free apartment in South Kensington at this price."

"I'm sure, but I'm not looking for an apartment, let alone in South Kensington."

"It was your mother's idea."

"I know."

"You need to buy, Juliet. You need to invest the money you earn," her mother interjected, and Juliet gave her a sidelong glance.

"You know we're not in Spain, don't you? On this side of the English Channel, people don't get obsessed with the idea of buying an apartment."

"You can't live your whole life renting."

"Why not?"

"Because a property is a safe investment."

"Yes, tell that to the victims of the housing bubble."

"Someday, you'll get kicked off the Barbican Estate. Then see what you do."

"I guess I'll have to look for another rental in the area because I love Barbican."

"In any case, thank you, Delilah. Give us two days, please, for her to think about it. It's a beautiful apartment in an unbeatable area. I'm sure she'll come to her senses."

"Sure, Gloria, I'll keep it for two days. Will you call me, Juliet? I can also look for something in Barbican."

"Thank you very much," she replied with a smile so as not to argue with her mother in front of third parties. They said goodbye to her on the street, giving her two kisses and thanking her for the trouble of accompanying her to see an apartment at that time of the evening.

She thought of calling Delilah as soon as she was alone to tell her not to hold anything for her since she didn't plan to spend a fortune in South Kensington. She followed her with her eyes until she disappeared and she could look her mother in the face.

"Why are you dragging me into this mess, Mum? I'm not looking for an apartment."

"It's a bargain."

"I don't have time for this. Seriously, why did you make me leave the office early to look at an apartment I'm not looking for?"

"It is an unbeatable price in an unbeatable neighborhood."

"An unbeatable neighborhood where sixty percent of my clients live. There's no way I'm going to live here. I have to go. I have a funeral close to home."

"I'll come with you, and we'll talk. Stop a cab."

"Do you want to go to a funeral? You didn't know Mrs. Stuyvesant."

"As if I knew her. You spent months talking about her. Come on."

"It is an Anglican funeral."

"I don't care. As if I only go to Catholic funerals. Juliet, a cab," she scolded.

Juliet reluctantly obeyed because she wasn't amused. She was meeting Michiel, who would be at Audrey's funeral. She sat next to her mother, looking at the landscape of London in February— a cold, beautiful, crowded London, as always.

"When are you going to the Oscars?"

"I'm not going this year. I've given my place to Andrea."

"She'll be thrilled."

"Yes, of course. You can't imagine how much work that is, but you have to get used to it. We left everything in advance on the last trip to Los Angeles. Now she will just have to finish it and try to come out of the battle unscathed."

"Iona is not going?"

"She is, but she doesn't work much, you know."

"Have you already got all the actresses' clothes?"

"Yes, theirs and ours. We signed everything at the end of January. Crazy, but everything is ready, thank God."

"When are you going to try on the dress? You're the only bridesmaid missing."

"I haven't had time, but I'll come as soon as I can. It looks very nice. Is Dad coming to pick you up from the center, or are you going back to Willesden by train?"

"Your brother will drive me back. He's working late tonight, and he's brought the car. I'll tell him to pick me up at the Barbican."

"Okay."

"Will you bring a date to the wedding, daughter?" She looked sideways at Juliet. "We're just starting to arrange the tables, and we don't have much room. You know that."

"I will come alone, as usual. If you assign me a stool in a

corner, it's enough for me," she joked as they arrived at St. Giles church. Her mother looked at her with narrowed eyes, starting to get angry. She grabbed her arm and pulled her into the church, trying to distract her. They walked down the center aisle admiring how beautiful the church was, being one of the few medieval churches that had survived the Great Fire of London in 1666 and was attached to the modern Barbican Estate. They decided to sit at a safe distance from the altar.

It was half empty. There were only a few people scattered in the front rows, but not a glimpse of the Glenn family or the Stuyvesants. Juliet scrutinized the few attendees and the corners of the church until she heard footsteps walking briskly on the marble and approaching them directly. She turned to see who it was, and before she could react, Michiel was settling in next to her.

"You're here. I was waiting for you outside."

"I didn't see you. We arrived a little earlier," she greeted him as he leaned over, determined to kiss her on the mouth. She was startled and avoided him, indicating her mother with her hand.

"This is my mother, Gloria. Mum, this is my friend, Michiel Lezer."

"The Dutch professor at the American School?" she asked with the enthusiasm of castanets, and he nodded.

"It is my pleasure, Mrs. Miller."

"Call me Gloria, please. I'm not *that* old."

"Of course, and you look like sisters. Now I understand from whom Juliet inherited her beauty."

"Oh, what a gentleman."

"*Zalamero,*" Juliet mumbled in Spanish, glanced sideways at him, and smiled.

He reached out, took her hand, and kissed it with a wink just before a murmur announced the arrival of Audrey's family at the church. Rosamund Glenn was in the lead, on the arm of her son Phillip, followed by a rather large group of people, including

Robert Hawksmoor. They solemnly walked down the center aisle.

"Look at that," Michiel whispered, pointing at the altar. Juliet saw a tall man appear through the rectory.

He was surrounded by bodyguards, among them Jack Lynch, who, upon discovering them among the attendees, stared at them with a murderous look on his face.

"One day, I'll smash that asshole's face in."

"Okay, let's go get him after the service," Juliet replied. Michiel stretched out his arm and rested it on her back, then kissed her ear, making her dissolve in giggles like a helpless sugar cube.

"My favorite couple!" Mrs. Glenn exclaimed. She recognized them when they came up to greet her after the funeral, and she reached out to grab them and kiss them.

Juliet introduced Mrs. Glenn to her mother, and when Michiel stepped aside to chat with Robert, she told them in detail about the wonders of Audrey's in-laws, who were very wealthy and willing to help all the Glenns without exception.

"Audrey left it up to them to take care of us, and they will. We are delighted, and all thanks to you, Juliet. It was a blessing that you came into our life."

"Mum, let's walk. It's getting very late," Phillip Glenn burst in and looked at Juliet very seriously. "Thank you for coming to the funeral, Miss Miller."

"You're welcome. Will Audrey's ashes be buried at Kensal Green next to Gregory?"

"No, they're going to the Glenn family vault in Highgate, northeast of Hampstead Heath," Rose hastened to reply.

"She has a site with her husband at Kensal Green, didn't you know?"

"We haven't discussed those details yet, Ms. Miller, but thank you for your interest. Now, if you'll excuse us."

"They cannot take her away from Gregory. That was not her desire!"

"Audrey's last will and testament is our business, Miss Miller," Phillip said tensely, emphasizing "Miss." She frowned.

"Do you have a problem with me, Mr. Glenn?"

"None, except that it has been explained to me that Michiel Lezer is not your husband, as you said when you came to my house. Such a lie!"

"I did not lie. You assumed that if I was accompanied by a man, it was my husband. What I did not do was correct you."

"It's all the same. Goodbye."

"Juliet," said her mother firmly, holding her by the arm. She had no choice but to follow them with her eyes, perplexed and very uncomfortable. It was a pity that it had all ended there in the hands of those people who knew nothing of Audrey, the wayward sister who had run away from England at the age of eighteen with her American sweetheart.

She felt terrible because it was all her fault for having handed them an inheritance and decisions that were not theirs, and she felt Michiel's hand on her back.

"What happened? Is everything all right?"

"He reproached me for lying to them by introducing you as my husband."

"I never!"

"I know, but it's fine. What bugs me is that they say they're going to bury her in Highgate, not Kensal Green."

"I don't think it's any of your business, dear," opined her mother. Juliet looked at Robert for support when he appeared at her side.

"We're still working on it, Juliet. Don't worry; we'll do the right thing."

"All right. This is my mother. Mum, this is Robert Hawksmoor, the lawyer who handles Audrey's family affairs."

"Pleased, can I steal her for a moment, Mrs. Miller? Juliet, can I have a word?"

"Of course."

She took a few steps away, leaving her mother with Michiel, and looked at Robert very attentively. He took a deep breath and fixed her with his dark eyes.

"Do you have Audrey Stuyvesant's diaries?"

"Yes, she sent them to me as a gift with a note to my Manhattan hotel after I visited her in November."

"The Stuyvesant family claims them."

"No way. They're mine."

"Does that note expressly state that they are for you?"

"Yes, and that I can do whatever I want with them. How did these people find out that there are diaries and that I have them?"

"I have no idea, but I will tell them that they are in a safe deposit box and that you are not going to part with them. The next step is for them to claim them in court."

"Let them do what they want. Do you think I should keep them in the bank?"

"We can make it easier for you to keep them safe in a safe deposit box. I think that at this moment, it is the most advisable thing to do. Michiel agrees."

"Mother of God, this is looking more and more like a Tarantino movie." She glanced sideways at Michiel and saw him chatting animatedly with her mother. "All right, I'll put them in a safe deposit box. I have one at HSBC."

"Great. I'm also at your disposal to take care of any litigation with these people."

"I think it's perfect. I prefer that, from this point onwards, you deal with my affairs with them."

"That's done. My secretary will contact you to formalize it. In the meantime, I'm going to talk to Mark Stuyvesant. He's waiting in the rectory and wanted to meet you."

He left them on the front lawn of the church, and Juliet stood frozen for a few seconds without understanding anything. She approached Michiel and his mother and paid attention to what they were talking about.

"Did you know that Willesden's new rabbi's name is Lezer?" she was telling him while stroking his arm. "He and his wife have become regular customers of my catering company. You don't know them?"

"I don't. Lezer is a fairly common Jewish surname."

"My mother-in-law was also Jewish. More like half-Jewish on her mother's side."

"Really?" Juliet asked in surprise, and her mother nodded.

"Of course, she was not religious, but her maternal family was. Her mother, Raisa, was the daughter of Russian Jewish immigrants. When she married a Protestant, your great-grandfather George, she pretty much abandoned her religion, yet she remained Jewish. Didn't you know that?"

"No, and I don't know why because it's very interesting."

Robert appeared behind them. "Mark Stuyvesant had to leave. He says he has an unavoidable dinner at the American Embassy. However, he says he would like to have a meeting with you in my office. Would you meet with him?"

<hr>

He opened one eye and reached out for Juliet but didn't find her because they hadn't slept together that night. The stark reality of the situation upset him.

He sat up in bed, looked at the time, and saw Romeo quietly entering his room. Juliet wasn't there, but her cat was because she had let him sleep with Daniel after the three of them had eaten Spanish food together, which she had prepared. He called him and petted him. Romeo watched him for a few seconds with his big green eyes, then ignored him and walked to his pillow to lie down to sleep there like a maharaja.

"Good morning, Romeo. Do you think your mistress would accept me in her bed at this hour? I'm afraid not."

He got up, remembering the reprimand he had given her the

day before for hinting at sleeping with him even though Daniel was home, and got under the shower, trying to relax his Morning Glory—his tremendous morning erection.

He closed his eyes, leaned with one hand on the shower tiles, and thought about her. About her soft and cozy body, her perfect hips and her smooth belly, her little belly button, round and tiny, her silky and abundant breasts in just the right size, her rosy nipples, her well-drawn and playful mouth, her scent, and that upturned and edible ass. Before he could blink, he had ejaculated. He missed her terribly.

He could not remember ever wanting a woman this much in his life.

Sure, he'd lost his mind over some girlfriend, especially when he was in his twenties, but it was nothing like the way he felt about Juliet Miller. She could give him a hard-on just by looking at him for thirty seconds.

She was dazzling, vehement, and passionate. She laughed heartily, kissed heartily, and loved heartily. She did everything with enthusiasm, whether it was talking about movies, literature, dancing, or running to hug you after a hard day's work. It was a bright light that had him enchanted and fascinated, and the most incredible thing was that he didn't care. He didn't mind living with the glitch in his usual routine of relationships because he could not help it and was unable to stop the frenzy of emotions they were sharing. Above all, because with her, he felt free and was not afraid to let himself go. On the contrary, he loved to let himself go because theirs was the result of a solid friendship and a blind trust, and that was priceless.

"Daniel, breakfast!" he called, looking at the time. He was worried because he was waiting for a purchase to be brought to him before he would leave for Buckinghamshire. They were going on a guided tour of Pinewood Studios. Juliet had invited them to spend Saturday with her, and the boy came out of his room with wet hair and Romeo in his arms.

"Did you take a nice shower? Did you make the bed?"

"Yes to everything. Do you have Romeo's food? Juliet says he's very punctual with breakfast. Come on, Romeo, let's eat. Do you think that when Juliet goes on her trip, she will leave Romeo for us to take care of him?"

"Normally, Romeo's friend Rocío comes to stay with him."

"We could offer it to her, and now that you are engaged…"

"I beg your pardon?" He poured the cereal and leaned against the kitchen counter, surprised.

"I've seen you kiss her secretly, Dad. I know you like her a lot and that she's your girlfriend."

"Huh."

"I like her. She's pretty and smart, and she doesn't play fake with me. On top of that, she knows a lot of actors. She's promised to introduce me to Henry Cavill or Richard Madden or John Snow, you know? How cool is Richard Madden in *Eternals*?"

He blinked, confused because he didn't know how to explain the relationship he had with her to his eight-year-old son. He realized that she was the first woman he had involved in his life, which was serious. He looked at Daniel without knowing what to say because he hadn't even thought about it, then thought it might be best not to say anything and take the heat off the matter. He took a sip from his coffee cup and the doorbell chirped, snapping him out of his bewilderment. "Go get Juliet, please. I need her to see what I bought. Let's go."

Daniel ran to Juliet's apartment, taking Romeo in his arms so he wouldn't run away, and Michiel went out into the hallway to wait for the surprise he had bought online.

"Hi!" Juliet greeted, appearing a few minutes later with Dani.

He winked at her. "Good morning. How did you sleep?"

"Very well. Has Romeo been behaving?"

"Perfectly. Look!" He nodded at the delivery people who were bringing his new bed and mattress, and she burst out laughing.

"You'll have no excuse now, *señorita*," he said in Spanish. "Do you like it? It's the latest in viscoelastic mattresses."

"Mother of God, Michiel."

"They're going to take all the old stuff, and I've bought a bunch of new sheets and two comforters."

"You are amazing."

"*You* are amazing."

He looked into her eyes and held her gaze. She shook her head and reached over to kiss him on the cheek.

"This does not guarantee you anything, my dear Watson, but I appreciate the gesture."

"What time are we leaving for Pinewood? Do you think Richard Madden will be there?" Dani interrupted.

She looked at him and ruffled his hair. "I called him, and unfortunately, he's not there today. He's not shooting, but Henry is there because he's shooting a new *Enola Holmes* movie. I texted him to come by and see us, and he said he's expecting us for lunch."

"How cool!"

"Yes, you're going to love him. He's very nice. The car picks us up in an hour. Do you think they'll be done by then, Michiel?"

"Sure, don't worry. Have you had breakfast? I have freshly brewed coffee."

"Thank you, but I can't. I have to make some work calls. When you're ready, let me know, okay?"

"Okay. In the meantime, we keep Romeo."

"Then we'll drop him off at my place." She smiled and went back to her apartment, and before entering, she looked at him with a shake of her head and blew him a kiss.

The guided tour of the famous Pinewood Studios, one of the most famous film studios in the world, where many movies were and are shot, was a huge surprise. Michiel considered himself a film buff. He loved movies, and for years, he had also been into TV series, but he wasn't a geek. However, seeing the sets of 007,

Robin Hood, *The Princess Bride*, or *Harry Potter* up close and personal and meeting very famous and very talented people who had been kind enough to attend them and spend time with them, thanks to their very close relationship with Juliet, had been a great experience and one that he would always be grateful for. Especially for Daniel, who had left excited with a tablet full of pictures and a bag of souvenirs and merchandise to share with his friends.

A Saturday spent visiting secret shoots with big stars who had not hesitated to take a break to talk to Juliet, have lunch with them, and spend time almost as a family because, if you saw it from the outside, she did have a large parallel family. A family that sincerely appreciated and loved her, trusted her opinion, and treated her with incredible confidence. Perhaps too incredible, he had thought while contemplating the constant displays of affection everyone lavished on her.

"Michiel, how many languages do you speak?"

"Huh?"

She spoke softly to him, and he stopped looking at the road to pay attention to her. They were passengers in one of her company's cars, very relaxed after Pinewood, with Dani sleeping between them. He reached out to caress her mouth with his thumb.

She repeated, "How many languages do you speak? I heard you speak German with Diane Kruger."

"Dutch, Yiddish, Hebrew, English, German, and a little French."

"Wow, that turns me on."

"Really?"

"Seriously, it's very sexy. Don't you remember Jamie Lee Curtis' character in *A Fish Called Wanda*? She would get all hot and bothered when Kevin Kline would talk to her in other languages."

"In what language do you want me to speak to you?"

"We'll see. I'll think about it."

"I'm turned on by your cadenced and sexy Spanish."

"Now, now. Don't be so smarmy."

"It's the truth." He tucked a lock of hair behind her ear, and she smiled.

"Now I understand why you are learning Spanish so fast. They say that once you get past two languages, the others come rolling in."

"So they say."

"I want you to know that the new bed was a great idea."

He took her hand and kissed it. "Anything to get you into my bedroom, Sherlock."

"Shhh," she scolded, pointing at Daniel.

He laughed. "He doesn't know anything. He sleeps like a log. Wait." He grabbed his cell phone, which began to vibrate insistently, and when he saw that it was Robert, he answered immediately. "Hi, Rob. How are you?"

"Are you with Juliet, or do you know where she is?"

"I'm with her. We just finished the tour of Pinewood Studios. Why, what's up?"

"Let me know how it goes. Now I'll tell you about something else. Can you put the speakerphone on?"

"Of course. That's it. What's it about?"

"Mark Stuyvesant just called me. He's finally back in London and says he can meet us in an hour in my office."

"On Saturday?"

"Yeah, it's a bummer, but he's had us on hold for ten days, and I wouldn't want to miss the opportunity. Are you coming? Fiona says she'll have a snack with Dani in a café near the office while we meet."

"Juliet?" He looked at her, and she nodded. "Okay, we're on our way."

"Great. I'll wait for you at the door of the building. Will it take you long?"

"No, half an hour," said Juliet.

"Perfect, so far."

———

Forty minutes later, Michiel introduced Fiona and left Daniel in her charge, then they went upstairs with Robert, one of his partners, his secretary, and two interns to the offices of Smithson, Hawksmoor & Phillips, Attorneys at Law, to wait for that capricious millionaire, the youngest son of Charles Irving Stuyvesant. Victoria Stuyvesant's ex-husband, who had been looking forward to meeting them on the weekend, although neither of them felt much like it.

Since Audrey's funeral in St. Giles, that guy had shown his interest in seeing them, and since then, for ten days, they had been waiting for a call from him to arrange the meeting. That had greatly deflated their expectations because with every day that passed, it seemed less interesting to them, but given Robert's enthusiasm and the effort he was making, they had agreed to listen to what he had to say and then forget it.

"Good afternoon."

At five o'clock sharp, Mark Stuyvesant and an entourage of eight people made a triumphant entrance into the meeting room. Everyone stood up to greet them except Juliet, who decided to stay in her seat with a frown on her face.

"Mr. Stuyvesant, welcome. This is Miss Miller and Mr. Lezer."

Robert shook his hand, and the guy, who was about fifty years old, dressed like a golfer and in very good shape, looked at them and smiled with unusual kindness.

"Please, we're not at a shareholders' meeting, I beg you. Hello, Michiel. Nice to meet you, Juliet. May I call you Juliet?"

"Of course. Delighted." She sat up and shook his hand.

"I'm sorry it took me so long to get back to London, but I had a lot of commitments in Germany and Switzerland. That's what happens when you don't come to Europe much. Could we have a coffee?"

"Miriam, please, coffee for everyone."

"Great, thanks." He sat down across from them and looked at them with his good-old-American-boy smile. "I won't take up too much of your time. I realize it's Saturday, and you'll have better things to do. I just wanted to meet you in person before I head back to New York tomorrow."

"Why is that?" Juliet asked, and he burst out laughing.

"Executive and to the point. I was warned about your brilliant personality, Juliet."

"I'm sorry?" She frowned, starting to get angry, and Michiel stroked her hand to appease her because it wasn't good to make things tenser.

"Why did you want to meet us, Mark? The truth is that Juliet and I don't understand this sudden interest in us. We have only raised suspicions in your family."

"Suspicions? Why do you say that?"

"Ask your head of security, Jack Lynch. He has always treated us like the enemy."

"He just does his job."

"What job? Threatening the neighbors of an eighty-three-year-old lady?" asked Juliet.

"Sharp. No, his job is to protect my family's interests. As far as we're concerned, you and Michiel were complete strangers when he caught you in our late Aunt Audrey's apartment. From then on, things got a bit out of hand, I admit, but we seem to have got it back on track now. We only have words of thanks to the two of you for accompanying and caring for our aunt during the confinement and afterward when you were concerned about her whereabouts."

"Perfect," said Robert. "What else can we help you with, Mark?"

"There is the issue of newspapers."

"You are interested in Audrey's diaries. That's why you wanted to join us, but as Robert must have explained to you, they are a gift from Audrey, and I don't intend to get rid of them. They are a treasure to me. I have a note in her handwriting expressing her wish for me to keep them, and that's what I'm going to do."

"Juliet, I don't know if you are aware that my family has a public legacy. We are an institution in the United States, and these diaries will become part of the sentimental and cultural heritage of the family and my country. They are not for me. They are a legacy for future generations. They will be exhibited to the public at the Stuyvesants' main house in Manhattan, where twice a year, they conduct guided visits for tourists from all over the world."

"They are of no cultural interest and are not a legacy, just the modest diaries of a very young girl telling her love story with an American boy she met while working as a box-office girl in a Leicester Square cinema. There is not much more."

"Isn't there much more? It tells intimate details of Stuyvesant's family life in the 1950s, of Gregory's relationship with my grandparents when they disinherited him, of the sad episode of their breakup and his estrangement from the family, of his 'exile' in Australia. In short, she talks about all those matters that the family has kept in the strictest privacy for more than six decades."

"If I give them to you, what are you going to do? Tear up the pages where she tells the truth about what happened before exposing her to the tourists? Destroy them?"

"I am willing to make a very generous financial offer for them."

"It's not a question of money. They were a gift from a good friend."

"That you are going to use to write a book."

"Partly yes, and with the blessing of Audrey, who asked me to do it and gave me her permission to write it."

"Here is a copy of the written authorization, legally valid in any country in the world." Robert slid a photocopy across the table, and Mark Stuyvesant read it.

"It's not enough. We can't allow it, and we will do everything we can to keep it from happening."

"I know that you coerced the man who was going to be my publisher, but it doesn't matter, I'm in no hurry, and there are thousands of publishers more willing than William Harrison. If not, there is self-publishing, which is the current trend."

"You shouldn't challenge us like that, Juliet."

"Is that a threat?" Michiel was fed up with his tone.

Mark Stuyvesant relaxed and leaned back in his chair. "No, for God's sake! Not at all. I'm just trying to talk some sense into her."

"Your position is clear, Mark," Robert opined. "If you want to, we'll go to court, and if not, you can let it go and forget about the juvenile diaries of an aunt-in-law you barely knew after sixty-five years away from your family."

"It is not about that. It is about the fact that no detail of any kind about any member of the Stuyvesant family, no matter how distant, should see the light of day through third parties. We are extremely discreet in that regard. We are driven by our interest in protecting the honor and privacy of the family."

"Your family's honor and privacy are in no danger from Audrey or me, believe me," Juliet mumbled. "As she asked, and as I promised, I will change the names. At no time will the name Stuyvesant be linked to the book. You have nothing to worry about."

"Not in the promotion of the play either?" asked the woman on her right, and Juliet shook her head.

"I'm not interested in linking it to anyone in particular, and I will not. You can take my word for it."

Mark Stuyvesant watched her for a few seconds in silence, and then, just like in the movies, he snapped his fingers at a bespectacled guy to his left. The man nodded and leaned his elbows on the table. "The Stuyvesant family would like to give you the apartment owned by Mrs. Audrey Rose Stuyvesant in the Barbican Estate," he read out of a folder, "in their names. Your lawyer can check it. Also a sum of money amounting to..."

"We want nothing from Audrey, much less from the family that took her from her home, manipulated her, isolated her, and left her to die alone far from her country."

"This is unacceptable." Mark looked at Robert in shock, then watched them narrowly.

"You'd better explain that in court."

"Michiel, please talk to her."

"That's enough. We're leaving." He stood up and grabbed Juliet's hand, and Stuyvesant gesticulated helplessly.

"Don't be offended, please. My aunt's wish was to compensate in some way for your concern for her."

"We have never been driven by economic interests."

"I know!"

"Look, Mark, if you want to buy goodwill with money," Juliet snapped at him before turning to the door, "you have the Glenns, who I'm sure will go along with anything. Neither Michiel nor I is like that."

"Do you not understand the meaning of the word 'compensation,' Juliet?"

"Surely better than you. Are you trying to make it up to us? Get rid of us for good? I'll tell you something else. Don't ever use that condescending tone with me again. Nobody talks to me like that."

"Also, see to it that your gorilla, Lynch, doesn't come near us again, or we'll have a problem," Michiel concluded, glaring at the whole group. He followed Juliet, and when they reached the elevator, he hugged her and kissed her.

CHAPTER TWENTY-FOUR

On the last Sunday in June, Michiel finished the school year according to the American calendar respected by his school, and although he still had a few days of work left, he was practically on vacation. He and Daniel had many plans for the summer.

Juliet, who had only her sister's upcoming wedding in Scotland on her mind, was still trying to make progress with her book. She had been able to invest a lot of time since the Stuyvesants had forgotten about them, they forgot about the Stuyvesants, and life had resumed its usual and placid normality.

Against all odds, after the meeting with Mark Stuyvesant at Smithson, Hawksmoor & Phillips Attorneys at Law, the dust had settled. Two days later, Robert had told them about the million-dollar settlement he had secured for the Glenns. It included money, a confidentiality pact, and a perpetual non-aggression pledge against the Stuyvesants. In short, they had paid them huge sums to avoid any future challenges, claims, or disagreements with them about Audrey's inheritance.

A pity because no one had taken into account Audrey and Gregory, who had suffered the rejection and contempt of their family for sixty-five years, much less thought of her alone in recent months, manipulated and isolated far from England. That had not mattered to anyone because, in reality, it had never mattered to her family.

As Michiel said, it was no longer their business, and they had better turn the page.

She took a deep breath and watched the rain pouring down on the other side of the window in Michiel's room. They were in bed and on their respective computers, working without interrupting each other or making a sound. She felt the weight of his body against hers because they had ended up shoulder to shoulder without realizing it, and she watched him carefully.

He was so handsome, she thought, looking at his disheveled hair, his profile, his beard, his strong forearms covered with beautiful brown hair, and his big, elegant hands typing on the computer. When he was wearing a white t-shirt, classic jeans, and had bare feet? Those feet and his long legs drove her crazy. He was working on his doctoral thesis because he had decided to take it up again seriously after many years, and she didn't want to disturb him, but he, noticing her shameless scrutiny, raised his head and fixed his eyes on her.

"*Zissele*," he whispered, taking off his headphones.

She said nothing, just stretched out her hand and stroked his hair, feeling many things. First, she wanted to kiss him, and second, she wanted to be able to utter the magic words she had wanted to say for weeks but did not dare. She took a deep breath and saved the "I love you" that her body was asking her to let out for later or for another life; she was not sure.

"Juliet, can I have some *tortilla de patatas*?" Daniel burst into the bedroom and pronounced "*tortilla de patatas*" in perfect Spanish. She nodded and left the computer on the bed to get up.

"Sure, I can make you an omelet sandwich. There's some bread left over from breakfast."

"Thank you very much."

"You're welcome, come on. Michiel?" She looked at him, and he turned his attention to her. "Do you want a snack?

"No, *Zissele*. I'm not hungry, but thank you."

She smiled at him and went to the kitchen to prepare a snack for the little boy who had just turned nine years old and who had become a fundamental part of her life five months earlier.

The good news was that the famous *carpe diem* had worked, or so it seemed and that since she had let herself live in the moment, her life had taken an impressive qualitative leap. She had only been making the most of the present without thinking about the future for about five months with Michiel, and she was already a different person. She had trouble remembering how she used to live without him when her orderly and stable life lacked butterflies in her stomach, passion, sex, and lots of love because she was utterly in love with him.

Sometimes she tried to remember what she had felt for Caden and laughed because it was nothing like a full and trusting relationship between adults. She had never felt safe and strong with Caden, from whom she had taken away the title of LOML. He had never aroused so many feelings, each one powerful, so she could consider herself a lucky and privileged person for having managed to change her life. She was very happy, so much so that everyone could see it.

They hadn't made their relationship official, a word that horrified Michiel, but they weren't hiding. They went many places together. He accompanied her to events and engagements, and they practically lived together between the two apartments in the Barbican Estate. She shared time with Daniel without any drama, even communicating with Fiona, his mother, on a regular basis. They had liked each other from the start, and her relationship with Robert, whom she now considered a friend, had contributed to their bonding and the occasional meal at their Regent's Park home.

In short, they had no apparent commitment, but they lived as if they had. She didn't ask herself questions. She didn't make herself crazy. She felt safe and at ease, and he seemed to enjoy the monogamy, as he called it, while laughing his head off that it was now his life.

Carpe diem, *Juliet*, she told herself daily while looking into his eyes or curled up on his chest. *Carpe diem* and "A vivir, que son dos días," which was something her grandmother kept repeating.

"Are you coming to Spain with us?" Daniel asked as he finished his sandwich on the kitchen counter. She poured herself a cup of coffee and looked into his eyes.

"I don't think so. This summer I have to concentrate on my sister's wedding. Maybe I can go to Cádiz for a few days to see my family, but not to Menorca."

"It's not that far away."

"No, but it's complicated because I also have a lot of work."

She cringed at the prospect of giving up seeing them for the entire summer, almost two months of vacation for Michiel, but she shooed the idea away and leaned over to change Romeo's water. He was roaming around as if he were at home.

"Where is your sister's wedding?"

"In Edinburgh, which is where she lives with her boyfriend."

"Dad says she's in the military. What does she do?"

"She is a career military officer, but she is also a civil engineer. She designs things needed by the army. She is sent to build field hospitals, bridges, or bases in the cities where the British Army moves."

"How cool."

"She loves it, and her fiancé does the same work. What do you want to do when you grow up?"

"I don't know yet. Maybe a video game tester."

"Wow, that's interesting."

"Is Dad going to the wedding?"

"No."

"Are you going alone? My aunt Mitzy says you should never go to weddings alone."

"Really?" She laughed at the witticism, and he looked at her very seriously. "I'm not going alone. I've invited a friend who is my sister's favorite actor. He's Scottish, and he'll be there on those dates. It will be a surprise."

"Who is it? Henry Cavill?"

"No, Henry is not Scottish. He's from the Isle of Jersey."

"What are you doing?" Michiel came into the kitchen, interrupting their conversation, passed her, and kissed her hair before going to pour himself a cup of coffee.

"Robert called and said he's coming to pick you up in half an hour, Dani. He feels like getting out of the house for a while."

"Okay, as long as the babies are not with him."

"Daniel!" His father shot him an annoyed look and he shrugged, picked up his plate, and took it to the dishwasher. Juliet reached out to caress Michiel's chest.

"Leave it. How are you doing? Have you made any progress?"

"The last stuff John sent me is no good to me, but I don't need it either. I've already discarded it. Shall we have dinner out today? It's stopped raining, and it's a lovely temperature."

"Okay. Wait, I have to answer."

She looked at her phone lighting up on the table, grabbed it, and stepped away to answer Sarah, who was freaking out with less than three months to go before the wedding in Edinburgh. She patiently listened to her complaints and her stories of tablecloths, napkins, and floral arrangements, and they chatted for quite a while. Then Robert appeared to pick up Dani and gave her the perfect excuse to hang up.

"Honey, don't worry. Everything will be fine. I have to go. I'll talk to you later."

"Mum says you have a date for the wedding. Who?"

"I'll tell you about it. I have to go."

"Okay, see you later."

She said goodbye, went into the living room to greet Robert, and caught him caressing Romeo, who was enjoying the attention. She smiled at him and he leaned against the back of a sofa, looking exhausted. He accepted a cup of coffee.

"How are you doing? How are the girls?"

"Imagine, Juliet. They are a month old, and it's already crazy. I can't wait to start my vacation. Fi is taking them to Holland next week. I'll pick them up a few days later, and we will all go to Cornwall. This year no beach, just countryside, peace, and grandmothers to lend a hand."

"A great idea."

"Yeah, and Daniel goes off and leaves me alone with a bunch of women," he joked and ruffled the boy's hair. "Don't be too long in coming back, buddy."

"On August first, you'll have him back," Michiel said. "Don't worry."

"When are you going to Amsterdam, man?"

"Tomorrow, but only for a couple of days to meet my new nephew and do some paperwork at the university."

"Very good." He took a sip of coffee and looked them in the eye. "We finally got Audrey's ashes to Kensal Green. Did I tell you?"

"No."

"I'm sorry. It's just that between paternity leave and being overwhelmed, I forgot to tell you about it. They were moved last Friday."

"At least it's good news."

"Yes, and let's hope that everything continues with a little peace and quiet. The Glenns have started to get paid, and they keep asking questions and pestering me."

"Mother of God."

"It's an occupational hazard, and we've earned a lot of money, so I'm not complaining. Daniel, buddy, shall we go? We have to go to the pharmacy to pick up some diapers."

They stood on the landing and watched them disappear. Michiel grabbed her and pulled her into the apartment, kicked the door shut, and cornered her against the wall.

"I've got you all to myself now, Sherlock."

"The same to you, my dear Watson."

She caressed his face and kissed him, and before they ended up doing it in the hallway standing up, she pulled away, grabbed him by the hand, and yanked him into the bedroom. She put him in front of the bed and pushed him onto the mattress to start removing his clothes.

"You are very impatient, Michiel Lezer. Let's see if you can relax a little."

"I don't know if I can. I like you too much."

She pulled off his shirt, ripped off his jeans, and slowly removed his underwear, not allowing him to move or touch her. Finally, she climbed onto the bed naked without brushing against him, and he snorted while staring at the ceiling.

"Don't do this to me, *Zissele*."

"At this stage of the game, we are supposed to be patient."

"Who says that bullshit?"

"Everyone knows it."

She trapped him between her thighs, held his precious erection carefully, guided him, and let him penetrate her with a moan that came from her soul.

She leaned over him to kiss him and bite his mouth, to feel his hot breath catch on hers, then pinned his arms. Her hips shot out in an instinctive and wild undulating movement that brought her to a first orgasm right away, but she didn't stop kissing him or moving and began to feel him dissolving inside her, laughing and calling her name until he grabbed her by the ass, spun her around, and got on top of her to bring her to another orgasm and another until they ended in a shared climax that made her let out a blissful laugh.

"Mother of God, Juliet! One day you're going to kill me."

"You exaggerate."

She reached down to comb his disheveled hair, then sat up and gave him a long, wet, delicious kiss before separating from him to go to the bathroom.

"I feel like going for a walk and having dinner at some Italian place. I'm going to take a quick shower, okay? Michiel?" she called to him when he didn't answer. He was still puffing, exhausted, and he nodded without moving. She went over to kiss him, then went to the bathroom to take a shower and put on something decent to go out to dinner.

"What about your sister's wedding?" he asked fifteen minutes later in a dry tone from the bathroom door, and she looked at him while closing her bathrobe.

"What do you mean, what about my sister's wedding?"

"Are you going to be accompanied?"

"What?

"Daniel just called me because he lost I don't know what video game, and he said to send him a message telling him who is the actor who is going to accompany you to your sister's wedding and that he will keep it a secret."

"Oh, my God! He doesn't miss anything. It's incredible. I'll write to him now."

"Juliet." He cut her off and forced her to look him in the face. "Did *I* miss something? Who are you planning to go to Sarah's wedding with?"

"With Richard M."

"Why didn't I know?"

"I didn't think you'd be interested with all the end of the school year mess, and anyway, I only decided to do it a couple of weeks ago."

"Did you decide all of a sudden?"

"What's wrong? What's the problem?"

"I thought you preferred to go alone."

"Yes, but my mother started to insist. I got overwhelmed, and then I saw Richard, who is Sarah's favorite actor. I told him about it, and he was delighted to sign up. End of story, it's a surprise for her."

"For me as well."

"I can't believe it."

"What can you not believe?"

"That you care since it doesn't matter."

"If it's not important, why didn't you ask me?"

"Because you are a no-commitment guy. How could I ask you to accompany me to an event where my whole family will be present? I would never think of putting you in that position."

"That guy, whom you hardly know, can go?"

"I've known him for ten years. We're close friends, and I know he has no problem with family commitments or inquisitive mothers or grandmothers." She tensed because he seemed very angry. She pushed him away from the door and went to get her clothes in the bedroom. "This is unusual, Michiel. I'm doing this for you, to not take you out of your comfort zone and respect your philosophy of life. Don't hold it against me. I *want* to go to the family party with you. I'm sick of going to everyone's weddings alone, and since I have the opportunity to have a companion, I've taken advantage of it. That's all."

"I repeat, if you wanted me to accompany you, you should have told me."

"I never contemplated the possibility of you accompanying me. I wasn't going to put you in that position."

"I care about you, Juliet. We've been in an exclusive and happy relationship for almost six months. I don't think..."

"Exclusive until it's over. I don't want my sister's wedding pictures, ten years from now, to show the guy who was monogamous with me for a while and then took off and left me hung up on him." As soon as she said that, she knew she had screwed up because, deep down, she thought that.

Her deep-seated rage had blinded her and spoken for her, and she supposed that, even if she didn't want to know him and thought she was living in the world of *Alice in Wonderland*, she didn't quite believe it. At least, her subconscious didn't quite believe it, and it had given her away.

She turned to face him, and he put his hands on his hips and lowered his head, resigned.

"Michiel."

"Are you aware that my choices of sentimental life or partner do not define me as a person?"

"I know."

"I'm not a monster, Juliet. I'm a normal person. I care about you, and if you want me to swim across the Atlantic for you, I will. Don't decide for me again. I'm not ten years old, and you should know that as long as you keep waiting for me to leave you hung up and dusty, we can't move forward. This is not how it works. It's not about living while waiting for disaster. It's about building positively, and at this moment, I have more chances of you leaving me hung up and in the dust than me leaving you, so do me a favor and stop judging me."

She stood mute with no retort. He put on his jeans and went to the living room to turn on the TV.

For a moment, she wanted to tell him everything, including that she loved and was in love with him and that sometimes fear spoke for itself, but she was unable to. She picked up her clothes, her backpack, her computer, and Romeo, who was always glued to her legs, and walked decisively to the door, then went out onto the landing in her bathrobe with wet hair. She didn't care; she slammed the door and went home alone, which was where she could be herself.

James Bond was theirs, and so was their villain and one of their Bond girls. They had made a full fifteen by signing the three main actors in the new film, plus a lot of the supporting cast. At Shaughnessy & McCameron, they were celebrating with bottles of champagne, hugs, and lots of confetti.

That was the news of the year: the best deal the agency had ever signed in its history. Juliet was as happy as everyone else since she had done her bit to get the multimillion-dollar contract, but she didn't jump up and hug everyone because she couldn't stop thinking about the big argument with Michiel the night before. It had ended with the two of them locked in their respective houses, not talking to each other even though he was leaving that morning for Amsterdam.

She was leaving for a few days too, and it was strange not to say goodbye. Not to hug him, not to know if she would see him again. What had happened the day before might have ended everything in one fell swoop, and that disconcerted her and broke her in two. If it was true that they had come that far, she would never forgive herself. Perhaps if she had been more conciliatory and less proud, she concluded, staring at the black computer screen... If she had been more understanding and a better friend and listened before spouting nonsense she didn't mean. If only...

The doubts were endless. The only thing she was sure of was that she did not know how to survive without him, not after the last few wonderful months they had shared, much less having him so close. The only thing she could think of was to turn on the computer to write to Delilah, the real estate agent, to ask her to find her an apartment far from the Barbican.

She found her email address and clicked on it, but she stopped herself before writing anything. She covered her face with both hands, trying to calm down, and took a deep breath, reproaching herself for not having followed her instincts and gone to look for him five minutes after getting into a fight with him. It had been a very long night of sitting on the floor of her foyer, deciding whether or not to go and talk to him. In the end, she hadn't done it so as not to make things worse, but mainly because she was harder than a rock.

"Juliet, come and have a drink. Don't be a bore," Fabio shouted from the door of her office, and she jumped up and forced a smile.

"You're working? Iona has given us the morning off, and they've gone to find James Bond to come and celebrate with us. Come on, Juliet!"

He grabbed her hand and pulled her forcibly into the lobby, where everyone was partying despite it being eleven in the morning. She smiled and accepted a glass of champagne, though she left it on a shelf and decided to call Michiel before he got on the plane.

"What's the matter? Are you all right?" Fabio approached her and looked at her. "Have you been crying?"

"I'm fine."

"What?"

"I had an argument with Michiel last night. I messed up big time, and I don't know how to fix it. I don't think he'll ever speak to me again."

"That is impossible."

"It's not impossible. You can't imagine."

"It's impossible because you have him right there." He nodded at the landing next to the elevators, and she turned and saw Michiel standing there, wearing faded jeans and a nice dark blue shirt. He was carrying a small suitcase and was watching every-thing with a frown on his face.

Her heart skipped a beat, and she ran to intercept him before he stepped through the glass doors of the reception area. She touched his arm.

"Hello!"

"What's going on here?" he asked, looking at the commotion.

"We have signed James Bond. We are celebrating."

"Congratulations."

"Thank you." She smiled at him, and he held her gaze. "I'm so glad to see you. I haven't slept at all."

"Juliet, I don't have much time, but I didn't want to travel without talking to you first. I wanted to see you."

"Of course." She felt tears well up in her eyes and took a step back, preparing to receive with some dignity and fortitude the worst news of her life.

"Last night we both said things that… I think I had a childish jealousy attack. It has never happened to me before, and I'm sorry for being so unfair, but I've learned that feelings can't be controlled."

"Juliet! Juliet!" the others called. She waved at them to be quiet and grabbed Michiel by the wrist.

"Let's go to my office. They are going crazy."

"No, I can't. I'm already too close to get to Heathrow with a safe margin."

"It's all right. It's all forgotten. I'm not very proud of what I said either. I'm sorry about that."

"I've never been where I am now, Juliet."

"Um…"

"I don't mind. On the contrary. I need to verbalize it."

"Okay."

"You told me one day that you just wanted to be someone's priority. You need to know that you've become my priority. I love you, and I've fallen in love with you, and I needed to tell you that before I take that flight to Amsterdam," he said, looking at her with those huge, sincere eyes. She felt her bones dissolve and her legs weaken, and tears and words caught in her throat. She opened her mouth to tell him that she loved him as well and he was her priority too, and that she was crazy about him, but a crowd of people came out of the elevator and someone ran up, grabbed her, pulled her into his arms, and started spinning with her.

"Juliet, Juliet, I'm 007! Julieeeet!" The flamboyant James Bond shouted in his euphoric way, and Juliet broke away and stomped away amidst the cheers and applause of everyone. She turned away from him angrily for having interrupted the most important moment of her life and looked for Michiel but could not find him. She scanned the reception area and the corridor desperately, and when she attempted to run into the lobby, the security guard gestured to her that her friend had gone down in the elevator.

She thanked him, went straight to the stairs, and ran down them at full speed, but had no luck since when she reached the street, he was leaving in a cab. She tried to call him, but she didn't have her cell with her, so she took a deep breath, rushed back in, managed to get to her office in the middle of the general revelry, and retrieved the phone from the desk.

"Off or out of coverage."

She got the automatic answer, and she wanted to throw it out the window. She repeated the call twice, and when it didn't work, she grabbed her purse and went to look for Andrea among the jumble of people and champagne.

"Andrea, I'm going to the airport. Stay by the phone in case I need you."

"To the airport?" her assistant asked with a surprised look on her face, but Juliet waved goodbye.

"Yes, I'll call you back."

Without a second thought, she went down to the street and caught a cab to Heathrow. She knew the plane was leaving around one o'clock, or she thought she remembered it was, and she called him many times because she didn't intend to let him leave without her answer. Without letting him know that she loved him too, that she had been madly in love with him for a long time, perhaps since their first talk in the takeaway store, or perhaps since the first night they had kissed at her house, or most likely, since she had been born because he was what she had been waiting for all her life.

The trip to the airport at Monday at noon was torture even before the left the city. She kept calling him without success and answering calls from Iona and other people, reprimanding her for leaving the party and from her mother and sister telling her about the wedding,

She began to hyperventilate and despair. She wanted to kill someone. She finally set foot in the airport and ran like crazy through the corridors to the boarding area…where she did not find him.

No one lingered in the departure area of an airport. Everyone went through the police checkpoints as quickly as possible to wait for boarding in the lounge corresponding to their flight, and she cursed herself while thinking about her options, even though she knew she had only one.

She retraced her steps, looked for the KLM counter, waited in line, and asked for a ticket on the first flight to Amsterdam.

"We have a flight leaving in forty-five minutes. I have one seat left in business class," the ground attendant assured her, and she pulled out her wallet. "That's six hundred pounds."

"Okay, thank you."

She paid the small fortune for a seventy-minute flight, grabbed her boarding pass, and ran to the security checkpoints. She flew past them because, thank God, they were half empty, and she sprinted through the duty-free to his gate, still calling him. He was probably taking off or about to take off.

He had made it clear that he was on a tight schedule, and she wasn't so lucky as to miraculously run into him in one of the aisles, so she planted herself at his gate, where people were already filing briskly into the plane. She assumed he was ahead of her.

"Andrea, I'm going to Amsterdam."

"What?" the woman shouted, and Juliet entered the machine, scrutinizing all the passengers who were already seated. "When are you coming back?"

"Tonight. I only have an hour's flight. Anyway, call Rocío, please, so he can come and see to Romeo."

"Okay. Is everything all right?"

"Yes, I'm just going to see Michiel and talk to him. Don't worry."

"Wasn't he here a while ago?"

"Yes, but he left in the middle of the party, and I need to see him. Okay? Talk to you later. Bye."

She arrived at Amsterdam Schiphol in exactly one hour and five minutes, with the decision made not to call Michiel anymore. At that point, she preferred to surprise him as he had surprised her that morning in his office. She had thought it was a beautiful gesture and wanted to return it, although when she stepped onto the street, she realized that she had no idea where she could go to surprise him since she had no idea where he was staying.

Juliet got into a cab, remembering that he had once told her that his family lived in the Jordaan district in the heart of the city, and asked the driver to take her there while she hurriedly thought about how she could find him without having to call him. She closed her eyes to focus and remembered that Michiel's mother was a psychiatrist and would probably have a practice. If she could find that, she could go there and ask her where he could find Michiel, and if the woman didn't think she was a stalker and told her where he was staying, she could go to wherever he was.

She googled Dr. Ruth Lezer, and in addition to many articles raving about her and her psychiatric work in various hospitals in the Netherlands, Juliet finally found the address of her private practice, which was, of course, in Jordaan.

The cab driver dropped her off on the corner right next to the office, which, according to Google, was in a building facing the Prince's Canal. She walked toward the doorway, getting nervous again. She approached the door, fixing her dress and looking at the time: three o'clock in the afternoon, four o'clock local time. She rang the bell at the main entrance with her heart pounding in her chest.

"*Wie is het?*" asked a female voice in Dutch, and she replied in English.

"Good afternoon. My name is Juliet Miller. I'm from London. I would like to speak to Dr. Lezer, please."

She didn't answer but opened the door with a very annoying creak, and she entered a nice narrow corridor that led to an old-fashioned carpeted wooden staircase. She looked around, and before she could move, someone opened the door to her right and peered curiously at her.

"Good afternoon. You do not have an appointment with the doctor. How can I help you?"

"It's personal. I wanted to talk to her."

"Juliet?"

Behind that friendly but rather dry lady, Michiel's mother appeared, taking off her glasses. She smiled at her and opened her arms to greet her.

"Wow, what a surprise. I didn't know you were coming to Amsterdam too."

"It's good to see you, Ruth." She hugged her and smiled. "I didn't know if I was going to get here."

"Oh, honey. Where's your luggage?"

"I didn't bring anything. I'm just passing through. Do you know where I can reach Michiel?"

"You don't know where he is?" She narrowed her eyes.

Juliet blushed, but she didn't flinch. "No, I came to surprise him. He doesn't even know I'm here."

She looked at her assistant first and they both looked at her doubtfully for a few eternal seconds. Then Ruth Lezer smiled and shook her head.

"The attic is his. He arrived about half an hour ago, so I guess he's still there." She pointed at the stairs and smiled from ear to ear, then kissed Juliet on the cheek.

Juliet ran up the steep steps, of which there were many, until she reached the attic.

She stopped to catch her breath, looked down to smooth out her summer dress, and arranged her hair a bit with her fingers before ringing the doorbell. She pressed it and waited for a few minutes without breathing until she felt muffled footsteps and someone opening the antique lock with much clattering. She stepped back, shaking like a leaf, then the door opened and she was face to face with Michiel, with his shirt wide open and barefoot.

"Juliet?" he asked, surprised.

"You left me with the words in my mouth."

"I can't believe it." He laughed, and she took a deep breath.

"You left without hearing what I had to say. That is not done, my dear Watson."

"Juliet." He reached out to touch her, but she stepped back.

"I love you. You are my priority too. I've been in love with you for a long time. I'm crazy about you, and if I haven't said it before, it's because I didn't want to scare you, but I love you. I love you more than I'm able to express."

"*Zissele.*" He approached her to hold her close to his body, and she wiped at her tears with his shirt.

She was crying from emotion and from sheer relief after hours of total stress. She snuggled into his chest until she sensed the presence of someone, turned away from him, looked inside the apartment, and saw a beautiful girl who was watching them very attentively. Without meaning to, she tensed, and all her alarms went off. Before she could say anything, Michiel looked her in the eyes, understanding what was going through her mind, grabbed her, and pulled her into the attic.

"Juliet, this is my sister Rachel. Rachel, this is Juliet, my girlfriend."

CHAPTER TWENTY-FIVE

September third was the day of Sarah and Jonathan's big wedding in Scotland in the ruins of St. Anthony's Chapel on the way to Arthur's Seat viewpoint, in the heart of Holyrood Park, with Edinburgh at their feet.

The site was spectacular, and many strings had to be pulled to make it happen, but finally, there they were, family and friends together, all celebrating the love of this couple who looked like something out of a fairytale.

Michiel watched them tenderly since they were lovely, then turned his eyes to his girl. To Juliet, one of Sarah's six bridesmaids, who had cried all through the ceremony.

She was very excited and happy for her little sister and had not stopped crying for four days since she had arrived in Edinburgh to help with the final preparations for the event. She had been involved to the maximum, which the bride and groom had thanked her for publicly on several occasions.

He ran his eyes over her tied-back brown hair, her dimpled ear with a tiny pearl earring, her very feminine neck, and her straight, smooth back, which stood out thanks to the wide neckline of her chocolate-brown dress. He continued his gaze down to her narrow waist, her pert backside, and the slender legs that looked great, thanks to a pair of strappy sandals. Gorgeous as always, he thought, and his mind flew back to June when she had shown up at the door of his Amsterdam home, leaving him stunned.

That very morning, sleepless after a night in which he had decided that he did not intend to lose her because he was crazy about her, and despite a bitter argument due to his childish jealousy, he had gone to her office to tell her how he felt, to talk about love for the first time in his life with a woman and to make a romantic and heroic gesture before flying to Holland. However, the celebrations for the James Bond contract had overshadowed the most momentous confession of his life, and, angry and impotent, he had given it up as impossible and left for the airport, planning to resume the conversation at another time.

What he could never have imagined was that she would react by taking a flight to come to his house, to look him in the eyes and tell him that she loved him too and that she was in love with him. It had been an incredible, precious gesture, and his love had grown. He was already quite devoted. Since then, they had hardly been separated.

Of course, after the unsurpassed romantic moment, he had convinced her to stay in Amsterdam with him. They went shopping because she had traveled with the clothes on her back, and they had enjoyed three unforgettable days. She had met his brothers, his brothers-in-law, his nephews, and his friends.

They came and went like a couple of tourists, and from that moment on, the summer had been a permanent honeymoon.

After her visit to Menorca, he and Daniel had traveled to see her in Cádiz for a week, and then the three of them had gone to Holland together. Although her work and the wedding preparations had kept her quite busy, they had not missed an opportunity to be together.

He sighed and ran his eyes over her again, and he felt that

surge of energy she provoked in him. It had had him half-stoned since they had first spoken in Amadeo's takeout place.

From then on, he had been a different person, and he was perfectly aware of it.

Since Juliet Miller had burst into his universe, nothing had been the same. He thanked God for the miracle because the changes had been positive. Everything had become more intense, more real, and more colorful. He had discovered that before Juliet, nothing had filled him, and there was no one like her because she was unique. She was the woman in his life, his accomplice, his partner, his lover, his best friend, his priority, his Sherlock.

He smiled at her as she turned to look at him, winked, and pointed at her left ring finger. He had been asking her to get married for days, and she responded by shaking her head and rolling her eyes.

He had never in his life considered that he would ever think of getting married, a procedure that was light-years away from his perceived lifestyle, but when he had assimilated that what he felt for her was love, that he was crazy about her and she felt the same way about him, the idea no longer seemed so bad, and he had begun to fantasize about the idea of marriage. He had even talked about it one serious night.

He was in La Línea de la Concepción with Lola, Juliet's grandmother, a wonderful lady with whom he could already communicate in Spanish. She had treated him like a son since he set foot in her house.

Lola, on whom Michiel had had a crush, said James, Juliet's father, had told her that in life, everything had to be done without regard for consequences. That half-measures were for cowards, and her granddaughter was one of those brave ones who would eat life in bites and that if he wanted to be at her level, he should marry her before someone else got ahead of him. He had laughed, but he had begun to think about it, and as soon as he had arrived in Scotland and taken in the general atmosphere, he had gotten serious about it. He had told Juliet about it, although she, like him a month and a half ago in Cádiz, had burst out laughing.

"Sarah and Jonathan, I now pronounce you man and wife. You may kiss the bride," said the military chaplain.

The bride and groom kissed, and everyone stood to applaud the newly married Snowdon couple who, after kissing, embraced their families first, then passed through the aisle of sabers held by their army buddies, who had solemnly guarded the entire outdoor ceremony.

"Come on. My cousins brought a band, and I want to see the looks on Sarah and my mother's faces when they arrive at the banquet," said Juliet, approaching Michiel. He had not moved from his chair, watching the guests disperse on their way to Holyrood Palace, and she held out her hand to him. He took her hand and stood up to kiss her on the mouth.

"*Coro Rociero?*"

"An Andalusian musical group. They will play *sevillanas* and stuff. It is a beautiful surprise."

"Wow, that's nice."

"I'm telling you."

"You're the most beautiful girl I've ever seen in my life, *Zissele*. Even today, with the bride's permission." He looked her up and down as they walked, and she gave him a sidelong glance.

"You're hot, my dear Watson. That suit suits you to a tee. With that hanger, you were born to wear a suit, I'm telling you."

"Do you like it? My girlfriend chose it."

"You have a girlfriend with very good taste."

"Of course. She goes out with me."

They arrived almost at a run at the famous Holyrood Palace that, making an extraordinary exception, had given them some rooms for the wedding lunch. When they stepped into the gardens, out of nowhere appeared Rocío's impressive band, twelve people in beautiful and colorful costumes with their instruments, singing the *Salve Rociera*, Juliet told him in his ear. It made the bride and the mother of the bride and everyone, even him, cry.

"I think this is the best wedding I've ever been to in my entire life," he confessed as they walked into the hotel suite three hours later. Juliet continued toward the bathroom.

"It has only just begun. There is still the party. The food was only an appetizer."

"I didn't know you danced *sevillanas*, *Zissele*. It was very sexy. It will take me years to recover."

"You're such a geek sometimes, Michiel." She laughed, leaned close, and kissed him on the mouth. He grabbed her and slid his hands down her backside to her hips. "You are the best companion in the universe. Everybody adores you, including my parents, my grandmother, my cousins, and even my brother, who has always been a pain in the ass about our boyfriends."

"*Novietes?*"

"You know what I mean." She laughed and continued kissing him. "We have a couple of hours to rest and change."

"Rest, Sherlock?"

He pulled down the zipper of her dress and kissed her eagerly, very excited. Her cell phone began to vibrate inside her purse. He tried to take it away, but she snorted and pulled away.

"I'm sorry, my love. It may be important."

"We said no cell phones until Monday, Juliet."

"I know, but I've got half the family spread out in Edinburgh. I'll just be a second."

"Hello." She pouted apologetically, then became serious. "Excuse me, hold on a second." She motioned for him to come closer, activated the speakerphone, and put the device on the bed.

"Speak up, please. Michiel and I are listening to you. Who do you say you are?"

"I'm Fran, Miss Miller. Fran Lopez, Mrs. Audrey Stuyvesant's nurse. Remember me? I just saw you entering the Scotsman Hotel in Edinburgh."

"Wow, what a coincidence. How are you, Fran?"

"Is she in Edinburgh?" asked Michiel with a frown, and Juliet shrugged.

"Yes, Mr. Lezer. We are in Edinburgh, and we are also staying at the Scotsman Hotel."

"We are? Who?" Juliet asked.

The woman answered.

"Mrs. Audrey and I have been living in the UK since April."

"I see you have fallen in love." Audrey Stuyvesant told them as they arrived hand in hand at her suite. Juliet didn't know if she wanted to kill her or smother her with kisses. She opted for the latter and went up to her to give her a big hug between tears of happiness and bewilderment.

"My goodness, how handsome you both are. May God give you many healthy children."

She gestured for them to sit in one of the beautiful armchairs in the spectacular Headline suite, the crown jewel of the Scotsman Hotel. Michiel took Juliet's hand again and gave her a sidelong glance before they sat down together across from Audrey, who looked great and healthy.

After receiving the unexpected call from Fran Lopez, he had been reluctant to go to meet her because everything seemed murky, like something out of a bad spy movie. Finally, after calling Robert to consult with him, Michiel had agreed to accompany her since he did not want to leave her alone, not because he felt like it.

Juliet smiled at him, stroked his hand, and returned to watching Audrey intently.

"I saw you enter the reception kissing, so elegant and attractive. 'A cinema couple,' I said to Fran. I was so happy to see you together, and we decided to call you."

"What's going on here, Audrey? Seven months ago, we went to your funeral at St. Giles."

"I know, Michiel."

"Did you fake your death? Juliet and I didn't know. We had a terrible time with your loss."

"I wish all that hadn't happened, but they left me no other options. I never imagined they would make a circus out of a funeral, let alone make you suffer. I'm so sorry. If I hadn't seen you today, you would have still thought I was dead. Maybe I was very selfish when I contacted you. Forgive me, but I couldn't resist. You know I love you very much, Michiel, both of you, and I would like to explain what ended up happening."

"The funeral was my fault since I was so insistent about the cemetery and all that," Juliet said, and Audrey smiled.

"I know you were very feisty, honey. I expected nothing less from you."

"So, to be specific. What's going on, Audrey?" Michiel asked seriously, and she sighed.

"By giving my diaries to Juliet, I signed my death warrant. I don't mind because, in the end, that impulsive decision got me out of a lot of things."

"Death sentence?"

"I don't know how to explain it better."

"You mean that when your in-laws learned of the existence of the diaries, they went ballistic," Fran interjected. "The Stuyvesant family demanded that she give them to them. She refused, and when one of the bodyguards discovered that she had given them to you, Miss Miller, they accused her of being a traitor, not worthy of the family. They accused her of many things and treated her very badly, and me too."

"She was fired," Audrey commented.

"Why didn't you call the police?"

"You know they had me in isolation. I couldn't talk to anyone. After I arrived in New York, after convincing me with lies and cajolery how much they wanted me to leave London, they made me sign a lot of things. One of those things was a confidentiality agreement. I didn't know about it because I signed blindly, happy to be collaborating with my nephews. Then I found out that it obliged me not to talk about anything about the family to anyone. I didn't have a phone, and I didn't leave that house. I was being held hostage, and by the time I realized it, it was too late. What could an old woman like me do alone in New York? I got scared and chose to keep quiet."

"When we came to see you?"

"When you came to see me, I had already realized that I was being used, but I didn't dare tell you anything. All the walls there have ears, you know, and that woman, Victoria, told me that if I spoke out of turn, they would hurt you. That they would make you lose your job and you would be out on the street. I knew they could do it. I knew very well. Look what they did to Gregory and me."

"*Mother!* Audrey, I'm so sorry."

"In that house, everything was threats. When I arrived, they took me out to dinner and introduced me to Gregory's nephews, but when I was no longer useful, they didn't know what to do with me and locked me in one of their houses. Thank God I had Fran."

"Are you aware that you ceded the entire estate that Charles had left you to them?"

"Yes, but he had left it to Gregory. I didn't care. I wouldn't know what to do with it. One day, after going through appraisers, after medical examinations to determine that he was in his right mind, after listening to a thousand talks about the Stuyvesant estate, and after signing his millions of transfer papers, I told Chuck, the oldest nephew, the worst of them all, that he shouldn't have made such a fuss to get me to transfer his damned treasure because I had never been interested in it, and he got really pissed off." Audrey burst out laughing, and Fran laughed with her. Juliet looked at Michiel, and he shook his head.

"So, you are aware of everything they did to you? How they used you, and what you signed up for? You are clear about what has happened in the last year?"

"Yes, my dear. I understand perfectly."

"You want to do something about it? We have a great lawyer."

"No. For God's sake, no. I just want to move on. I just want to turn the page. I am eighty-four years old, and I want to live my remaining years enjoying my money and my peace of mind."

"What money?"

"When the scandal with the newspapers broke, they said they would disown me. That they would wipe me off the face of the earth, and I was no longer of any use to them. That it was better for me to die at once. I told them, 'I will disappear if you finance me.' Gregory always said his family got everything by paying and that you could get the pounds out of them as long as you had something good to offer them, and that's how it was. I told them to let me go free. I transformed myself into someone else once, and I could do it again. If they would give me money, they would never hear from me again.

"From that day on, I signed other agreements giving up everything in the present and the future, and one of their employees helped me get Fran back. We got on a plane and left everything behind. By January of this year, I was Mrs. McCrory again. First, we went to Austria to see old friends, and in April, we came to the UK. We have not stopped traveling. I used to come to Edinburgh a lot when I was a child. You know, my father was born here."

"Despite everything, they paid a lot of money to your family."

"Ah, that's none of my business anymore, Michiel. They made up that I died at Christmas. They told you, you told a lawyer, and all hell broke loose. It got out of hand, and they had to keep up the lie. So much so that they had to compensate my horrible family to avoid more trouble. It was all ridiculous, even the funeral, but that's up to them. They have been coercing and hurting people all their lives. Whether they paid a lot or a little, I don't know, but screw them."

"According to her people, what they paid the Glenns was a pittance, considering what they have," Fran said.

"Yes, and although they don't deserve it because they have never been a family to me, may they enjoy it." She looked at them attentively. "I gave you the apartment on the Barbican Estate. The apartment has one more room than yours, and I wanted you to keep it. Has it been delivered to you?"

"They offered it to us, but we didn't take it. We couldn't do it, Audrey."

"What do you mean, Juliet? Don't you live together?"

"We share the two apartments. We have not yet settled on one."

"Do you want the Stuyvesants to keep it, who are sure to abandon it?"

"We'll talk about it." Michiel took a deep breath. "Are you sure the Stuyvesants have forgotten about you and don't know that we're talking to you right now?"

"They don't follow me. They got rid of me like they got rid of Gregory sixty-six years ago."

"Are you sure? I don't want us to be immersed in another chapter of this plot that has already taken up so much of our time."

"I swear to God, Michiel, they don't know where I am, and they don't care. I have a very important contact within the family who has taken care of it personally."

"Who is it?"

"Jack Lynch. His name is really Jack Aleijem. He is a former Israeli army officer. He's been the head of security for the family for ten years, but he was on my side from the beginning. If it hadn't been for him always looking out for my welfare, I wouldn't have come out of it alive, nor would I have recovered Fran, nor would I have been allowed to disappear. He was always very good to me. He picked up my things from the Barbican Estate and left them in storage. He calls me from time to time to check that we are still okay, and he has sworn to me that he has stopped any surveillance operations with me, Fran, or my entourage. He schedules those stakeouts, so we took his word for it. He just told us to keep a low profile, and everything would be fine."

"Jack Lynch?" Juliet looked at Michiel and laughed. "He has always been very rude to us. A nightmare."

"I know, he told me. I was just trying to protect you and keep you away from the Stuyvesant spotlight, but you guys were up in arms and sticking your noses everywhere. I know he's sorry. He was just doing his job. He's good people. I'm telling you the truth."

"Israeli army?" Michiel mumbled, and Audrey nodded.

"Yes, he's from your town, dear."

"So, you plan to continue traveling?"

"Yes, Juliet. As long as my health permits, we will travel. When it doesn't, I will stay in a nice part of London. Fran has no family either and is willing to stay with me for as long as it takes."

"I hope so." Michiel stood up, closing the meeting. "I'm glad to hear you're well, Audrey, but they're waiting for us, and it's getting very late."

"Wait, one last question." Juliet got up and grabbed his arm. "In your diaries, you go back to London after living in Australia, which was when you got your family name back."

"When Gregory's father finally died, we returned to England, and Charles let us take the family name back."

"That was my question. Did you always keep in touch with his brother?"

"I always have, although they wanted to keep it a secret so as not to arouse the family's sensitivities. Charles and Gregory corresponded until the end of his days. He assigned him a monthly allowance for our support and always cared about us. The proof is that in the end, he tried to make up with his brother by giving it all back to him."

"Didn't he know that Gregory died a year ago?"

"Yes, he knew. Of course he knew, but he kept to his intentions, and in the end, he bequeathed it all to me. It was a big surprise because, unfortunately, since we had no children, it made no sense to leave it to me, but he did. One of his best friends in Manhattan told me one day that he had done it for justice, but above all, he had done it to spite his offspring, whom he could not stand."

"What a mess it unleashed."

"It's true. In the end, it was a selfish act, but he had his reasons."

"Why didn't you ever tell us about this, Audrey? If your father-in-law had been dead for decades when we met and Charles was on your side, why didn't you tell Juliet and me?"

"By habit and inertia, Michiel. We had spent our whole lives hiding and lying so as not to unleash the wrath of old Peter Gregory II. Eventually, you get used to it and lie to everyone. Juliet, did you write the book?"

"I'm working on it, but I haven't had much time lately."

"When you publish it, send a copy to me. I hope we'll keep in touch from now on, but please don't include this last meeting after returning from the grave." She laughed. "I wouldn't want to stir the waters."

"It's okay, although this is an anticlimactic ending." She went over to kiss Audrey. "We have to go. My sister got married today. We are here for her wedding, and we are expected at the party."

"Michiel, honey, look at me. Don't be angry with me. I know you're very upset about all this, but I give you my word of honor that I never thought I'd get you involved. I never imagined that you would come looking for me, let alone go this far."

He nodded and hugged her, then pulled away.

"It's a little bit beyond me, Audrey, because it's not normal, and we've been involved in a drama that we didn't want to be in," he said. "However, I will overlook it because, thanks to you and the Stuyvesants, I met Juliet."

"That's the spirit, Michiel. I hope you will be very happy. You deserve it since you are both wonderful people. Fran?" she called to her friend, who approached solicitously. "Give my details to Juliet so we can meet again. Right, guys?"

"Of course."

"Congratulations to your sister, darling, and don't forget to claim the Barbican Estate apartment. It's yours. In my mind, I've always seen you there together, raising a bunch of beautiful children."

The two looked into each other's eyes without saying anything, said goodbye, and left her with Fran in her luxury suite. They went out into the hall and did not open their mouths until they entered the elevator.

"Even if we could tell, no one would believe us. This beats any Netflix series," Juliet whispered, still a little shocked. She reached out to stroke his hair. "What are you thinking?"

"Mainly, that we should accept the flat."

"Really?"

"We deserve it after this past year."

"It has been the best year of my life."

"Mine too, but we could improve it with an apartment. It has three bedrooms and a great terrace. Romeo loves it."

"Are you going to use my cat to convince me?"

"Zissele." He stopped her on the landing when they got off the elevator, stood in front of her, and took her hands. "We practically live together. The most reasonable thing to do would be to accept the gift, hand over our rented apartments, and move in there. We can redecorate it, and it will be perfect. Do you know how much a property in the Barbican Estate is worth?"

"I know."

"We can also sell it and invest the money in another neighborhood, but we both love Barbican."

"Yes, but I don't know. Isn't it strange that a non-family member gives us an apartment as a gift?"

"Before, I thought it was bad because I believed it was a maneuver by the Stuyvesants to buy us, but now that we know that Audrey is alive and well and the decision was hers, why not?"

"That is true."

"Don't you want to live with me officially?"

"I already live with you officially."

"Great. I'll ask Robert to manage it."

"Okay." She smiled at him and went up on tiptoe to kiss him. "Do you have the feeling that we have finally come full circle?"

"The truth is, I do."

They hugged and went straight to the street to catch a cab.

"We could also get married and save a lot of paperwork. I'm sure it's easier to turn the apartment into a community property."

"Mother of God, Michiel."

"I'm just trying to be practical."

"It's not that. It's just that I think my grandmother has driven you insane."

"Why do you think your lovely grandmother has done that?"

"You have gone from polysex to marriage. I'm sorry to say, but it's a bit incoherent, my dear Watson."

"I'm tempted to wear a wedding ring."

"I find men who wear a wedding ring very sexy. If you want, I'll give you one."

"I'm thinking about our future, Sherlock. Don't tease me."

"I think you should not think so much about the future. Enjoy the moment."

"Juliet!"

"*Carpe diem,* Michiel. *Carpe diem.*"

EPILOGUE

One year later

"Do you like it, honey?" Iona stood in front of her. She was very excited because they had made a huge effort to welcome her into her new office after six months of absence.

Juliet took a step back and read the letters on the glass door again. Juliet Miller-Lezer, Managing Director for the UK and Ireland.

"Do you like it?"

"I love it. It's very nice. Thank you very much."

Everyone started clapping, and she instinctively covered the ears of her six-month-old daughter Hazel, whom she was carrying in a baby sling. The little girl shook her head and watched them all with her wide blue eyes.

"That little girl is a cutie." Iona put a hand to her chest with a smile. "Come on in. You're going to love what they've made for the two of you."

Juliet glanced sideways at Andrea, who was still her right-hand woman on the management floor, and walked into the huge office overlooking Mayfair. She saw her things and a children's corner so she could have Hazel with her. They had decided that as soon as she was off the breast, she would not take her to the office, but Iona didn't know that.

Juliet went up to her and kissed her. "It's beautiful. Thank you! You didn't have to do all this, but I like it very much."

"We want you back and as comfortable as possible. It's a pleasure, and this way, we'll have the little princess close by. Won't we, sweetie?"

"Aren't you coming to work with Aunt Iona?" Iona touched her little face with a finger, and Hazel smiled at her. "Oh, she's such a sweetheart."

"She is very sociable."

"We'll leave you alone to get settled in. Come on, guys. Everybody back to work."

"Thank you all a thousand times."

Juliet smiled at them as the boss sent them back to the second floor, then looked at Andrea, walked over to her new chair, and slumped into it, overwhelmed by the massive reception after her maternity leave, the last two months of which she had spent working from home.

"I hadn't even thought about Miller-Lezer," she whispered.

Andrea shook her head. "I said that, but Iona said that when a woman becomes a mother, she usually takes her husband's last name. In the end, Fabio said he had heard you use the Miller-Lezer thing on occasion, and it stuck."

"He must have heard me, but in my personal and family life, not in my professional life. Anyway, I'm not going to be bitter about it. Actually, for the last six months, I've only been Hazel Lezer's mother. Haven't I, my love?" She looked into the eyes of her precious little girl and smiled at her before kissing her. Hazel let herself be pampered. She was quiet because she was a *kalye*, her father said, or "*mimosa*" in Yiddish. "For professional purposes, I'm still Juliet Miller, and we'll keep it that way."

"I think it's perfect. Do you want to have a drink?"

"No, honey, thank you very much. I'm going to check the mail and finish the report on the new script for Lily."

"All right. I'll be back in fifteen minutes so we can go over what's pending."

"Great, thank you."

She turned on the computer and glanced at the children's area set up for Hazel. It had a rocking chair for adults and another for babies, a playpen that could be used as a crib, a lovely hypoallergenic rug, a small table with toys, a changing table, and a closet full of pink diapers. It was very much in the style of Iona, who had surely hired an interior designer to make everything perfect.

The truth was that since her boss had found out about her pregnancy, she had been great with her. She had gone out of her way to support her and make her life easier. She said she felt like a surrogate grandmother, and she was acting like one, which Juliet would be grateful for all her life.

Something else to thank her for all her life because, from giving her a job to making her her right-hand woman, to appointing her general manager for the UK and Ireland to organizing the most amazing wedding party in the world, Iona McCameron had done almost everything for her in twelve years of mutual collaboration. That was why she respected and appreciated her, and that was also why she had asked her to be Hazel's godmother for a Catholic baptism that they had celebrated in private to reassure her grandmother.

She had explained that it was their intention to raise the child in a Jewish cultural environment. It was fundamental to Michiel and his family, and it reinforced his Hebrew roots on his father's side.

Never in her life would she have imagined that matters of faith or religion would one day mean something important to her because, when you are half-Catholic, half-Anglican, and you are not interested in religions, everything seems to be from another planet. However, when you fall in love with someone who cares about his culture and his people, and on top of that, you have a daughter with him, everything changes. A world of possibilities opens up, and suddenly, you are forced to inform yourself. To learn and make decisions.

Fiona, Daniel's mother, had never been involved with Judaism because she was not interested in it. She wasn't opposed to following certain customs to respect Michiel's principles, but she didn't participate or support or intervene. On the contrary, she was agnostic and preferred that her son stay away from any indoctrination, but Juliet saw it differently because she had learned that it wasn't simply a religion, rituals, or visits to a synagogue. It was a culture and genetics and a way of life that she thought was enriching and positive for her daughter. At least until she grew up, formed her own criteria, and decided for herself.

She kissed her little blonde head and thought it was time to take her out of the backpack and put her in the playpen because she had fallen asleep, but she stroked her back instead, thinking about her unexpected and happy arrival.

Although she hadn't suspected it, she was pregnant before she went to Sarah's wedding. As the gynecologist and the ultrasound had confirmed in mid-September, she had become pregnant in mid-June, before Michiel's declaration of love and her whirlwind trip to Amsterdam to tell him that she loved him too.

She had been using oral contraceptives for years because of a hormonal issue, but she had taken a break, and against all odds, she had gotten pregnant the first time. No withdrawal period. At the first glimmer of hope, the magic had worked, and they had conceived their precious baby. They had confirmed the news while sitting on the edge of the bathtub after going together to a pharmacy to buy a pregnancy test.

When she came back from the wedding, she realized that she had missed at least two periods and that she was due for her third, but she had put it down to the stress of the last few months. When her breasts had started to feel swollen and tender and she'd thrown up after smelling a latte, she'd panicked and talked it over with Michiel. He, with that calmness of his, had shown up to pick her up at the office, and they'd gone off to get a pregnancy test.

It hadn't taken them five minutes to confirm that they were going to be parents, and although they had been speechless and disconcerted at first, they had immediately embraced each other with tears of happiness because neither doubted for a second that this was wonderful news. Unexpected, unscheduled, and hasty, but perfect. With that same joy, they had communicated it to their families and friends, their co-workers, and everyone because they could not feel more fortunate.

On November fourth, a month after her thirty-third birthday and after putting aside the jokes and accepting that it was unavoidable, she married the love of her life in an intimate and discreet civil ceremony at the Dutch embassy. A friend of Michiel's parents had arranged everything very quickly and very much to their liking, without a wedding dress and without any fuss.

They had said "I do" with only their parents and siblings in attendance, plus Daniel and her grandmother, who had come from Cádiz. Nobody else until they had arrived at the romantic hotel in Windsor at which Michiel had insisted on spending the wedding night. They had walked into the most amazing and crowded party of their lives. Iona, Fabio, and Andrea, supported by Michiel, his brothers, and a top wedding planner, had moved heaven and earth, and in a matter of weeks, they had managed to put together a dazzling surprise party that had attracted every-one. From her most famous actors to the lesser known, their respective co-workers, their friends, their cousins from Cádiz, Michiel's family and friends from Amsterdam, all the people who mattered to them. They had enjoyed the best wedding party in the universe and their love and all the good things that life was giving them.

"We should enter the Guinness Book of Records. Two daughters married in two months," her father had said the next day as he left the hotel tired and satisfied. Everyone had said he was absolutely right, and it had been worthy of making the newspapers.

With the marital status established, just as Michiel had predicted, the matter of Audrey's apartment in Barbican had been re-settled quite simply. By the end of November, it was theirs, considered to be the Lezers' joint property, and they had begun renovations.

In principle, the renovations were minor, but they had lasted almost four months until the birth of Hazel, who had come into the world by natural childbirth on March twenty-second at St. Mary's Hospital in London.

The contractions had almost scared her to death because they had caught her working in the office, and she had been rushing at a dizzying pace from the minute she had started the contractions. Once in the clinic and with Michiel holding her hand, everything had gone smoothly, and she had welcomed with tears her beautiful baby girl with blue eyes like Michiel's, whom they had named Hazel Rose. Hazel, a very old Hebrew name whose meaning is "she who has seen the Lord," which Michiel especially liked, and Rose for Audrey Rose Stuyvesant, who had united them forever.

With their daughter in the world, they had started a new stage and had at last moved to Audrey's apartment, as they both called it, where they had three bedrooms and a very nice terrace. Daniel spent a lot of time with them. He had no trouble getting involved with his new baby sister, but he still preferred the company of Romeo, who had also taken the baby's arrival in stride.

To be fair, Michiel said Romeo had been the first to detect the pregnancy. Before the drugstore test, he'd been following her around the house very intently, and at the first sign of a change, he'd nipped at her belly. So it had gone for the nine months until Hazel had come home. Then he'd become her official watcher. He rarely left her crib and occasionally sniffed her to make sure everything was okay. He never touched her, but he kept an eye on her, and the little one loved him. Family life aside, professionally, things had changed quite a bit. Michiel had finished school in July and taken a one year leave of absence to finish his doctorate at the University of Amsterdam. With a couple of scholarships from his government and support from his school, he was determined to finally finish his thesis, which he had almost completed. While he was working on it, he also took care of Hazel.

With him at home and lacking a schedule, she had been able to announce her return to work after six months of near-retirement.

Of course, she had never stopped answering calls and putting out fires, especially in the last two months she had worked from her living room via video calls, but she could no longer resist going back to the office. Michiel had made it easy for her since he was an exceptional father. So, while it hurt to leave the warmth of home and be away from her little girl, she knew she was leaving Hazel in the best hands in the universe.

In short, she had finally returned to Shaughnessy & McCameron and a new position as Managing Director for the UK and Ireland. It was an even better position than her previous one. She maintained the nature of her job, but she would do it without as much travel. For that, she had Andrea, who was a great fit, and Claire, a new assistant whom Andrea had trained in her absence and who would cover for her when she had to fly to Bulgaria or Northern Ireland or wherever was necessary to take care of her actors and actresses.

She watched Andrea through the glass, chatting with Claire at the computer. Apparently, she was a very tough boss, Fabio had informed her. Juliet liked it that way because she was efficient and knew the job very well, which gave her immense relief.

She looked at her computer screen and saw a message from John Tompkins in the inbox. He was asking about Hazel and telling her that his latest biography of the Stuyvesants was still in the top ten of the New York Times bestsellers. A real success. She smiled, thinking about what John would do with the juicy information about Audrey's "undeath." Unfortunately, she couldn't tell him anything, so she wrote back congratulating him and sending him the latest picture of Hazel in the park.

Regarding Audrey, they heard from each other quite often. They messaged each other through Fran's phone, and once they had gone to visit her at an apartment she had bought in Piccadilly Street opposite Green Park, where she had settled in like a queen to enjoy her later years as she wished.

Thank God the Stuyvesants had left them alone. They had never heard from any member of that family or any of their employees again. Even Victoria Stuyvesant, who had not withstood even two rounds in the difficult London auditions, had vanished from the city, which she was also grateful for because she was a mediocre actress.

For his part, Robert, who had become a little richer thanks to the agreement signed with the Stuyvesants, said that the Glenns were squandering their money hand over fist, which usually happened when it had cost you nothing to earn it. Although he did know about Audrey's unexpected "resurrection," he kept the matter a professional secret.

They only discussed it when they met at home in private, and they remembered the madness that the now-famous "Stuyvesant case" had meant for the three of them. A great madness, she thought every time she went over everything they had lived through, especially when she had time to work on her book, for which she had already found a publisher—her brother James and her sister-in-law Siobhan, who had founded a small independent publishing house where such a story could be published.

She continued going through the emails and saw one from Caden Brown, whom she had met about eight months ago while walking in Camden Town. She, very pregnant, was with Michiel, and he was with a girlfriend he had introduced as Mary. The famous Carola had passed into history. She had not paid him ten seconds of attention and had politely said goodbye to him, wishing never to see him again in her life. With any luck, she wouldn't because soon after, he had written to her to inform her that he was living in Australia again.

She opened the message out of curiosity, found that it only contained information about an exhibition he was planning in Sydney, and deleted it. At the same time, she heard Michiel greeting Andrea and Claire.

"Good morning, ladies."

"Hi, Michiel. Your girls are in the office."

"Thank you."

She looked up to see him enter the office and smiled like a fool because she couldn't find him more handsome or more manly, or more edible, or more...

"Hello, *Zissele*. How are you, my love?"

"Hi! I was starting to miss you. Thank goodness I have Hazel."

"Didn't you leave her in her crib? Wow, this place is great!" he interrupted himself to admire the new office, and Juliet took time to spy on his faded jeans, his boots, his dark blue shirt, and his beautiful, long, disheveled hair, and she sighed with love. "It's a knockout."

"It is, yes. How about Dani?"

"Fatal, but we've fixed it."

"What do you mean, fatal?"

"Nothing serious, it's just that when he got to school, he remembered that he had to bring food to donate to the Food Bank. He went the whole weekend telling no one. I was going to leave him hanging so Chris could give him a good talking-to, but I couldn't. I bought some stuff in Tesco and took it to his class. That's why it took me a bit longer."

"No one told us we had to bring food."

"They didn't want to notify the parents so they could take responsibility for the children. How are you, *Zissele*? How are you doing?"

He approached the table to kiss her many times, then spoke over her mouth: "You are the most beautiful girl in the world. I don't know whether to leave you alone in this nest of movie stars."

"*Zalamero.*"

"I'm not a flatterer. Hi, honey!" He took Hazel from her and kissed her. "*Meyn kalye malke.*"

"I changed her forty minutes ago, and she ate very well."

"Perfect, I'll take her for a walk. We'll go get some books in Covent Garden, and then I'll bring her back to you. Will you be okay?"

"I don't know, but I have to. Go before I regret it." He stood up and hugged them both after adjusting his backpack.

"Your mother called me and confirmed that they are coming on Saturday to stay with the girl, so I will make a reservation for a romantic dinner at Amadeo's Italian. Okay?"

"Why did she call you? Why didn't she call me?"

"Because she didn't want to interrupt your first day at the office. Okay, we're leaving. We'll walk close by. If anything happens, call me, and I'll come right back. I love you, *Zissele*."

"I love you too."

They kissed again, and Juliet watched them walk down the street after they got downstairs. Her heart and her whole body ached, but she pulled herself together because it was time to start being more independent from her daughter. She looked at Andrea, who was gazing at her with a tender face, and waved her in.

"Tell me, what do we have?"

"In half an hour, a meeting with HBO. At one o'clock, the executive producer of DreamWorks comes to see you. Spielberg wants all the actors in his new project to be British."

"Rita told me about it. I have a professional proposal. I'll give it to you so you can make copies."

"Henry wants to talk to you. Richard M too, and also, Lily, Jen, Sam, and Billy H. Naomi says she doesn't plan to accept Remi's without signing an addendum agreement about nudity that you review. So far, that's it."

"Perfect! Here we go."

Claudia Velasco, Madrid, June 2021

THAT FLIGHT FROM LONDON TO MADRID

If you enjoyed this book, you might also enjoy *That Flight From London to Madrid*, from Claudia Velasco.

Grab your copy today!

A chance encounter will change the lives of two strangers forever.

Daniela Mendoza makes a snap decision to get away from it all after a betrayal makes her reevaluate her life.

She meets Edward Dankworth on her flight from London to Madrid. Her unexpected traveling companion offers the comfort she needs, then disappears from her life when their plane lands.

Two years later, coincidence reunites them in Rome. Edward does his best to distance himself from Daniela, but fate has other plans for them...

Their chance encounter unleashes a series of events that immerses Daniela in Edward's world. She finds herself caught in the tangled web of smuggling and spies, secrets and lies that has prevented Edward from letting anyone in.

As their thrilling adventure takes them through Rome, Madrid, and London, Daniela and Edward discover more than the source of the international mystery and espionage that brought them back together.

Can they learn to trust and rely on each other? Or will their pasts get in the way of falling in love?

Grab your copy today!